JENNIFER S. ALDERSON

Death by Oxcart

An Independence Day Murder in Costa Rica

First published by Traveling Life Press | Amsterdam 2024

Copyright © 2024 by Jennifer S. Alderson

All rights reserved. No part of this publication may be reproduced, stored or transmitted in any form or by any means, electronic, mechanical, photocopying, recording, scanning, or otherwise without written permission from the publisher. It is illegal to copy this book, post it to a website, or distribute it by any other means without permission.

This novel is entirely a work of fiction. The names, characters and incidents portrayed in it are the work of the author's imagination. Any resemblance to actual persons, living or dead, events or localities is entirely coincidental.

Jennifer S. Alderson asserts the moral right to be identified as the author of this work.

First edition

This book was professionally typeset on Reedsy.
Find out more at reedsy.com

Contents

1	Snuggling with Seymour	1
2	The Way to San Jose	8
3	Snippy Tour Guide	12
4	First Impressions	19
5	The Mysterious Spheres of Costa Rica	28
6	Live Music at Ram Luna	33
7	White Lies	44
8	Stick to our Story	48
9	No Place For Lovers	54
10	Zip-lining through Cloud Forests	57
11	Horses and Hanging Bridges	61
12	Hummingbird Café	67
13	Unwanted Kickbacks	71
14	Casa del Mar	75
15	Visiting the Site	81
16	Exit Through the Gift Shop	86
17	Alone Time at the Dig	92
18	Exposing Lies	96
19	A Two-Ton Carreta	101
20	Building an Oxcart	106
21	A Terrible Accident	113
22	Romantic Fireworks	117
23	Independence Day	119
24	A Painful Reminder	127
25	What Sam Knew	130
26	Hiking an Active Volcano	133

27	Shark Teeth	142
28	Bad News for Lana	145
29	Investigation Time	148
30	Change of Plans	150
31	Suspects List	152
32	Googling the Suspects	155
33	Fat Cat	158
34	Lana Reaches Out	161
35	A Sore Backside	165
36	Alex the Planner	167
37	Tarnished Reputation	169
38	Confronting Xavier	175
39	Hanging with Sea Turtles	179
40	Not an Accident	182
41	Robbery Gone Wrong	185
42	A Neat Solution	189
43	A Monochrome View	192
44	Going Kayaking	196
45	Jeremy Calls Back	198
46	Going For A Swim	201
47	Case Closed	203
48	The Tour Must Go On	208
49	Home is Where You Are	211
Acknowledgments		214
About the Author		215
Collecting Can Be Murder		217

1

Snuggling with Seymour

Wednesday—Seattle, Washington

"How is your jet lag?" Dotty Thompson asked as she plopped down into the deck chair next to Lana Hansen. Her two canines, Rodney and Chipper, lay down at their mistress's feet, exhausted from their long walk from Dotty's Fremont home to Lana's houseboat on Lake Union.

Lana pulled the woolen blanket tighter around her shoulders, considering her friend's question. She'd just returned from a glorious month-long trip around Southeast Asia, scouting out potential routes for a new line of adventure-oriented tours that Dotty was considering adding to her company's agenda next year. Not only was Dotty her friend and landlord, she was also the owner of Wanderlust Tours, the company Lana worked for.

It had been wonderful to backpack around on her own, without having to worry about a group for a change. Yet after being away from Seattle for so long, right now Lana was glad to be home with her cat, Seymour—currently snoring softly in her lap—as she gazed across the peaceful lake and listened to the waves gently crash against her low-lying dock. From their perch on the houseboat's deck, they had an uninterrupted view across Lake Union, with Gas Works Park on their left and downtown Seattle on their right.

"Not too bad, I guess. It is only day nine, and they say you need a day per time zone to recover completely, which means I have six more to go—at least, if that old wives' tale is true. I did sleep for most of the night and didn't feel completely exhausted when I got up this morning, so that's a win. I just can't get warm. It is so much colder here than in Thailand, I guess my body needs more time to get its internal temperature readjusted."

"Excellent, I'm glad to hear that," Dotty replied.

Lana regarded her boss, wondering what had prompted that strange response. Despite her advancing age, Dotty was still as sharp as a tack. Ideas about why her boss would react like that raced through Lana's mind, but none made sense. "Are you glad to hear that I can't get warm, or that the jet lag is almost over?"

"Both." After her cryptic comment, Dotty chose to look out over the water instead of meeting Lana's gaze.

Boy, she is going to make me work for this, isn't she? Lana thought.

Yet before she could push her boss for an answer, the dogs began yapping at a low-flying duck, coming in for a landing close to her deck. Seymour raised his head to see what all the commotion was, but didn't seem to be further bothered by their barking.

When the dogs raced over to the edge of the dock, Lana held her heart fast. Before she could spring up or they could fall in, Dotty snapped her fingers twice and held out a hand to Chipper and Rodney. Both the pug and Jack Russell immediately forgot about the duck and raced over, knowing their mistress would have something tasty for them.

Sure enough, Dotty pulled out two strips of dog jerky, which the canines wolfed down before sitting contently between the two deck chairs. Lana scratched at Rodney's ears, receiving a tongue-lolling grin in reward. When Chipper pushed the pug aside and maneuvered his head under Lana's hand, she couldn't help but laugh. Instead of scolding him, she scratched under his chin, to Chipper's obvious delight. After giving herself a moment to enjoy how the Jack Russell's tiny tail thumped against her leg, Lana looked over at her boss. "What's going on, Dotty?"

When her boss finally responded, her voice quivered. "Sweetie, you know that when I told you to take off as much time as you needed, I meant it, don't you?"

"Yeah, I suppose I do."

Lana was officially taking a break from leading groups through Europe, in order to help her clear her head and conscience after a string of deaths had plagued her last few tours. That was why Dotty had sent her to Asia for the month. Although she had finished her scouting assignment and turned in two potential itineraries through Thailand, Vietnam, and Laos for her boss to consider, Lana still didn't feel ready to lead another European tour because the deaths still weighed heavily on her mind. In fact, just yesterday she'd expressed her concerns to Dotty, who had repeatedly assured her that she could take another month off, guilt free, before diving back into tour duties.

When her boss remained suspiciously silent instead of explaining herself, Lana asked, "Where are you going with this, Dotty?"

The older lady clicked her tongue against her teeth and let out a sigh. "I truly hate to have to ask you this, but there is a situation that needs fixing, and you are by far the best person for the job. But it would require that you help an in-progress tour get through its last nine days together."

Lana could feel her back curving, just as her cat's did when he was angry with her. "Wait, just yesterday you assured me that you had enough guides to cover all of the tours for the coming month. I'm still jet-lagged from my flight home from Bangkok—why are you putting pressure on me to lead a group so soon?"

"Before you get upset, know that I have a good reason for asking. It's not that I need you to cover for another guide…" Dotty's voice trailed off for moment, and she averted her gaze, as if she was embarrassed to have to tell Lana the rest. "It's Alex. He's on his second tour—as part of his training—but it is not going well. In fact, I'm afraid he's either going to give up and fly home before the end of the week, or I'm going to have to ask him to step aside and let the other two guides handle the rest of the tour."

Lana sank further into her chair and ran her fingers through Seymour's thick fur. His purrs increased in intensity and volume while she thought back on Alex's last few messages. Her boyfriend had sounded so upbeat and positive—so what had gone wrong?

"I don't understand. He didn't say anything about there being stress on the current tour in Costa Rica, or his first, for that matter. In fact, he said that the tour in Mexico had gone far better than he had expected."

She had been quite jealous when Alex had told her that he would be assisting on a scouting trip in Central America, as well as group tours in Mexico and Costa Rica, as part of his training. Both were trial runs of the new line of adrenaline-filled excursions Dotty was considering offering. Instead of European trips focused on experiencing a city's cultural highlights and tasting the finest local cuisine, these would be aimed at a younger generation and built around outdoor adventures—kayaking, hiking, zip-lining, surfing, horseback riding, snorkeling, and the like.

Dotty shook her head slowly. "Well, honey, he either has pretty low expectations, or he was lying to you. I wouldn't blame him for doing so, since you took to the job like a fish to water. In fact, I was joking the other day with the ladies in accounting that you must have been a tour guide in a former life. So I can imagine he'd be embarrassed to admit that he is having trouble getting the hang of it."

Lana felt her stomach knot up as her friend's words sank in. Lying to each other was something they had promised never to do again. Alex's lies about his participation in an environmental organization's radical protest actions had almost landed him in jail and had put their relationship in jeopardy. They'd gotten through it eventually, and Lana thought their relationship was stronger for it, but now she wondered whether it was all a ruse. Yet as angry as she was that Alex may be trying to deceive her again, she couldn't bear to hear her boss speak ill of him, either.

"What is he doing wrong, exactly?"

"It's not just one thing. According to George, the senior guide, Alex seems to be having trouble making any meaningful connections with his guests, and instead seems to be antagonizing them with his snippy comments. I've already received a few complaints from guests on both tours about his grumpy behavior."

Lana began to protest, but Dotty held up her hand. "Let me finish. After talking it through with George, I decided to send down an extra guide for the Costa Rica trip, in case Alex struggled again. It cost me a pretty penny to do so, but I need to ensure that the tour goes on, with or without Alex leading it. As you well know, our guests pay a whole lot of money to take one of my tours, and they expected to be treated as royalty, not to be talked down to or made to feel as if they are dumb. I know these are trial runs, but I expect them to be identical to a real tour, otherwise there's no point in testing them out."

"Have you talked to Alex about the complaints? It could just be a clash of personalities, or perhaps George is misinterpreting Alex's actions."

Dotty pursed her lips. "Yesterday Alex made one woman so mad that she called the office and demanded he be fired on the spot."

Lana's face paled. "That doesn't sound like my boyfriend."

"No, it does not, and that's what concerns me. George said Alex was enthusiastic and fun to be around during their two-week-long scouting expedition, and that he made a professional impression on the tour operators that they'd met with. So the travel bit doesn't seem to be the problem. But Lana, George told me the last time we talked that Alex was being so rude to the clients that he doesn't want to leave him alone with them anymore."

"Oh, no. That's not good at all."

"I know. It must be that he's having trouble getting a handle on how to deal with all of the diverse personalities on a tour. Or something completely different is going on that he refuses to talk with George about. That's why I want to send you down there—to see if you can figure out what's blocking him from doing his best."

Lana chewed on her lip as she considered Dotty's request. She loved Alex too much to let him flail around, but as much as she wanted to help him find his way as a tour guide, she wondered whether she was really the right person for the job.

"I don't know if this is a good idea. He is my boyfriend, and I would hate for this to damage our relationship. What about his brother—could Randy fly down? I know he hasn't led a tour in quite a while, and that the bed and breakfast is super busy…"

Randy Wright had been her favorite colleague at Wanderlust Tours, until he'd gotten married and chose to manage Dotty's Seattle-based bed and breakfast, instead of leading international tours. Lana couldn't blame him; traveling to Europe on a regular basis didn't make it easy to sustain a relationship with his new wife.

Dotty cleared her throat, cutting Lana off as she grabbed her hand. "Randy is the guide that I sent down to Costa Rica at the last minute. We both thought he could help his brother get back on track, but it doesn't seem to be working out like we'd hoped."

Lana pulled her hand out of Dotty's grip, as her eyebrows knitted together. "That's not possible; I had dinner with Randy and Gloria last week, and he didn't say anything about flying to Costa Rica."

She thought back to that fun night and how they were all in a jovial mood, thanks to the great company and the wonderful lasagna his wife, Gloria, had made. Why would Randy not have told her he was about to embark on a tour with his brother?

"I only asked him to join the tour a few days ago, after I heard about how badly things went in Mexico. Honestly, Randy did me a favor by flying down at the last minute. Yet it seems that even brotherly love isn't working—Randy said he's been quite irritable and not open to constructive criticism from either him or George."

Lana blew out her cheeks, searching for another way out. "Four is a lot of guides for one tour. How many clients are there?"

"Only nine. You make a good point, though. Once you get settled into the group, maybe you can send Randy back to Seattle. I kind of pressured him to go, and I know Gloria was not pleased that he agreed to help me out with this. It has been ridiculously busy at the bed and breakfast, and they are short-staffed, as it is."

"This is a big ask," Lana finally said.

"Lana, let me be real blunt with you. If Alex can't figure out how to be a guide worthy of Wanderlust Tours before the end of next week, I will not be able to hire him. I need to trust that the guides I send out are able and willing to provide the high-quality customer service our guests pay dearly for."

"Oh, it is really that serious."

Lana let her eyelids flutter closed, considering the situation. If Randy couldn't get through to his brother, who was more of his best friend than just a blood relative, then Lana didn't know what Dotty expected her to do.

Yet the thought of poor Alex possibly losing his job because of whatever was going on was enough to get her on that plane. It had taken him months to finally quit his soul-sucking job in the corporate world, and Lana knew he only dared to do so because he was convinced that being a tour guide was the perfect career for him. But if he failed at this, the blow to his ego would be immense.

As reluctant as she was to agree, for fear of damaging her relationship, she felt as if she had no choice but to say yes. If she let him fail without even trying to help him succeed, she'd never forgive herself.

Lana leaned down to whisper into Seymour's ear as she scratched his head. "Well, buddy, it looks like you are going to spend some more time with Aunt Dotty."

Her boss's shoulders sagged as her face lit up with a smile. "Thank you, Lana. I really do appreciate this. Trust me, I want Alex to succeed, otherwise I wouldn't be asking you to fly down."

Lana clasped Dotty's hand. "I know, and I appreciate that. We all want him to do well. If Randy can't get through to him, then I can't guarantee that I'll be able to, but I'll do my best."

Dotty squeezed back. "I know you will. But before you go, I better tell you everything that he's said to upset the clients. It ain't pretty."

The knot in Lana's stomach drew tighter. As much as she wanted to throw her hands over her ears, she knew she had to be adult about this. "Okay, tell me everything."

2

The Way to San Jose

Wednesday—Day Four of the Wanderlust Tour of San Jose, Costa Rica

The nine-hour flight down to San Jose from Seattle had not been relaxing, but a roller coaster of emotions and a stream of questions. In what state were Alex, George, and Randy going to be? What exactly had happened on that river that made Alex think it appropriate to call a guest such a nasty name? After hearing all that Dotty had to say about her boyfriend's performance and the specifics of the complaints made against him, she was frankly shocked that her boss was giving him another chance. If it had been any other trainee, they would have been fired on the spot.

Lana thought back to how pumped up Alex had sounded during his scouting trip with George. It had been ages since she'd heard her boyfriend so excited about anything work-related, and hearing the enthusiasm in his voice gave her the feeling that things were going well.

Granted, she hadn't spoken with him much during his first week-long tour as an assistant guide because she'd been traveling through Vietnam, Thailand, and Laos, exploring the many fascinating cultural monuments and natural phenomena that Southeast Asia had to offer. Not only was cell reception pretty poor, overseas calls were also obscenely expensive, so they had agreed to stick to short text messages until she'd gotten back to Seattle.

Yet since she'd been home, they'd only spoken briefly twice, and both times had been interrupted by a client's question. In neither case had he called her back. And his replies to her messages had been quite delayed, as well. She had figured that he had been busy and didn't want to pressure him into calling her back by repeatedly messaging him. But now she wondered whether he had been avoiding her.

On the plane ride down, she had scrolled through his messages, examining them for blatant lies. Based on what Dotty had told her, his texts were snippets of fiction and not at all a true rendition of how the tour had been going at the time.

Yet as mad as she knew she should be, Lana still couldn't decide if Alex had intentionally lied to her for the sake of brevity, figuring he could explain himself properly once he got back home. Or did he actually think that she would not find out about his poor performance?

When she pulled out her phone and re-read his upbeat messages once more, another thought entered her mind, one that terrified her even more than the idea that he'd intentionally deceived her. What if Alex truly believed that he was doing his job well? That would make this situation infinitely worse, if he couldn't see for himself that things weren't working out as they should.

All she knew for certain was that one of the guests had been so upset by how Alex had treated her that she had reached out to Dotty yesterday and demanded that he be fired on the spot.

For the life of her, she could not imagine what had pushed her normally level-headed boyfriend so far over the edge. Lana shook her head and told herself to let it go. She'd find out soon enough.

To distract herself, she looked outside, taking in the streets of San Jose. Her taxi driver had kept the gas pedal pressed to the floor from the moment they'd zipped away from the airport. They'd already whizzed by the industrial outskirts of the city center and were now approaching downtown.

The capital seemed to spread across a wide valley, circled by the Irazu and Barva Volcanoes in the north, and the Talamanca Mountains in the south. The city center was a hodgepodge of modern, skyscraper-style concrete boxes and glorious old neocolonial structures with tiled roofs painted in warm shades of red, yellow, and green.

Best of all, the city was dressed up for Costa Rica's upcoming Independence Day celebrations, to mark the country's liberation from Spanish colonial rule. Hanging off of streetlights, overhanging wires, trees, and buildings were an abundance of festive streamers and a plethora of flags in red, white, and blue. Lana had read that the country's flag was an expression of its values, with blue representing perseverance; white, peace; and red, a reminder of the bloodshed in achieving its independence. She couldn't wait to experience the celebrations firsthand during this tour.

The taxi driver kept up a clipped pace as they traversed a busy city street until he slammed on the brakes and turned into a private parking lot. Lana could hardly believe the charming building with a turret on one end and colorful orange sunshades adorning each of the many windows was where she would be staying the night.

After paying her driver, Lana turned to the entrance, wondering what she would find on the other side of the doors. According to their itinerary, the group should be at the hotel, taking a short rest break before meeting back up for dinner. She hadn't yet texted her fellow guides to let them know she was on her way down, because she knew Dotty had already done so.

When she arrived at the airport, she'd debated calling Alex, but decided against it. If he knew she was on her way to the hotel, he might choose to act differently than he had been. And if she was going to help him, she needed to see and hear what he was doing wrong.

Unfortunately for Lana, she didn't have to wait long. As soon as she entered the neocolonial hotel, she heard Alex's voice wafting through the lobby. Its high pitch alerted her, even before she spotted him and a guest across the room, to how stressed out he was.

"As I said before, the minivan will be here at nine a.m. sharp, and the breakfast hall is open at seven. You have more than enough time to eat a leisurely meal, as you call it. Just don't sleep in."

"There's no need to be snippy with me," the older man chastised. From the descriptions and passport photos that Dotty had sent her, Lana guessed the man was Xavier Johns, a respected archaeologist and guest on the tour.

"Boy, Dotty must be short on guides this season if she hired you," Xavier grumbled as he turned on his heel and stormed off, before her boyfriend could even utter a response.

It was probably for the best. Based on Alex's clenched jaw and livid expression, it would not have been client-friendly.

Lana sucked in her breath, wondering what had happened to make him act so. This wasn't the relaxed and friendly Alex Wright that she knew and loved. He seemed even more stressed now than when he had been leading corporate workshops at those international conferences.

She followed him to the elevator, watching as he practically tore his gorgeous hair out of his head in frustration, hoping her presence would make him relax a smidgen and not worsen his mood. When she caught up, Lana tapped him on the shoulder. "Excuse me, sir…"

Before she could complete her sentence, Alex cut her off. "What do I look like—" he groused as he turned around to face her. "Lana!"

His arms encircled her so tightly, it felt like he was squeezing all of the air out of her lungs. "Boy, am I glad to see you. Wow, you got here fast."

"Oh, good. I'm glad you're relieved that I'm here, and not angry."

He pulled back and searched her face. "Wait a second, did Dotty send you down here to take my place?"

Before she could respond, Alex leaned against the wall, his head already hanging. "You're here to fire me, aren't you? I know Dotty's not pleased with everything that's happened so far, but I had hoped for a little more leeway."

The panic on his face made her stomach clench up. This was not the way she wanted to start things off. She snapped her fingers in front of his face.

"Hey, earth to Alex—it's me, your girlfriend, whom you haven't seen in almost two months. Can we have a little 'us time' before we dive into the work stuff? I really missed you. Shall we grab a drink? I hear Costa Rica's got some great coffee."

His warm smile melted her heart. "Sure, that sounds great. My treat."

3

Snippy Tour Guide

After a half hour of chitchat, Alex finally seemed relaxed enough for Lana to broach the elephant in the room. She lay a hand over his as she looked him in the eye.

"My love, it's great to catch up, but we need to have a serious talk about work. Dotty told me that there have been complaints about your behavior, but she didn't have all of the details. Which means I need you to fill me in on everything that has gone wrong during your first tour and this one so far, okay?"

Alex hung his head. "Fair enough. Although we might need to order some snacks. There's a lot to tell."

"Okay, but before we order, let's start with what was going on in the lobby when I arrived. It looked as if you were having some sort of altercation with an older guest."

When he pulled a face, she cocked an eyebrow at him. "You were pretty snippy with the man. Even you can admit that."

Alex ran a hand through his hair, signaling to her that he was going on the defensive. "I had just finished a stressful phone call, and Xavier was the last guest I wanted to run into. That guy can't seem to tie his own shoelaces, let alone remember what day it is. I'm honestly shocked that he is such a well-regarded archaeologist."

"Even so, you can't take your frustrations out on the guests. These tours are ridiculously expensive, and our clients expect to be treated like royalty. Dotty takes customer satisfaction seriously, and even our being in a relationship won't save your job, if too many guests complain about you."

Instead of admitting he had been in the wrong, Alex clenched his jaw, to Lana's irritation. "Okay, but Xavier's not a normal guest. Randy told me that he and his two assistants didn't have to pay for the tour."

"Alex, no one is paying for this tour—that's the only reason why you haven't been sacked already. From what Dotty told me, this is a trial run of the itinerary George submitted for Costa Rica. She handpicked all of the guests and offered them a free trip, in exchange for their feedback. We expect there to be problems with the itinerary that might irritate paying clients, one that will need to be fixed before Dotty puts it on Wanderlust Tours' official agenda. That's why she values their feedback more than their money on this one."

Alex leaned back in his chair. "Oh, I thought only the three archaeologists had a free ride. I guess I didn't understand Randy correctly then."

"Even so, just because they are here for free is no reason to treat them differently than you would a paying guest. And so you know, these tours may be trial runs, but she expects it to mirror the real experience as much as possible so our guests can better critique George's itineraries."

Lana dipped her head, unable to meet Alex's eye when she added, "This is a trial run for you, too. Dotty needs to know that you take your responsibilities seriously, otherwise she won't be able to send you out on a real tour."

Alex's eyes flew open. She could tell the steam was quickly building up behind his ears. "Is that why you are here—to judge my performance?"

Lana sighed and fiddled with the handle of her coffee mug. "In a way, yes. But I am also here to help you figure out how to do your job better. However, I can only do so if you tell me the complete truth. What can you tell me about the incident with Jersey yesterday? She apparently thinks you should be fired for it, which is what prompted Dotty to send me down."

When Alex tensed visibly, she rushed to add, "Just so you know, Dotty thinks Jersey sounded completely irrational—in her phone calls, emails, and voicemails. But she has to take the complaint seriously, and until she knows what really happened, she can't just discount the woman's comments as ridiculous."

"I thought I explained myself clearly to both Dotty and Randy yesterday, but apparently not." He took a deep breath, blowing it out violently. "We had just started rafting down the Pacuare River, and things were going well until we began to approach the first series of serious rapids. Our guide specifically warned us not to stand up for the coming minutes, and to hold on to a rope running along the side of the boat, so that we didn't fall out."

Alex paused a moment, clearly trying to get his anger under control, before continuing. "That's when Jersey started screaming that she didn't want to get wet. The moment she got splashed, she stood up and started yelling that she wanted out of the raft. The guide told her to sit back down, but she refused. Before we knew it, the whole raft tipped over, and we all fell into the river. Only after we got it flipped back over did we realize that we'd also lost a few of the bags because Jersey hadn't tied them down properly."

"And that's when you yelled at her?" Lana pushed, needing him to admit what he'd done.

"Yes, but it wasn't intentional, it kind of slipped out. She'd already been messing up the group's rhythm because she couldn't get the hang of paddling in sync with the rest, so I guess I was already irritated with her. But after she started yelling about not wanting to get wet and then tipped us all over, I guess I'd had enough. I mean, who expects to stay dry during a whitewater rafting trip? Isn't getting wet the whole point?"

Lana couldn't help but smile. "True, but did you have to yell at her? Couldn't you have made a mild joke at her expense, instead? Something silly like, 'thanks, Jersey, now I don't have to take a shower.' Making light of something can be a great way to defuse a nasty situation."

Alex's shoulders slumped further. "I suppose that's what you would have done."

"Yeah, I would have because the client is always right. That's pretty much Wanderlust Tours' motto."

When he rolled his eyes at her, something snapped inside of Lana. "Alex, I don't care what they do, you can't call a guest a 'flipping idiot' and berate them in front of the others, even if they are clumsy and acting a fool. You're lucky that Dotty wants you to succeed at this, otherwise you would have been fired already."

"Great, that makes me feel even better," Alex huffed.

"Hey, I was happy to be home and hanging out with Seymour for a change. Don't expect me to spare your feelings. If you weren't my boyfriend and Randy's brother, there is no way Dotty would be so lenient. But she truly believes that you'll be a great guide, once you figure out how to handle the guests. But if you can't do that during this tour, then you are out of a job."

Alex paled. "Oh, so it's that serious."

Lana's brows knitted together. "Yes, it is. Why do you think she sent me down? I'm not here on a volunteer basis; my being here is costing Dotty money."

He dropped his head for a moment before peeking back up at her, as if he was afraid to meet her eye. "So the incident with Jersey is the real reason why Dotty sent you down, not because of what happened to George?"

Lana frowned; she was sure that in her recent conversations with Dotty, her boss hadn't mentioned anything about George beyond that he was the lead guide on this trip, which he'd scouted out with Alex. She did remember that Dotty saw this recent hiring as a coup, because he'd spent the previous five years leading adventure tours in Central America for rival companies. Though Lana hadn't had the pleasure of meeting him in person yet, she was already impressed with him, as Dotty had raved about how George tapped into his existing network to quickly create several different tour itineraries crisscrossing the region.

"I have no idea what you are talking about," Lana admitted. "What happened to George?"

Alex ran a hand over the back of his neck. "That's why I was so stressed out when you arrived. I'd just gotten off the phone with the hospital about George's condition, and his leg is worse than we initially thought."

Lana felt her heart tighten. "What's wrong with George's leg? Can you start at the beginning, please?"

"This afternoon George fell into a pothole during a walk around downtown

San Jose and broke his leg in several places. It was pretty horrifying to see. He wants to be airlifted back to the States, but the doctor won't release him yet because the fractures are too severe."

Lana covered her mouth to suppress her gag reflex. "Alex, darling, I boarded my plane early this morning, so I was in the air when George had his accident. The incident with Jersey was reason enough for Dotty to send me down."

When Alex began to babble, she knew something was wrong.

"I did think it was strange how fast you got here. When Randy called to let Dotty know what had happened, she said that you were on your way. I figured she meant it figuratively, but then you appeared here so quickly."

Lana blew out her cheeks. "Dotty couldn't have known what was going to happen to George when she asked me, but the timing is serendipitous." She paused a moment. "Wait—did you say he fell into a pothole? Like in the street? Or did I mishear you."

"No, you heard right."

"How is that even possible? Why was he in the road?"

Alex snorted at her question. "It wasn't the road, but the sidewalk. You won't believe the terrible state many of them are in. I swear some of them are deep enough to lose a child in. To make matters worse, thieves steal storm-drain and manhole covers, too. You really have to remain alert when you're walking around the center."

"It doesn't sound like him breaking his leg is your fault, just a silly mistake and some bad luck. It's not like you had anything to do with his accident..."

The way Alex cringed made Lana's words catch in her mouth. "Oh no, what happened?"

"The holes in the sidewalks are hazardous, and we all knew that because he'd warned us repeatedly to watch our step. But he and I had gotten into an argument about how we could best reach a café, and when he turned around to snap at me, he fell into one. I didn't mean to distract him. If I had just let him decide how to get the group to the restaurant, instead of trying to force my opinion on him, he would not have fallen in."

That is probably true. Lana grimaced internally, not wanting to be too harsh with Alex, for fear of him closing down completely. "Darling, you're blaming yourself for no reason. It sounds like it could have happened to anyone. Does Dotty know how George's accident occurred?"

"I'm pretty certain she does. Randy had called to update her after we got him to the hospital. That's why I figured Dotty had told you already. I had just gotten off the phone with his doctor when Xavier began pelting me with questions, and then you arrived."

Lana shook her head. "No, Dotty hasn't messaged me about it. I guess she'd figured I would hear about it soon enough. Either way, it's a good thing I'm here now. So how can I help?"

"Well, now that George is down for the count, there's only you and Randy to lead the tour."

"And you, Alex!"

Her boyfriend pulled a face. Before she could call him on it, Randy's voice reverberated through the hotel café.

"Alex! What are you doing sitting around? It's time to get the group to dinner."

Though Lana couldn't see Randy's face, the tension in his voice was unmistakable. What the heck had happened this past week to make these two friendly and easygoing brothers act so crazy?

When Randy rushed into the restaurant and got a look at who Alex was sitting with, Lana swore his whole body seemed to react. His legs froze midstep as his eyes cast downwards and his cheeks flushed pink. "Hey, Lana. Dotty texted to let me know you were on your way. Man, you got here fast."

Instead of leaning in for a hug as she'd expected, Randy stayed well away. So Lana did the honors, carefully wrapping her old friend up in a warm embrace.

"Hey, Randy, it's great to see you. Dotty said you'd done her a big favor by flying down to help out with this tour. That was mighty nice of you to do that, especially since I can imagine Gloria was not thrilled with your decision."

Her words seemed to defuse the tension building up in Randy's body, and his rigid posture relaxed as his embrace tightened. "It's great to see you,

Lana." When he pulled back, his smile was warm and welcoming.

"So, I hear you two are in a bit of a jam, now that the senior guide is incapacitated. I'm here to help."

"Yeah, well, right now we need to get the guests into a minivan so we don't miss our dinner reservation. Would you join us? It's an easy ride over, and the dinner includes live music, so I doubt we'll need help wrangling the guests once we get there. Most importantly, it's supposed to be one of the best traditional restaurants in the San Jose area."

Lana's stomach grumbled its answer for all to hear. "Yes, please."

4

First Impressions

It was a short ride to their destination in Tarbaca on the outskirts of San Jose. According to the restaurant's website, Ram Luna prided itself on offering the best traditional cuisine, music, and dance that Costa Rica had to offer. Lana couldn't wait to dig in.

The sun was starting to set when they entered the establishment. Instead of taking them to a table placed inside, the server led them outside to the restaurant's rooftop terrace overlooking the city center.

When Lana stepped out onto the balcony, the sight before her momentarily took her breath away. To call the views of San Jose from the restaurant's terrace amazing was an understatement. They were just in time for sunset and watched as the buildings in the city and outlying areas changed color and hue as the sun slowly set. The massive field of clouds that stretched out over the city center lit up like slow-motion fireworks, gradually morphing from a sea of reds and yellows into pinks and purples.

The large, half-moon-shaped terrace provided plenty of space for the diners to enjoy the show nature provided. Most of her guests crowded up to the stone wall holding them back from tumbling off the steep cliff. Several vied for a place under the official "Ram Luna Viewpoint" marker, with the expansive view perfectly framed behind them.

From up here, it was easy to see that they were in the middle of a wide valley, with volcanoes and a mountain range flanking them. Once the sun set and darkness descended, the city's lights sparkled like diamonds, far off into the distance. It was a magical experience, one Lana was glad to have enjoyed firsthand.

After the sun was well and truly under, a waitress escorted them to a long table set at the back of the terrace. Lana was glad to sit outside tonight. The temperatures were still in the high seventies, and the breeze felt great.

After they got their guests seated in the dining area, Randy snapped his fingers. "Lana, I need to schedule our taxi ride back to the hotel and would like to show Alex how to do so. Do you mind watching over the group for a minute? I promise we won't be long."

"I know how to call a taxi company," Alex grumbled.

"Sure thing," Lana rushed to answer, seeing as her boyfriend's face was flushing red pretty fast. She stood on her tippy-toes and pecked him on the cheek before turning back towards the guests. Randy and Alex had to work out their own issues, she figured.

Lana stood for a moment inside the doorway to the restaurant, wondering what she was getting herself into. After a rough few months in her personal life and several deaths occurring on back-to-back tours, Lana had experienced a sort of mini-breakdown and ended up fleeing to Iceland in the hopes of clearing her head. That hadn't worked out how she had hoped, but the experience did make her realize that she was cut out to be a tour guide, after all. Dotty's invitation to scout out a few Asian routes before leading groups around Europe again was a gentle way for her to get back onto that travel horse without worrying about guests' safety.

But now she was back with a group and expected to lead them around a country she'd never visited. Lana knew one of the best ways to get to know the guests on a tour was to observe their interactions and listen to their conversations during a group dinner. Considering there were only nine guests, she figured one meal would be enough to get a feel for their personalities and quirks.

Instead of formally introducing herself straight away, she decided to top up their water glasses and listen in on their conversations first. Thanks to Dotty's descriptions of the guests—an unusual mixture of older scientists, students, and adventure-seeking marketers—she could easily put names to faces.

She started with the far end of the table, where four corporate-looking twentysomethings, all dressed in similar khaki shorts and T-shirts with designer logos, were seated. Lana wasn't certain how they had spent their afternoon, but they all smelt strongly of whiskey. Their rowdy laughs and random shoulder punches told her that it was time to get dinner on the table, pronto.

The quartet were employees of a technology company located in Fremont, close to Wanderlust Tours' offices. Dotty had asked their human resources manager, a good friend of hers, to suggest four of their twentysomething employees to participate in the initial run of the Costa Rica tour. So many had volunteered, they'd ended up drawing straws to decide who got to go.

According to Dotty, the four were the ideal target audience—wealthy, childless yuppies who loved to push themselves on their vacations so they had adventurous stories to tell at parties. Her hope was that they would love the Costa Rica tour so much, they would recommend it to all of their co-workers and friends.

Lana took her time filling their glasses, listening to their slightly slurred banter and drunken one-upmanship. Brad, Mike, Chet, and Dave—the four marketing gurus who'd won the trip—were unsurprisingly corporate in dress and attitude, and seemed to be talking primarily about their work and mutual co-workers. *I guess that's a disadvantage to traveling with colleagues; work is all that really binds you*, Lana mused. Yet by the way they'd positioned their bodies in relationship to the rest, it was clear they were not interested in mingling with the others, either.

Two empty chairs separated them from the geologists, Gregory and Cecile. The married scientists were sharing a bottle of chilled sauvignon blanc and were clearly trying to enjoy a romantic meal, despite their boisterous table companions.

Yet instead of ignoring the younger foursome and getting lost in each other's eyes, Gregory and Cecile glared at the group each time another round of laughter pealed out. The twentysomethings, on the other hand, didn't seem to notice the older couple.

Are they intentionally antagonizing the geologists? Lana wondered. Yet as she watched them interact, she didn't think the four marketers were acting maliciously. They were simply having a good time and were clearly not interested in taking the geologists' hopes for a romantic meal into consideration. Lana couldn't really blame them. It was probably just the age difference that was causing the problem, though it did highlight how different generations preferred to unwind, as well as the difference between traveling as a couple or with a bunch of buddies.

Lana wondered again about the target audience her boss wanted to entice. Once these "adventure tours," as Dotty loved to call them, had gotten off the ground, she assumed they would be only accessible to a younger crowd. At least, she hoped the adrenaline-infused trips would be marketed solely towards groups of buddies and colleagues, rather than couples seeking a romantic outing.

When Gregory started to make another fuss, Lana snuck a glance at the scientist. Dotty had informed her that the rather dapper looking fifty-something gentleman had become quite wealthy after inventing an app that proved invaluable to geologists worldwide. All Lana knew for certain was that it was some sort of database containing information about minerals found around the world, in turn making it easier for geologists to identify and classify them. Since he no longer needed to work to pay the bills, Gregory spent his days traveling the world and researching gemstones, accompanied by his wife and fellow geologist, Cecile.

She was dressed similarly to her husband, in a pair of khaki shorts and a cream-colored T-shirt that seemed to be tailored to her body. When Lana looked to Cecile's armpits, she was shocked to see that they were dry.

Lana had opted for a sundress in order to give her arms and legs a chance to breathe. San Jose was considerably hotter and more humid than Seattle, and her whole body was covered in a sheen of sticky sweat. But at least she wasn't trembling from the cold.

She ran her eyes over the couple again. It wasn't Gregory's neatly pressed and expensive-looking polo shirt or designer shorts that held her attention, but the age difference between him and his wife. She couldn't tell for certain, but would guess that Cecile was at least twenty years younger than her husband. According to Dotty, the pair had started dating shortly after his first wife—an archaeologist named Rowena—died last year. The pair married soon after.

When Cecile seemed to turn towards her, Lana averted her gaze, afraid of being caught staring, just as Xavier's booming voice grabbed her attention. There was one empty chair between the archaeologist and geologist, but that didn't stop him from projecting his voice, as if he was on stage.

While Xavier talked, Lana regarded the pudgy scientist. She knew Xavier was a respected archaeologist and university professor who had been leading digs in Central America for many years. He was obviously used to being out in the sun because his skin was deep brown, not tinged with red. His hair was thin but long and tied back in a tiny ponytail that ran down his back. His shorts and T-shirt were at least one size too small, forcing his belly to bulge out over the waistband. Even worse, the shirt was flecked with food stains and sweat marks, making her wonder when he had washed his clothes or body last.

Sitting across from Xavier were his two assistants, Sam and Jersey, both PhD students he was mentoring. Based on his gestures, he seemed to be explaining something to them, Lana presumed about this dig. The pair were dressed in khaki shorts and beige T-shirts similar to Xavier's, but theirs were clean.

Dotty had mentioned that the pair had already been in Costa Rica working on Xavier's site for a few weeks, before this tour began. Both were staying for the summer season, meaning they would be here until August.

While he spoke, Lana studied his two assistants. Sam was long and lanky, with shaggy blond hair framing his face. A chain of shells circled his neck, while his T-shirt told the world to "Just Chill." If she hadn't known he was here for a dig, she would have assumed he was here to surf.

The longer Xavier rambled on, the more Sam's relaxed smile turned into a smirk directed at Jersey. At first, Lana thought the young woman was listening intently to their boss. Yet after watching her a few seconds, she realized Jersey's eyes—almost hidden under the thick bangs of her short bob—were darting around the table. Lana hung around Jersey longer than necessary, because she wanted to get a feel for the woman who'd lodged such an angry complaint about her boyfriend. Unfortunately Jersey hadn't said much while Lana had made her way around the table.

Instead, Xavier held the floor. Though Lana had initially thought the senior archaeologist was lecturing his assistants, when she homed in on his words, she realized he was actually rambling on about the necessity of attracting more sponsors to his dig. The two younger people squirmed in their chairs as if they wished they could be anywhere else but here.

Yet Xavier didn't seem to notice and continued with his monologue. Lana was confused as to his reasons for doing so, until she realized he was rocking back and forth in his seat as he spoke, repeatedly glancing over at Gregory as he described the work his two assistants still had to complete this summer.

Dotty had told her that Xavier had decided to specialize in the stone spheres of Costa Rica after unearthing several in the Diquís Delta. When he'd had the chance to buy a plot of land that was supposed to be full of them, the university hadn't been able to extend him enough funding, forcing him to search for private donors and sponsors to help him further.

That was when he had reached out to Dotty—Lana's boss and his second cousin through marriage. The two distant relatives had briefly reconnected at a funeral, where Xavier had approached Dotty with his proposal as they were walking out of the church service. Emotionally raw from grieving her favorite aunt, she had agreed to help him out and had regretted that decision ever since.

Dotty had told Lana that he was back in Costa Rica to continue excavating a series of fields he'd purchased for the university he worked for, where the UNESCO-protected spheres had been found. Over the course of the past three years, he had unearthed hundreds of those stones and was now concentrating on preparing the site to be a cultural center dedicated to the Diquís people.

Despite all that she had already done for him, Xavier's dreams kept getting bigger, and his requests for more funding became increasingly frequent.

Three years on, Dotty was ready to cut the cord, but hated leaving him in a lurch. He was family, after all.

Which was why she'd convinced Gregory and Cecile, casual acquaintances she'd recently run into at a mutual friend's cocktail party, to join the tour. Dotty had told Lana that after the couple had told her about their upcoming research trip to Costa Rica and Nicaragua, she'd begged them to go on the trial run of this trip and evaluate it. Not only did they have extensive experience traveling through Central America, Dotty hoped that Xavier would charm their socks off to the point that they would want to invest in his project.

However, by the way the couple were making a point of ignoring the archaeologist, Lana was pretty certain Dotty's plan was backfiring so far.

After she'd made her way around the table, Lana chose to sit in between Sam and Cecile, and across from Xavier and Gregory. The archaeologist was still dominating the conversation and now talking loudly about the gift shop his team had recently begun construction on.

Dotty had told her so much about him and his fieldwork that Lana had already created a mental image in her mind. Yet now that she sitting here across from Xavier, she was having trouble separating her expectations from reality.

Unfortunately, her optimistic boss had failed to mention that in addition to being an esteemed archaeologist, Xavier was also a first-rate jerk. His tone dripped arrogance, and his posture made clear that he considered himself to be superior to those around him. No wonder his two assistants appeared to be uncomfortable.

Xavier snapped his fingers at a passing waitress. "One beer," he barked before leaning farther over the table and into Gregory's field of vision. When the geologist cringed, Lana cleared her throat loudly, hoping to distract Xavier's attention. It didn't work.

"As I was saying, once we get the gift shop finished, we can open the site to visitors. It's only a matter of time—and money, of course." He laughed boisterously as his table companions looked away.

Only after Lana cleared her throat for the second time did he deign to look in her direction.

"Who are you?" The way he glared at her was disarming. Was Xavier so self-centered that he had failed to notice her in the minivan? She wouldn't be surprised if that was the case. Still, Lana kept her most professional smile plastered on, in spite of his insolent tone.

Yet instead of answering him directly, she stood back up and raised her voice to address the entire group. "Hello, everyone! For those I didn't speak to on the ride over, I'm Lana Hansen, and I'm a guide with Wanderlust Tours. I'm here to help out with the rest of the tour, now that George has been injured."

"Wow, you got here fast. It's a good thing, too. That tall guide, Alex, has a real attitude problem. I already complained about him to your boss. Did she tell you?" Jersey said in an irritatingly high-pitched voice.

Lana groaned internally, grateful that Alex wasn't present to hear this. "She did mention that a raft had tipped over. Thank goodness everyone is alright. On past tours, there have been serious injuries as a result of similar incidents."

Luckily Lana didn't need to mention Jersey by name, or even that her carelessness had caused the situation in the first place. The young lady's mouth snapped shut, and her face reddened so quickly that Lana had to suppress a chuckle.

At the same time, Sam raised his beer glass to hide a grin.

Xavier nodded to her, as way of acknowledgment. "Well, Lana, I was just explaining to Cecile and Gregory what we are planning on selling in our gift shop. It's quite a diverse selection of locally produced crafts, but the focus is on the Diquís spheres, of course."

When the geologists remained silent, Xavier leaned over farther, butting his rotund belly against the tabletop. "I have the utmost respect for geologists. You wanna know why? Geologists and archaeologists are quite similar in the sense that we are the most patient, attentive, and detail-oriented of the exact sciences, traits required for those in our chosen professions to succeed." He raised his water glass in a toast, but neither geologist responded in kind.

Why does everything that comes out of his mouth sound degrading? Lana wondered. When she noticed Xavier was about to speak again, she intervened, hoping to stave off a verbal argument.

"You are excavating stone cannonballs, correct?"

Xavier slammed a fist onto the tabletop, rattling their drink glasses and cutlery. "No! Not correct. They are made of stone and are round, but that does not make them cannonballs."

Lana put one hand under her chin and leaned on it, in an attempt to look interested. "Huh, okay, what can you tell me about them?"

He narrowed his eyes at her. "This is exactly why I always travel with a small sphere in my luggage—it's easier to show one to an amateur such as yourself than try to explain their worth. It's a waste of my time, otherwise."

Xavier burped loudly before pushing his chair back from the table. "Tell you what, I'm going to hit the can. Sam and Jersey can tell you all about them. They might as well do something to earn their keep."

Lana felt her eyebrows shooting up, but managed to hold her tongue. She'd only just met the man but already felt sorry for Dotty that she was related to him, even if only by marriage. He was truly horrid.

5

The Mysterious Spheres of Costa Rica

As soon as Xavier was out of earshot, Cecile held out her hand. "Hi, Lana. I'm Cecile, and this is my husband, Gregory. That was a terrible way to be indoctrinated into our group. Most of us don't bite."

Lana laughed as she took her hand, glad that Cecile was able to make light of the situation instead of complaining about it. It was too bad that Alex hadn't been here to hear her response; he could have learned from her example.

Speak of the devil, Lana thought as she spotted Alex and Randy Wright shuffling out onto the terrace, heads close together. Based on their grim expressions, Lana bet that they'd had another disagreement. She sighed softly, telling herself that now was not the time to tackle the Alex problem again—not here in a busy restaurant in front of their guests. That conversation would be better held behind closed doors.

As soon as she waved them over, both men gave her smiles, albeit forced ones, and joined the group. The two brothers sat in between the four marketers and the geologists. Cecile nodded hello to the both of them, then turned her attention back to Lana.

"It's nice to meet you two. Dotty had mentioned that you are geologists—that's rather exciting."

Gregory laughed. "I don't know if exciting is the word I would use, but we do find it exhilarating to make a new discovery. Since my app took off and I no longer needed to work, we now travel the world for fun and do research into geological phenomena that interest us, instead of what would bring in the most sponsors and grants. It's liberating," Gregory said, quite breezily.

Lana's eyes lit up. "Is that why you were already in Costa Rica?"

"Indeed. We arrived a few weeks before this tour began so that we could get our transportation and housing organized for our next expedition. After this tour, we are heading out to a recently excavated jade mine used in pre-Columbian times. It could be where the jade imported into Costa Rica through trade was mined from. If we can test the chemical composition of the gems found there and compare them to those found in archeological digs in Costa Rica, we may be able to prove it."

Apparently Lana's reaction was too lackluster, because Cecile added, "There are no jade mines in Costa Rica, so proving that the jade found in ancient settlements originally came from Nicaragua would help prove the existence of a pre-Columbian trade route, similar to the Silk Road. It would be quite the coup in our world."

Gregory grabbed her hand and kissed it. "Cecile is an incredibly tenacious researcher and the only one brilliant enough to keep up with me. That's why I married her."

Though he said it as if it was a compliment, his words felt like a slap in the face. Yet Cecile only smiled. "I was lucky to have the best PhD supervisor that there is—you."

Gregory went pale and still until Cecile leaned over the table and puckered up. Gregory met her halfway and pecked her on the lips.

Lana wasn't one to judge love, but did wonder whether Gregory's being a multimillionaire had any influence on Cecile's decision to date a much older man.

"Of course, well done. At least, I hope it works out for you."

"I am certain it will. We met with the director of the Jade Museum on our first day in San Jose, and he is interested in sponsoring our research. Not financially—I don't need the money. But for the museum to publicly endorse our research would help open doors and ensure our findings reach a wider audience."

Sam sniggered behind his drink. When Gregory whipped his head up to face him, the assistant archaeologist didn't avert his eyes but seemed to challenge him to say something. Instead of doing so, Gregory looked away and took a swig of his drink.

"Rowena was right—you are a pompous jerk."

Gregory's face turned bright red. "Excuse me? How dare you speak to me like that. And how did you know my wife?"

Sam jutted out his chest, causing his shell necklace to rattle softly. "I'll speak to you however I please. She was my mentor during my master's degree, and I got to work on her last dig. Boy, did she talk a lot about you. It was quite an illuminating experience, in more ways than one."

Gregory held up his drink. "I'm glad to hear she was a good mentor to you."

"Oh, yes, we had many long talks about my research and our personal lives. We got to know each other pretty well. It's too bad they never arrested her murderer." Sam locked eyes with Gregory, almost as if he was challenging the older man to respond.

The geologist's eyes narrowed at him. "I know what you are trying to do, but it won't work. I had nothing to do with my wife's death. I loved her; why would I hurt her? Besides, you know she died of an infection; she wasn't murdered."

"You may not have killed her directly, but you hurt her more than you know with your actions," Sam hissed.

"Stop it, Sam! You have no idea what you are talking about," Cecile snapped.

"Is that true? Are you certain, Cecile?" he said, in a taunting voice.

Gregory pushed his chair back, screeching its legs across the tiled floor. "Excuse me, I must use the restroom."

"You can't run from the truth!" Sam called out as the geologist scurried away.

What is going on between them? Lana wondered. Hoping to end this dinner on a high note, she turned to face the young pair. "You must be Sam and Jersey. Is that right?"

Both nodded. Sam glared in Gregory's direction for a moment before turning to Lana. "Would you like to know more about the spheres we are excavating?"

"Yes, of course!" She picked up her water glass and swirled the ice blocks around, curious to hear more about the spheres Xavier had spent years of his life studying.

Sam leaned over the table. "Had you heard of the Diquís spheres before you came to Costa Rica?"

"No, never. I know very little about Central American or pre-Columbian cultures, but hope to rectify that situation during this trip."

"The Diquís were an indigenous culture that flourished between the years 600 and 1000 AD, before the Spanish conquest. Shortly after the Europeans arrived, the Diquís civilization disappeared. Anthropologists believe new diseases wiped them out, though the conquistadors' lances and swords may have played a part. Little remains of their chiefdom settlements, expect for their odd contribution to art—round spheres or orbs made of *gabbro*, a local stone similar to basalt. Locals called them *las bolas*—the balls."

"How intriguing. What makes them so special?" she responded cordially.

His eyes lit up. "Considering they were created by a civilization that's been wiped out, it's all speculation as to how they carved *las bolas*, and why. It's their unique and mysterious story that caused UNESCO to place their chiefdom settlements and spheres on their World Heritage list. Technically, they aren't allowed out of the country." Sam blushed and dipped his head, as if he was embarrassed by what he'd said.

Concerned she wasn't showing enough interest again, Lana pepped up her tone. "Are they decorated in any way? Or do you think they may have once been painted, like all those Greek and Roman statues?"

"No, they are free from any decoration or embellishment, which makes them even more of an achievement. Their makers had no way to disguise any faults, so each sphere had to be perfect."

"What do you think were they used for?"

"Some archaeologists believe they were maps of the heavens, used to read the stars and predict the seasons. Others believe they were nothing more than decorations for their homes and temples. Here are some photos of a few spheres we dug out last week. There is a small display in the Museo Nacional in the Bellavista Fortress in San Jose, but we have better ones at our site."

He picked his phone up off of the table and swiped past several images of a massive, perfectly round stone, half buried in a red-brown field. Jersey stood next to it, and it almost came up to her shoulder.

"Isn't that incredible?" Sam enthused.

"Oh, my, it is gigantic." Lana tried her best, but couldn't get behind his enthusiasm. Yes, it was quite large and round, which was in one sense impressive. But it didn't look like anything more than a gigantic shot put or cannonball to her.

Yet Sam smiled at the photo like a proud papa. "Many are, but they do come in all shapes and sizes. Some are small enough you could fit them in your pocket. The spheres are even more impressive in person, especially when you can see how perfectly round and smooth they are. I'm glad Xavier has decided to focus on preparing his site for visitors before the end of the season, but we have quite a bit of work to do before it will be ready to open."

"Oh, like what?"

"You'll see soon enough," Jersey sniped, joining the conversation in a strangely aggressive way. "We aren't really supposed to talk about our work; it's part of the confidentiality agreement we signed when we accepted the job. Remember, Sam?"

The young man blushed red. "Oh, yeah, I forgot. Sorry, Lana."

She felt duly rebuffed, but figured this was a good moment to switch subjects. She'd learned enough about the Diquís spheres for one night. "It's no problem. Thanks for showing me what you are excavating."

6

Live Music at Ram Luna

After Xavier returned to the table, the archaeologist tried once again to engage the geologists in a conversation about his dig. The way he described it, it seemed as if the pair didn't invest soon, they would miss out on an incredible opportunity.

Lana failed to see how. Dotty had poured money into Xavier's dig for three years, but so far he had accomplished few of his lofty goals. That was why she'd pushed him to start building the cultural center, as a way of generating income. Dotty had meant for him to do it with the money that she'd already donated, but Xavier apparently saw it as a green light to ask for more. Though she'd repeatedly said no, Lana feared that if her boss couldn't find another sucker to invest in his dig, she would feel compelled to continue her support.

Yet the chances that the geologists would be the ones to take over were growing slimmer with every word that came out of Xavier's mouth.

Thankfully a team of waitresses served them dinner before the scientists could get into a verbal tiff. The scents of spicy paprikas and slowly cooked beans made their way up to Lana's nose, causing her to salivate automatically. One waitress quickly named the many dishes, but she only caught a few of them and instead looked to the menu for enlightenment. Healthy portions of creole salad, beet salad, beef stew, chicken fajitas, fried cassava, and chicken empanadas filled their table. She still wasn't certain which dish was which, but it didn't really matter. Everything looked delicious.

After her guests had filled their plates, she scooped up a spoonful of everything. Yet before she could take her first bite, Xavier started up again, causing Gregory to groan loudly. Just as Lana wondered whether the geologists would ask to move to another table, a live band began to play, making conversation impossible.

She breathed a sigh of relief, glad to be able to focus on their scrumptious meal instead of having to play referee. Several bites later, her plate was clean, and she was ready for more. The spices used were so tangy, it made every bite a sensation for her taste buds. From their appreciative nods and delighted expressions, she dared to say her group agreed.

Once the band finished their second song, two dancers joined them on the terrace. The pair wore white frilly tops, blue belts, and long red skirts that reached the floor, fringed with white and blue stripes. Each held a sparkly blue fan, and they were adorned with choker necklaces and earrings in red, white, and blue. A glorious hairpiece made of flowers in the same color combination topped their tall buns. Lana watched appreciatively while they swung around the small space dancing the samba and then the macarena, their hips timed perfectly with the rhythm.

After wowing the diners with their skills, the pair descended the stage and began weaving through the crowd, pulling random diners out of their chairs to dance along. The professionals made the passes look so easy, but when they pulled a few guests up to dance along with them, none could keep up with the rhythm for long.

As soon as dessert was served, the act wound down and waved their goodbyes, to a resounding round of applause. Lana was thrilled to see that most of their guests were clearly enjoying the meal and entertainment. Only Xavier and Jersey wore sour expressions, but thankfully neither complained openly. Lana had a feeling neither was easy to please.

After they'd returned to the hotel and had all stepped out of the minivan, Xavier looked over at Alex. "When does the restaurant open for breakfast?"

When her boyfriend's jaw clenched, Lana lay a hand over his arm and responded for him. "At seven, and the minivan will pick us up at nine. You have plenty of time to enjoy a leisurely breakfast," she said as sweetly as she could.

"Excellent," Xavier grumbled before striding off into the hotel.

As she watched him waddle away, Lana couldn't help but think about how each tour group was a mixed bag of personalities. Whether or not everyone would get along was often the luck of the draw. In rare cases, the group meshed together so well, they almost preferred to lead themselves around and ignored the guides. Yet on most tours, there were a few clients who couldn't seem to read a watch, let alone a map. This kind of person tended to seek the guide's advice for pretty much everything—from when they should set their alarm clock, to which souvenir shops they should visit. It appeared this was one of the more typical tours.

After they'd gotten everyone into the hotel, Alex grabbed Lana's hand. "Fancy a drink?"

She pecked him on the cheek. "I do, but before I join you, I need to talk to Randy. We can still have a drink afterwards, if you want. I'll see you up in the room in a few minutes, okay?"

When Alex's lips pursed, Lana added, "Randy and I need to talk about the guests and several tour details—not you."

He nodded in agreement but didn't look happy about it. As much as it pained her to see him upset, now was the time to have a chat with her friend and fellow guide, not to worry about her boyfriend's fragile ego.

She rushed to catch up with Randy, thankfully still in the lobby and checking the reservations for tomorrow's minivan. After he'd received confirmation from the hotel's receptionist that everything was scheduled, he turned to her and raised an eyebrow.

Lana couldn't recall seeing such dark circles under his eyes before. "Hey, Randy. If you aren't too tired, could I buy you a drink? I'd love to talk about the guests and tour for a few minutes, so I can get a better grip on the group and agenda."

He ran a hand through his hair, but smiled as he did. "Sure, I'd like that. Why don't we grab a beer in the hotel bar?"

"Sounds great."

After they'd both been served a Cerveza Imperial, Lana began, "There seems to be quite a bit of tension within the group. What's happened so far to make everyone so edgy?"

"Oh, Lana, this tour is a hot mess. It's no wonder Alex is having trouble getting into the groove. But before we talk about the guests, I feel like I owe you an explanation. I didn't tell you that I was coming down to help Alex out, because he'd told me he hadn't been entirely truthful with you about how badly the first tour had gone. He lied because he didn't want you to know that he needed help."

Lana felt herself tensing up when she realized that not only had Alex been lying to her, but that Randy knew that he had. Yet this was a conversation she needed to have with her boyfriend, not his brother. So she sucked up her anger and set it aside for later, then waved a hand over her beer. "It's okay. I was surprised you hadn't mentioned that you were coming down, but Dotty said it was all so last-minute, I figured it had slipped your mind."

"Trust me, I didn't want to because things have been crazy busy at the bed and breakfast, but Dotty didn't feel comfortable sending Alex on this tour without my supervision. She figured brotherly love would solve everything, but I think it's making it worse. He is my older brother, after all, and he is definitely not appreciating me constantly correcting him. It doesn't help that I've been leading tours either up Mount Rainier or for Wanderlust for most of my adult life. Leading groups comes naturally to me, but unfortunately not to Alex. His customer service skills stink."

Lana cringed at his comment. "Do you think he could be a good guide, once he gets into the swing of things?"

Randy took a long swig of his beer, instead of answering immediately. "Honestly, it's hard to tell. From what George told me, he did just fine during the scouting trip and got along well with their business contacts. But the guests' repetitive questions are clearly grating on Alex's nerves, and he's having trouble making small talk with any of them. Frankly, I get the feeling that he loved the freedom that the scouting trip offered, but is far less interested in being tied to the same group of people and following a set agenda."

"Oof. That's going to be a problem. Those are two key components to keeping the group happy—answering their sometimes frivolous questions and sticking to the itinerary."

"Exactly. Based on his behavior so far, I'm not even sure if Alex really wants to be a guide. Your arrival down here should be a wakeup call for him. It is important for him to understand that what he did was wrong and that Dotty isn't discounting Jersey's complaints, despite the fact that they are rather absurd."

Lana let her beer fall to the table with a thud. "I'm glad you brought that up. Alex told me the gist of what had happened, but did you witness their tiff firsthand?"

Randy chuckled. "I'm afraid we all did. The rafting guides had split our group up into two boats, but we were pretty close together. I was with the geologists, and Alex was in the same raft as the three archaeologists. If you haven't already noticed, Jersey is downright clumsy and uncoordinated. She couldn't get the hang of rowing and kept banging her paddle into the others, when they were trying to row in sync. Alex had made a few comments, yet nothing that could be construed as rude. But after she tipped over the raft, he lost it."

"And that was when he called her a 'flipping idiot.'"

Randy blushed. "Yep."

Lana blew out her cheeks, knowing she didn't have to point out the stupidity of Alex's remark to him. Yet discussing her boyfriend's mistake really wasn't why she'd wanted to meet up with Randy. "That is a bummer. Thanks for explaining why Alex exploded, although I do agree that Jersey's clumsiness does not justify his remark. Now, can you enlighten me as to why the geologists seem to dislike Xavier?"

"Oh, that's easy. Xavier has been pushing them to sponsor his dig and gift shop since he arrived. They are clearly not interested, and the more he talks about it, the more irritated they seem to get. During our day trip in San Jose, they made a point of avoiding him—I mean literally standing up and leaving the room whenever he entered. Since then, it hasn't gotten much better."

"That's too bad. Hey, speaking of which, what did you think of the capital?

My taxi driver was auditioning for Formula One, so most of it was a blur."

Randy chuckled. "San Jose is pretty nice. It's a sunny, bustling capital city with that Spanish colonial-era style of architecture. It is always satisfying to see palm trees growing in a city center. I liked all of the fountains because it's nice to cool off in their spray. And there is a ridiculous amount of statues—I can't recall the last time I saw so many in one city center. But most are well-executed so it wasn't a torture to keep running across them."

Lana grinned, knowing that Randy was not particularly fond of artwork. However, she was already looking forward to wandering around the city center and seeing the many statues—at least, as long as she kept an eye out for holes in the sidewalks.

"That sounds pretty great. I can't wait to see it, when we go back for the Independence Day celebrations."

"Yeah, that's going to be a hoot. The city center is already covered with red, white, and blue decorations, and the parades are supposed to be a riot of color and music."

"Fantastic! Now you're getting me excited about it, too. I guess we'll just have to watch out for potholes while we party."

Randy grimaced. "You heard about George already?"

Lana nodded.

"It was pretty gruesome. I do hope the city makes a point of covering them up before the celebrations begin."

"Me, too. What did the guests think of San Jose?"

"They seemed to enjoy themselves. Gregory, in particular, loved San Jose—or at least his visit to the Jade Museum. He wouldn't stop talking about it after we met up again. We all visited that first, then he and Cecile met with the director while we went over to the neighboring National Museum. That's where they housed some of the stone spheres Xavier has been excavating. It was his request to go because he wanted his two assistants to see the displays, and so that we could learn more about their cultural significance."

Lana thought back on Sam's photos, wondering whether they were more impressive in person. "What did everyone think of them?"

Randy frowned, something he rarely did. "There is a row of six large stones in the museum's garden and a small information board about them. That's it. To be honest, after all the buildup, the display was rather mundane, and even the two assistant archaeologists seemed underwhelmed. The four bros chuckled when they saw the display, which put Xavier in a bad mood instantly. Yet, I couldn't fault them for it."

"That's good to know."

"I do have to say that it was probably better that the geologists weren't there to make snide remarks about the spheres. Frankly, this entire tour would be far more pleasant if Xavier would stop rambling on about needing more sponsors for his dig. I mean, we get it already."

Lana nodded, taking in what Randy had to say. "And what about the four marketers—Brad, Mike, Chet, and Dave?"

"The four bros?" Randy chuckled again. "They call each other 'bro' so often, I've kind of dubbed them that. They seem nice enough and do get along with Alex, which is refreshing. The only problem is that they keep getting injured."

Lana cocked her head at him. "Do you mean that they keep having bad luck, or is there something else going on?"

"No, it's more that during every activity they either pull a prank on each other that goes horribly wrong or push themselves too hard, and then they end up with nasty cuts and bruises. I keep having to restock the first aid kit, just to keep up with their injuries."

Lana's eyes narrowed. "What have they done?"

Randy puffed out his cheeks. "Quite a bit, actually, but the best example I can think of happened during a hike up a steep trail that we'd taken after the rafting trip went wrong yesterday. At some point, Chet pushed Brad into a tree—he claimed as a joke. But he pushed him so hard, Brad ended up missing the tree and sliding off the trail and down a sharp incline, instead. It took us an hour to get him back up, and then another thirty minutes to pull out the many thorns he'd managed to pick up and bandage his wounds. Chet apologized profusely, but that doesn't change the fact that he pushed his buddy down a hill covered in thorny shrubs."

"Oh, jeez, that's not really good for the group comradery," Lana grumbled.

"No, it is not, and they are pushing our limits as guides, too," Randy said, emphatically. "I have no medical training; none of us do! Sure, Dotty requires us all to take first aid and CPR training, but that doesn't qualify us to set broken bones or recognize a fractured limb out in the field. I think Brad may have torn a ligament in his arm during his tumble down that hill, but he may have fractured it. We won't know for certain until he gets it checked by a doctor. Which he refuses to do in Costa Rica, so he's on his own, as far as I'm concerned."

"Why does he refuse?"

"In his eyes, it's a third-world country, and he just assumes the medical care will be inferior to what he'd receive in America."

Lana's jaw dropped. "What a snob. There are so many Americans who fly down to Central America to receive medical treatment because they can't afford the same operation in an American hospital."

"I know, but these guys are only used to the finest of everything. Brad says his arm doesn't hurt that much, and I can't force him to receive medical treatment. Frankly, I'd be happy to send him on the next plane home—him and his buddies. Unfortunately, they remind me so much of the corporate groups I used to get on the Mount Rainier trips."

Lana cocked an eyebrow at him. "What is that supposed to mean?"

"The hikes I led were popular with employees of several local tech companies, and I ended up guiding quite a few groups of young men who remind me of the four bros. Because they got rich by being great with computers, they seem to have this idea that they can succeed in anything—including climbing a mountain without training for it first."

Lana gasped. "You're kidding, right?"

"I wish I was. We required a basic knowledge of climbing equipment and practices, and we made them sign waivers attesting to such, but there was no way to really test their fitness levels before we set out. To make matters worse, those kinds of guests generally didn't listen to my orders and pushed themselves too far. On several, none made it to the top."

"Yikes, that's not a good sign. From what Dotty told me, the four bros are pretty much the ideal target audience for these new, adrenaline-filled tours."

"I know; that's what worries me. Honestly, up on Rainier if someone got hurt because they didn't listen, I had a hard time feeling sorry for them and could easily shrug it off as their own stupidity. It was when they brought other clients into problems that I got angry. So far, the four bros haven't put anyone else in harm's way, but it almost feels like it's sheer luck that it hasn't happened yet."

"If we get more of these kinds of groups, we may have to require additional travel insurance."

Randy chuckled. "That might be the best solution."

When he tried to hide a yawn with the back of his hand, Lana knew it was time to wrap this conversation up so they could both hit the sack.

"One more question, then I'll let you sleep. What can you tell me about Xavier's other assistant—Sam?"

The smile that instantly appeared on Randy's face when she mentioned the young man's name told her enough.

"Sam seems like a great guy, just a little young and overly enthusiastic, is all. He's still got that naiveté of youth that makes him see the world as black-and-white, and tends to say whatever comes up in his mind. I don't mind so much, but he has rubbed a few of the guests the wrong way. It's a trait that might get him in trouble someday, if he doesn't grow out of it."

Lana chuckled, thinking back to how passionate she'd been in her twenties, and how age had mellowed her out. "I'm sure he will."

"But it is refreshing to meet someone so honest and sincere. He's a sharp contrast with Jersey and Xavier. Those two act as if all of their conversations about their dig are top secret. Which is silly, considering they usually hold them in the hotel lobby where anyone can listen in."

"That explains a lot. However, I also noticed some tension between Sam and the geologists during dinner. Do you know anything about that?"

Randy's gaze turned upwards, as if he was trying to recall anything untoward or unusual. "Gosh, now that you mention it, when we met up in the lobby that first night, Sam seemed surprised to see Gregory, but I didn't have the idea that Gregory recognized him."

"Did you ever find out why Sam reacted like that?"

"Yeah, I did. If I remember correctly, Gregory's first wife was Sam's supervisor for a research project and they were quite close."

"That's odd. Sam made it clear at dinner that he doesn't think much of Gregory, though he didn't specify why," Lana said.

"That is strange. His dead wife must have said some pretty nasty stuff about Gregory."

Lana thought back to the dinner and how Sam had done his best to bait Gregory, who in turn had ignored him. "Okay, that's good to know. Hopefully they will come to some sort of truce before the end of the tour."

When Randy tried unsuccessfully to hide another yawn, Lana put a hand over his and squeezed. "Thanks for catching me up. What do you say we head back up to our rooms? I can be on call tonight, if you want."

In Lana's experience, guests tended to have unusual emergencies in the middle of the night, usually the kind that needed to be solved immediately. Which was why one guide was always "on call."

Randy's smile lit up the room. "That would be wonderful. Gloria's ticked off that our FaceTime conversations keep getting interrupted by needy guests. I know she'd appreciate it, too."

"Then it's settled. Now, should we take the stairs or elevator?"

"I'm pretty pooped. Would you mind if we took the lift?"

"Not at all."

After they had said their goodnights, Lana turned left down the hallway towards Alex's room. When her boyfriend answered her soft knock, she draped herself over the doorway and smiled coyly up at him. "Dotty assumed that I could bunk with you. Do you mind?"

His wolfish grin as he pulled back the door was answer enough. "Not at all!"

She kicked the door closed with one heel and fell into his arms. When Lana nuzzled against his chin, the stubble sent tingles down her spine. "I know we should talk about the tour and the guests, but it's been too long since I've seen my boyfriend. Can we forget about work for a few hours? If we can get up early and talk before breakfast, I'd be satisfied."

"I'll set the alarm for six a.m. Is that acceptable?"

Lana wriggled out of his grip and sprung onto the bed. "More than. Now, come here, you."

"Yes, ma'am." Alex grinned that adorable lopsided grin of his, before joining her.

7

White Lies

Thursday—Day Five of the Wanderlust Tour, Diquís Cultural Center and Sarchi

The next morning, Alex was in a much better mood than he had been the previous day. Lana only hoped he remained so, once the guests showed up.

When they'd slipped into a booth at the back of the breakfast hall at seven, she was glad to see that none of their clients were present. This was a chat she'd prefer to keep private.

After finishing their first cup of coffee, Lana tried to figure out how to start the conversation, but luckily Alex did it for her.

"I think I need to tell you what really happened during the first tour, before we start to deal with this one."

Lana leaned back into her chair, wondering what she was about to hear. Hopefully, it would be the truth this time. She kept her voice even, despite the feelings of betrayal that surfaced, thinking about how he had lied to her again. "That sounds good. I must say, because you'd said that the scouting trip went well, I was shocked when Dotty told me that you were so stressed out during the first tour that George didn't think you were fit to lead this second one."

Alex ran a hand through his wavy hair. "Yes, well, there were mitigating circumstances. The clients on that first tour were a group of young environmental activists that George knew. It was our trial run of the new tour in Mexico that he'd sketched out, which is why Dotty had asked him to invite his friends, instead of having us leading around paying guests."

Lana nodded along, signaling that she was listening. When he dropped his head and stared into his coffee cup, she had a nasty feeling that she wasn't going to like what he had to say next.

"They were as fanatic as many of the younger Earth Warriors were, which wouldn't have been a problem, except one of them figured out that I'd taken part in some of the Earth Warriors' more daring actions and tried to recruit me to their cause. When they acted like they weren't going to take no for an answer, I guess I got a little freaked and lashed out verbally. With George's help, we were able to talk it through, but I didn't really feel comfortable around them after that, and I got the sense that they felt the same way."

"That's horrible! No wonder you were stressed out during the tour." Yet, underneath her outward concern, Lana was fuming. They had recently worked through a lot of issues, almost all of which revolved around Alex not being able to tell her the whole truth about a situation. Specifically, he'd gotten sucked into working with a militant environmental organization called the Earth Warriors several months earlier, and that had ended quite badly.

Lana tried to suppress her anger, knowing she needed to get to the crux of the matter before Alex clammed up, but she couldn't contain her frustrations any longer. "Why couldn't you have trusted me enough to tell me the truth about Mexico? After all you'd gone through with the Earth Warriors and the police investigation, I would have understood."

Alex sighed but didn't make eye contact. "Technically, I didn't lie; I just didn't tell you everything that was going on."

"No, let's not play semantics. You tried to deceive me into thinking everything was fine and dandy, which qualifies as lying."

Alex hung his head. "You're right. I'm sorry. It was my first gig, I felt like I was messing everything up, and I couldn't bear to tell you. I wanted you to be proud of me, not have to deal with another one of my messes."

Lana blew out her cheeks, knowing she couldn't let herself get into a tizzy right now. In a few minutes' time, she expected the first guests to roll in.

"Alex, during the altercation with the environmental group, did you call any of them nasty names or say anything that could be deemed as inappropriate?"

"No! I did manage to hold my tongue during that trip. But that was why I avoided them after our argument; I was worried I might say something I would regret if we did get into another quarrel. Unfortunately, George then got upset with me for not interacting with them, as I should have if they were paying guests. Looking back, George did have to carry the whole tour, because I wasn't able to handle the bookings or administration. That must be why he complained to Dotty about me, and why she decided to send Randy down to try to help me."

"So why aren't you letting Randy help you?"

"He's my little brother! And to make matters worse, Randy is so caring and considerate of the guests—he's the perfect tour guide, which makes me even angrier that I can't emulate him. I know Dotty meant well, but he's the last person I want telling me what to do. Nor do I want to have to learn the ropes from my girlfriend. Honestly, Lana, it might have been better if Dotty had sent a stranger down, instead of you two."

Lana could feel her blood boiling. "Alex, listen to me very carefully. Randy and I are literally your last hope. Unless you can figure out how to treat our clients with respect before this tour ends, your career with Wanderlust Tours will be over before it even begins. Do you understand?"

Alex paled as he nodded.

"I think the first topic we need to tackle is customer relations—that seems to be the crux of the problem. I know at your past job, the workshop participants raved about your winning personality. Don't laugh, I saw it mentioned in several reviews. So what's going on during these tours that is making you crazy?"

"It's the guests asking the same question over and over again. Especially when it's something simple like what we have planned today. Even when I email them the itinerary again or print them off another copy, they still find it necessary to ask me, instead of looking it up themselves."

Lana threw back her head and laughed. "That's because they are on vacation, not at work. This is a whole different kind of client than those you gave corporate workshops to. They were there on orders from their bosses to take your course and report back. Of course they were attentive and interested—their job depended on it."

Alex's face was a wash of emotions. Clearly he had not yet considered that possibility.

"And I hate to tell you, but it's not going to get better—most guests ask me the same questions on a daily basis. It gets under my skin sometimes, too, but I know there's no point in calling them out on it. They usually pay absurd amounts to be able to travel with Wanderlust, after all."

"I bet you smile and politely answer them, as if it was the first time they asked, don't you?" The hostility in Alex's voice set Lana on edge.

"Yes, of course; that's what tour guides do."

His laugh was bitter, worryingly so. "I can't do this right now."

Before she could react, he pushed back from the table and strode out of the dining room, just as the first guests arrived for breakfast.

"Great, that went well," Lana mumbled as she watched Alex disappear into the lobby. Instead of chasing after her boyfriend, she stood and smiled at her clients, before offering Gregory and Cecile coffee, as Dotty would expect any Wanderlust Tours guide to do.

8

Stick to our Story

The moment Lana stepped outside the hotel, the sun pricked at her skin, reminding her of the necessity of applying suntan lotion. Because she'd left Seattle so quickly, she hadn't had time to shop for any. *Come to think of it, a one-piece swimsuit and shorts would come in handy for the sea kayaking and swimming stops listed on the itinerary,* Lana realized. A shopping trip was definitely in order.

She hid a soft burp behind her palm, hoping she wouldn't feel so bloated for the entire bus ride. She'd eaten far too much breakfast, but didn't regret it. The plate of *gallo pinto*—a traditional breakfast of black beans, sour cream, egg, and rice—was a sensation of flavors and spices, and she'd savored every bite.

After breakfast, she and Randy had circled the hall, asking the group to grab their day packs and meet them outside. She spotted most of the guests already standing next to a makeshift bus stop a few feet from the hotel's entrance. Lana presumed it had been placed there as a meeting point for the many minivans shuttling tourists from one destination to another.

Standing at the back of the group was Alex, doing his best to not make eye contact with the others. Lana had to suppress a wave of irritation when she caught sight of him. He hadn't shown his face since he'd stormed off, and she was beginning to wonder whether he was even going to join the tour today. As glad as she was to see that he'd showed up, she did hope that his mood had improved; otherwise this was going to be a long and trying day.

The only clients missing were the four marketers. They'd gone clubbing last night and had returned at around three in the morning, singing off-key as they wandered the hallways in search of their rooms. Based on how low their heads were hanging and the amount of coffee she'd seen them consume during breakfast, Lana figured they were all nursing major hangovers. Before she could go back inside and call up to their rooms, the foursome shuffled outside, groaning and moaning. Luckily they had three hours to sleep on the bus before they reached their final destination for the day—the Monteverde Cloud Forest.

Now that their group was complete, Lana moved on to her next task. While Randy confirmed their hotel reservations and tickets for the tour they were planning on doing that evening, she and Alex were supposed to check that everyone had brought a daypack with them because they were going to spend the night at an eco-hotel in Monteverde. Considering she couldn't really rely on her boyfriend to do his job at the moment, she quickly scanned the group, noting that everyone seemed to have a backpack or small suitcase with them.

Her tasks now complete, Lana looked up the road to check whether the bus happened to be heading their way. She didn't see their transportation but did notice that Xavier had answered his phone, then shot off into the parking lot. After a few seconds of silence, he screamed into his phone, "They have no right to audit me!"

His two assistants, Jersey and Sam, both looked quite concerned as they watched their boss pace the asphalt.

"Do you think they are going to officially interview all of us?" Sam asked Jersey, his voice trembling.

"Probably. Just stick with our story and you'll be fine."

Lana's ears pricked up at Jersey's words. What did she mean by "stick to our story"?

"Of course I recall the possibility of an audit being mentioned in the contract that I signed, but I had expected the university to have more faith in me and this project," Xavier bellowed.

After listening for a few more seconds, his face flushed. "Your suggestions are ludicrous, and the audit will prove that." He hung up so suddenly that Lana doubted that his conversational partner had had a chance to respond.

Xavier seemed to momentarily turn in on himself, pinching his nose and hunching his shoulders. Lana could only assume he was trying to process what sounded like a nasty conversation. Her curiosity piqued, she made a point of remaining close to Sam and Jersey, hoping he would explain to his assistants what had happened. Sooner than expected, her patience was rewarded.

When Xavier walked back over, the color had returned to his face, and he stood a little straighter.

"What was that all about? Is the board of directors going forward with the audit?" Sam asked.

"Yes, they are. It's an enormous waste of time and resources, of course, but they have already started the process."

Sam and Jersey looked to each other, their expressions grim. Yet before either could respond, a 4x4 minivan pulled up to the hotel curb. Lana hadn't seen anything quite like it. It seemed to offer the roominess and comfort of a van, but with a wider chassis and larger wheels that could presumably handle any terrain.

The driver shut down the engine and sprung out, yelling as he did. "Wanderlust Tours?"

When Lana raised her hand and waved, he bowed his head as he crossed over to her. "I apologize for being so late. Traffic is terrible today because they've closed off several roads in preparation for the Independence Day celebrations."

She put on a comforting smile, wanting the driver to be calm before he drove them across a series of hectic freeways and mountainous passes. "That's fine, we're not in a rush. Everyone is here, and we're ready to go whenever you are."

He nodded once, but Lana could see his expression mellow as he took in her words. Satisfied their driver was relaxed enough to do his job, she waved for her group to get in.

The van was quite spacious and offered seating for twenty. She relaxed into one of the plush chairs at the back and sighed in satisfaction. Alex plunked down next to her, but he still seemed to be in a funk and didn't make eye contact. Instead of stressing about it, Lana decided to forget about him and enjoy the ride.

However, Xavier had other ideas. As soon as they pulled out of the driveway, he turned to address Gregory, seated in the row behind him. "Did I mention that we've already received funding from several private investors, as well as a few governmental organizations? Last I checked, we have seventeen sponsors on board. So if you and Cecile want to talk to any of the others before investing, I can put you in contact with them."

Lana frowned at his words. Dotty had repeatedly mentioned that she was his sole patron, which was why she was so desperate to find another investor to help lighten her financial load. Yet if he had already secured a plethora of sponsors, as he was clearly implying that he had, then why was he still pushing Dotty to give him more? And where was all this money going to?

When Xavier launched into a monologue about the five main reasons why Gregory and Cecile should invest in his dig, instead of another Central American archeological site, the couple finally let their pent-up frustration free.

"Will you give us a break? No one in this van is interested in investing in your dig—especially not Cecile or I," Gregory clarified.

Xavier sucked on his teeth as he stared at the geologist. Lana could almost see the wheels of his mind turning as he sought the perfect comeback, before he popped out with, "Did they ever figure out how your first wife died?"

His concerned tone didn't mesh with the twinkle in his eye.

Gregory recoiled. "How did you know my wife? I don't recall ever meeting you."

Xavier smiled. "I don't think we ever did meet. Your wife and I were colleagues; she sat in the office two doors down from mine. We weren't close, but considering where I worked, I was privy to all the gossip surrounding her mysterious death. Are you certain you don't want to invest in the gift shop, perhaps in her memory? The story died down, but I never did hear if her death was an accident or not."

"Those horrid rumors aren't true—I did not harm my first wife!" Gregory declared, half rising out of his seat.

Before their quarrel could escalate, Lana decided to intervene. "Gentlemen. Who is looking forward to the zip line tour of the cloud forest?"

Gregory looked down at the plump archaeologist and sneered. "Is there a weight limit? I don't know if Xavier will be able to ride it."

"Why, you slimy little—"

When Xavier leaned over the chair, as if he wanted to throttle Gregory, Lana clapped as loudly as she could. Both men looked at her in shock, startled by her unexpected action. "Say, Xavier, what do you think of the hotel in San Jose?"

"It's adequate for our needs."

Lana suppressed a snort. Adequate? The hotel was one of the most expensive in San Jose. She wondered where he was used to staying and whether he was using the other sponsors' money to pay for his lodgings. "Oh, my boss, Dotty Thompson, told me your budget was quite sparce and left no room for luxury. That was why she invited you and your team on this tour—as a treat."

Lana knew it really wasn't her place to speak to Xavier in that way, but his haughty attitude was really grating on her nerves, and she couldn't help but knock him down a notch.

"The old girl must be mistaken. It was nice of Dotty to organize this, but the hotel is quite similar to the accommodations we've been staying in."

When Sam burst out in laughter, Jersey elbowed him.

Sam must think Xavier is acting pompous and ungrateful, too. I wonder what Dotty will think when she hears about the other sponsors and Xavier's luxurious lodgings, Lana thought. Not pleased, she bet.

"Dotty also mentioned that she had funded the dig we are going to visit tomorrow. What did your other sponsors contribute to?"

Xavier smiled. "Dotty *helps* to fund the site, that is true. She's one of several investors who are helping me to bring my vision to life. It's expanded somewhat since I submitted my original plan to the university, which is why

I've reached out to other parties over the years."

Lana cringed inwardly, knowing this information was going to make her boss quite unhappy. As much as she wanted to call Dotty now and tell her everything, Lana knew it would be better to do so after she'd seen the site. She wondered again how far along Xavier really was with the excavation and construction of the cultural center. Her gut told her that he was probably lying about more than just the number of sponsors.

9

No Place For Lovers

After defusing the scientists' argument, Lana poked Alex gently in the side and wriggled her eyebrows. When he suppressed a chuckle with his palm, she couldn't resist pecking him on the cheek.

Seconds later, a shriek rose from the back seat. "No wonder you keep defending him—you're lovers! He should have been fired immediately for talking to me like that during the rafting trip."

It was Jersey, now standing up in her seat and pointing back at the pair.

When Alex's jaw tightened, Lana groaned in frustration. "I'll take care of this."

She moved up the aisle towards Jersey, yet before she could speak, the young woman held up her palm. "I'm not interested in hearing your excuses. At least now I know why my complaint has not been taken seriously."

"That's not true, Jersey. Dotty did take your complaint seriously, which is why I was sent down to help out on the tour. Unfortunately, there were no other guides available. Although Alex shouldn't have reacted so forcefully after the rafting incident, there were mitigating circumstances, which is why he has not been fired. Our being in a relationship has nothing to do with it."

Jersey blew out her cheeks. "It's a good thing this trip is free; otherwise I would lodge a protest with the Better Business Bureau about Wanderlust Tours."

When she threw her arms over her torso and dropped into her seat again,

Lana turned back to Alex and rolled her eyes.

"Is our being in a relationship a reason for her to complain again?" Alex whispered, once she'd rejoined him.

"She can complain all she wants, but Dotty knows we are in a relationship."

"True. Though it might be best if we don't kiss in front of our group again."

Lana laughed, then covered her mouth with her hand to suppress the sound. "Agreed. From now on, kissing and cuddling are only allowed in the privacy of our hotel room."

She resisted laying her head on his shoulder and instead focused on the spectacular views outside their window. On the way to Monteverde, they caught glimpses of waterfalls, cavorting monkeys, many exotic birds, and towering trees the likes of which she'd never seen.

The mountain passes were hairier than she'd expected, forcing their driver to take it slow on some of the sharper turns. Their van climbed higher and higher, until tendrils of mist began to float by their window.

"Oh my gosh, we are really driving into the clouds, aren't we?"

Alex squeezed her hand. "I guess we are. It's pretty amazing."

Too soon, Randy leaned over his chair's backrest and nodded at his watch. "We're about twenty minutes out."

"Great. I'm going to grab another bottle of water from the cooler at the front. Do either of you want one?"

Both brothers shook their heads.

"Okay, be back in a jiff."

The bus hit a deep pothole just as Lana stood, causing her head to bonk against the roof. Randy had mentioned that many roads were poorly maintained, but she hadn't realized just how bad they were. She stumbled a few steps forward before stopping to rub at the swelling bump.

When she did, Lana could overhear Jersey, Sam, and Xavier's conversation. The two assistants were leaning over the backs of their chairs so they could see what Xavier had in his lap as they talked. Lana assumed they were discussing their next steps on the dig, but this conversation didn't sound like the rest.

"The Costa Rican government has sent over another list of addresses. We are going to need a flatbed truck, a crane, and lots of rope. We have six sites to visit, but luckily they are all located in the same region. A week should give us enough time to excavate everything and transport them back. The government barely pays enough to cover the rentals, so try to keep it cheap, okay? Let's start by asking our local connections if they can help us get a good deal."

Xavier's words didn't make any sense to Lana. Had he said *transport the spheres back*? Wasn't the point of excavating a site to leave as much as possible in place? Lana was pretty certain scientists called that *in situ*. And what did the Costa Rican government have to do with this?

Whatever it was, she doubted Xavier would answer her honestly if she did ask him about it. Which was why she decided to try to get a look at whatever was in the archaeologist's lap.

Lana kept rubbing her head as she shuffled closer. It turned out to be a map of Costa Rica with several red dots marked on it, clustered together in the south.

Unfortunately, Jersey must have noticed, for she sprung up and blocked Lana's path. "Excuse me, what do you think you are doing?"

"Going to get a bottle of water?" Lana answered in as innocent of a tone as she could muster.

"Then why are you standing there listening in on our conversation? Are you a spy for another university?"

"No, I really am a tour guide, and I don't know anyone who would be interested in hearing about your site. Your secrets are safe with me."

Jersey studied her intently, until Sam sighed. "Give her a break, Jersey. You'll have to forgive my colleague, Lana. Archeological excavations are fairly cutthroat because there is only so much funding to go around. That's why we prefer to keep our intel to ourselves," he explained.

Lana nodded solemnly. "I understand. I promise I won't tell anyone about your dig."

10

Zip-lining through Cloud Forests

Lana readjusted her helmet and shifted her legs, trying to get used to the tight straps now circling her thighs and waist.

The group was standing close to a wooden platform built atop a small outcrop, ready to start its first adventure of the day—a zip line tour of the cloud forest of Monteverde. Lana gulped as she looked out over the canopies of these skyscraper-tall trees they were about to zip through.

Soon after arriving at the eco-lodge, the group had walked over to the zip line company's headquarters. After a short safety lecture, they'd gotten geared up fairly quickly. Her guests were amazed at the complexity of the harnesses they were required to wear, and by how difficult they were to don correctly. Three straps on their waistbands connected to one C-clamp, which was attached to another long strap that would clip onto the zip line. Their guides had checked that everything was correctly placed and connected before leading them out of the hut and to the starting point.

During the short yet glorious walk to the first platform, Lana could already see the guests relaxing. The jungle was so beautiful. Thanks to the sounds of monkeys screeching and birds singing, Lana felt as if they were walking through a nature documentary.

By the time they'd reached their starting point, everyone was smiling. It may have helped that Xavier was trailing far behind as he huffed and puffed his way towards the first platform, making it impossible for him to dominate the conversation.

One by one, they ascended a short flight of stairs up to a wide wooden platform built against a massive tree trunk. From up here, it looked like the thin black cable they were supposed to clip onto disappeared into the clouds.

The geologist had rushed to be the first, dragging his nervous-looking wife behind him by the hand. The guide helped Gregory clip onto the zip line, explaining to the rest how to open and close the clamp as he did. When the geologist pushed off from the platform, he yelled out a "wahoo" so loudly, birds of all sorts took flight, squawking their displeasure as they went.

Cecile followed suit, albeit more quietly, barely letting out a peep as she flew through the leafy branches before disappearing into the mist.

Next up were the four marketers, all jostling to be the first of their group to go. After they'd all zipped off into the distance, the archaeologists were up.

When the guide got a good look at Xavier, his eyes hovered over the older man's wide torso before he added an instruction. "You will need to stretch your arms out to slow yourself down when you see the other platform approaching. Okay?"

"Why me, and not the rest?"

The guide blushed and mumbled something in Spanish that had Sam giggling. When Xavier reddened yet remained silent, Sam translated it for the rest. "Because he's too fat and the guide is afraid he'll fly across the zip line and slam into the other platform."

Xavier moaned about it not being safe and tried to climb back down to firm ground, but the guides weren't having it. After much convincing, he did eventually allow them to clip him onto the zip line, yelling out in fright when a guide gently pushed him off of the platform.

As soon as he was away, Sam stepped up and clipped himself onto the line. "It's not my first rodeo," he announced before taking flight. His screams were of pure delight.

Jersey was the last guest to go, before the three guides were to follow. Despite having witnessed the rest of the group clip in, she fumbled with the C-clamp, seemingly unable to secure it onto the main line. One of the guides attempted to assist her, but she just waved his hand away. After it looked as if she had finally succeeded, Jersey stepped forward to the edge and leaned back, about to launch herself off of the platform, when the guide's bloodcurdling scream made her freeze.

"Stop!" He grabbed onto her harness, preventing her from falling forward. When she whipped around to yell at him, the guide held up the other end of the rope she'd clipped onto the zip line. Only one strap was attached to it, instead of three.

"I had already checked your gear, and the three straps were was securely fastened to this clamp. Why did you remove two of them?"

"They were causing the waistband to rub against my belly piercing," she whined.

"This single strap cannot support your weight. If you tamper with your gear again, I will not be able to allow you to join in."

"Fine already. There's no need to be so dramatic."

"Without this clipped in, you would have fallen to your death," he whispered. The poor man looked to be scared out of his wits.

"No, I wouldn't have—I'm not that heavy."

Lana was beginning to understand why Jersey irritated Alex so. She'd almost zipped herself to death, and yet, instead of thanking the guide properly for saving her life, she acted as if he was in the wrong.

The guide began to retort, but when he looked over to the rest of the group, he apparently decided to let it go. Instead, he muttered something in Spanish to his co-workers, who shook their heads sympathetically. Only after he had triple-checked all of her gear did the guide step out of the way and allow Jersey to fly off into the distance.

As Lana watched her disappear, she couldn't help but think that Jersey was not very attentive or detail-oriented, exactly the traits that Xavier had touted as essential for an archaeologist. So how had Jersey of all people secured a paid position on his dig for the past three years in a row?

"Ma'am, would you like to go next?"

Lana knew the smiling young guide meant to be polite. But what wouldn't she give to be call "miss" again!

"Yes, thanks." She let the guide clip her onto the line and check all of her straps before he waved her forward. She flexed her hands, feeling the gloves stretch as she grabbed onto the line. She was suddenly glad for the extra protection, required to help minimalize the friction from cutting through her skin.

Lana could feel her stomach drop as her feet tried to stop her from approaching the platform's edge. Yet she pushed aside her fear of heights and instead sucked in her breath and kicked off with her heels, immediately feeling the strange sensation of nothing under her feet.

The line made a high-pitched whizzing noise as she cruised through the abundant foliage far too quickly to see if any monkeys were watching her, or perhaps covering their ears against her squeals of delight. Seconds later, when her feet touched down on the next platform, Lana felt a grin splitting her face.

Sam looked over at her, a smile also firmly planted on his. "So, what did you think?"

The sensation of being in flight—albeit briefly—was incredibly freeing and so addictive. "I want to do that again!"

11

Horses and Hanging Bridges

After the group made it across the thirteen zip lines, the members were giddy with excitement and adrenaline. Despite all of their previous squabbling, they were now high-fiving each other, congratulating themselves on having dared to complete the entire course.

Lana felt the same. She'd never experienced anything quite like it, and the sensation of flying through the leaves and mist would stay with her for quite a long time. Seeing all of the animals in their natural habitat was the cherry on top of this incredible excursion.

Once the conversations petered out, Randy reminded them that they had to make a choice as to how they wished to spend the rest of the afternoon. He patiently explained the three options of taking a horseback ride, hiking over the hanging bridges, or relaxing in a café.

Earlier, she and Alex had played rock-paper-scissors to decide who got to accompany each group. Lana had won the bridges tour, which did sound wonderful. She only hoped her mild fear of heights wouldn't hold her back from truly enjoying the walk.

After a few minutes of decision making, the guests finally picked a destination. The four marketers were to join Alex for a horseback ride, Lana would accompany the two young archaeologists and geologists on a rainforest hike, and Randy would walk with Xavier to a café where he could have a cool drink. The older archaeologist was clearly wiped out after the zip line tour and kept wiping a handkerchief along his brow as he waited for Randy to lead the way.

Lana knew that Randy wanted to go to the café because he had to confirm several reservations before dinner. Since George's accident, Randy had taken all of the injured guide's tasks onto his shoulders, without asking either Lana or Alex to help. As much as she appreciated it, she also knew that it could be a lot to deal with, especially considering the rather chaotic itinerary George had submitted.

She knew it was a new kind of tour and that there were bound to be kinks that still had to be worked out, but there sure seemed to an excessive amount of driving on this trip. Given the number of spectacular-looking eco-lodges dotted around the country, she didn't understand why George had chosen San Jose as their base, when they could have made a loop around the country and seen more of Costa Rica.

But she also knew that now was not the time to discuss this with Randy; they needed to get their clients to their next excursion. Alex and the foursome had to hurry up to make their scheduled ride. Her boyfriend waved as he passed, afraid to actually blow her a kiss, she suspected. That was okay with her. Thanks to this experience, Lana now knew why Dotty had already said she would prefer not to schedule them on the same tour, if Alex did get the job.

Lana gathered her small group together, and then they set off for the starting point of the self-guided tour. As they walked, she asked, "What did you think of the zip lines?"

"That was incredible. I really felt like I was flying on a few of those lines," Sam gushed.

"It was okay. Those guides were kind of pushy, but otherwise it was worth it, I guess," Jersey grumbled, no doubt still ticked off that the guides had made a point of triple-checking her lines at every stop. The first one must have told the rest that she was a client to watch out for.

"I must admit that I was terrified the first time, but it felt so freeing that I couldn't wait to do the next one!" Cecile enthused.

"It was worth making the drive up, that's for sure," Gregory added.

They soon reached the trailhead, well-marked with a depiction of the six hanging bridges that crossed the cloud-infused canopy of Monteverde's forest.

Once there, Lana looked to her small group. "It's a self-guided tour in the form of a loop and should take an hour to complete. But we aren't in a rush, so please do take your time. The views from the bridges are spectacular, and I expect us to see quite a bit of wildlife."

Gregory and Cecile made a point of speedwalking over the first bridge, putting distance between themselves and the rest. By the way they held hands and nuzzled up against each other, it was clear they wanted to be alone. Lana didn't mind. Instead, she made a point of distracting Sam and Jersey by pointing out a monkey, in order to give the couple more of a head start.

Neither of the two young archaeologists was in the mood for mindless chitchat, which Lana appreciated. It was rare that she could just enjoy excursions, because there was usually a guest or two who needed to be either pampered or entertained the entire time. Not that Lana minded; she was paid well to travel the world and experience, at least in part, the same high-end outings that they did, but for free.

She breathed in the damp, earthy scents, as she looked out over the leafy canopies partially enshrouded in mist. Everything seemed to drip with moisture. Leaves in all shades of green waved in the breeze. Exotic birds with colorful feathers squawked as they flew close by the hanging bridges, almost as if to see who dared cross through their territory.

Toucans, with their tiny bodies and gigantic heads, eyed them curiously, strangely unafraid. The crying of monkeys was so frequent that it soon became part of the background. Howler monkeys swung through the abundant foliage, using branches and vines to propel themselves forward. Other primates cavorted in the treetops, eating and resting on large, hammock-like branches. Flowering vines crawled up the tree trunks, their blossoms hanging down like party streamers. Wild orchids and dainty fernlike plants filled in many branches' nooks and crannies.

During their walk, they seemed to dip in and out of the clouds, hovering at canopy level. It was a magical experience, albeit slippery.

Lana was glad that Xavier hadn't joined them. Not only because of his attitude, but thanks to the ups and downs in the trail and slipperiness of the path, the pudgy older man would not have done well on this hike.

She trailed behind Sam and Jersey, reveling in the beauty of nature as she half listened to them chat about their dig and upcoming tasks. There seemed to be quite a bit of large machinery needed, which surprised her a little. Lana thought that archaeologists usually worked with precision tools, but in this case, they apparently didn't need to be as careful.

When their conversation wound down, Sam looked back to her, as if he was suddenly interested in mindless chitchat after all. Uncertain where to begin, Lana figured their accommodations was a good start. "What do you think of the hotel in San Jose?"

"It's incredible!" Sam gushed. "I've never stayed in such a fancy place in all of my life."

Lana stumbled at his answer. "I thought Xavier had put you all up in luxurious hotel rooms."

Sam's laughter startled a flock of large green parrots, causing them to fly close overhead, screeching in protest. "I wish! No, we're sleeping in leaky tents pitched behind the gift shop, not in a fancy hotel. It was really nice of Dotty to treat us to this trip. I'm not sure why Xavier lied to you earlier. Maybe he's embarrassed that he hasn't found us better lodgings by now."

"What are you doing, Sam? Xavier doesn't want us talking about the dig with strangers. That's why we signed confidentiality agreements, remember?"

Sam blinked. "For the work we do, not where we sleep."

"Still, I don't think our boss would appreciate you badmouthing what he's provided for us, especially in front of one of our sponsor's employees. He did pay for our airplane tickets out here and is still working on finding us a better place to sleep."

"The university budget includes provisions for the return flights, all meals, and hotel accommodations for two assistants. Tents are not what I was expecting, nor is being told to do my own shopping whenever I ask Xavier when he's going to buy groceries."

When Jersey noticed Lana's shaken expression, her face twisted into a grimace. "If we stayed in a luxe hotel, we wouldn't get any stipend, I bet."

"Some stipend. Two hundred dollars per week is pretty skimpy. The university budget dictates that it be five hundred per week. I don't understand where the rest of the money went."

"It's skimpy only if you don't count the rest he's providing," Jersey protested.

"You mean the leaky outdoor shower and compost toilet? Or the camper-style gas stove we use to cook?" Sam teased.

Why is Jersey defending Xavier's strange choices every chance she gets? Is it simply because I work for Dotty? Lana wondered.

"I just hope he's going to pay for our flight home," Sam grumbled.

Lana couldn't keep her astonishment to herself this time. "Xavier only paid for the flight out? That doesn't seem right."

"We don't have a definitive end date yet, so there was no point in booking the return flight yet," Jersey rushed to explain. "It all depends on how many more spheres we find this summer and how long it takes to complete the museum building."

"I already told Xavier that I can't stay past August. If I miss any more lessons, I'm going to have to retake a few classes, and I can't afford to. It's not like the spheres are going anywhere," Sam groused.

"That's not fair! If we don't figure out how to protect the stones we've excavated, the site is going to be robbed or vandalized before we can get back here next year. The Costa Rican government doesn't have enough money or resources to protect them all."

"Are they really a target for thieves?" Lana asked. She thought back on the massive stones she'd seen in the photos. She couldn't imagine that there was a great demand for them. Then again, she knew nothing about the trade in, or value of, pre-Columbian artifacts.

"Yes, they are. Yet there are so many, it's impossible for the Costa Rican government to protect them all. It's dedicated professionals—like us—that should be doing all we can to keep them in the country and safe for future generations."

The ferocity in Sam's voice was surprising. Before she could work out why he was so concerned, he pointed to a group of monkeys swinging their way towards them.

"What kind of monkeys are those, Lana?"

12

Hummingbird Café

After they had completed the loop, Lana led them to the Hummingbird Café where Randy and Xavier were waiting. She had expected that Alex and the four marketers would have returned before them, but they were nowhere in sight. Only Xavier sat contentedly watching hummingbirds in iridescent colors buzz around the terrace in the canopies. The condensation from his cold beer, clutched in one hand, rolled over his fingers and dripped onto the table, forming a small pool by his wrist.

Randy sat at the back of the café, talking on the phone with one finger in his free ear. When she noted the stressed-out expression on his face, she decided to leave him alone and question the senior archaeologist, instead.

"Hi, Xavier. Are you enjoying the views?"

He nodded happily. "Yep. It's wonderfully quiet here and so peaceful. I don't think most tourists know about this place."

Lana was shocked. This was the first positive thing Xavier had said since she'd arrived. "That's great, I'm glad to hear you are enjoying yourself."

He tipped his beer at her before taking another swig. Based on his jovial expression and surprisingly good mood, Lana figured that wasn't his first cerveza.

She turned to her group, figuring her clients would want to quench their thirst, as well. "So, gang, what would you like to drink?"

Sam nodded at Xavier's beer. "I'll take a cold brewski. That looks good."

"Me, too," Gregory added.

"I'll have a Spa Red with ice blocks," Cecile said.

"That sounds good—the ice, I mean. I'm pretty sweaty from that hike. Can you get me a Coke, Lana?" Jersey asked.

"Coming up." She quickly placed their order, adding an iced tea with ice for herself.

After she'd served the drinks to her guests, Lana crossed back to Randy, now off the phone and staring into the distance. She could imagine that it was all quite overwhelming for him right now.

"Hey, Randy, how are you doing?"

"Hey, Lana. Okay, I guess. This whole Alex situation is exhausting me, but George's itinerary isn't making life easier. We're constantly on the move, making me feel like a conductor leading an orchestra of chauffeurs, excursion operators, restaurant owners, and hotels."

"Yeah, about that. What do you think of George's schedule? There seems to be quite a bit of driving that could have been avoided if he'd booked hotels along the way, instead of using San Jose as a base. I still don't understand why you all drove three hours out to the Caribbean Sea for a rafting trip, and then back to San Jose on the same day. You could have easily booked an eco-lodge there, then made the short drive to Panama for the snorkeling excursion the next day. It would have saved many hours of driving."

Randy shrugged. "I thought so, too, but George said he had to accommodate several last-minute requests to visit Sarchi, Xavier's dig, and the two museums in San Jose. That's why he chose to use the capital as our base. Plus, he said the views from the highways were so spectacular that no one would be complaining about spending a few hours a day in the minivan. So far, he's been right about the views; however, a few of the guests have already noticed the long drive times in the coming days and asked about them."

"Do you think we have the right to change anything around?"

"This tour is supposed to be our chance to try out George's itinerary as he set it up. And even if Dotty was okay with us changing his itinerary, it might be difficult to do so, considering the hotels are already booked and I don't think they would give us refunds. But we should take notes on other properties that we think might suitable for future tours."

"It's too bad George didn't provide Dotty with a list of reserve hotels. I thought that was the whole point of him and Alex scouting locations, so we had several options to choose from."

"Maybe he did and she forgot about it. I hate to say it, but Dotty has become a bit forgetful as of late. Not to the point where I'm worried about dementia," Randy rushed to add when he noted Lana's face constricting. "But she's juggling so many balls right now because she wants to add all of these new tours and insists on micromanaging everything. It's too much and she just can't retain it all, I'm afraid."

Lana nodded, trying to recall any similar incidents. She couldn't offhand, but she hadn't really been home long enough to have noticed. "I'll keep my eye out. Thanks for letting me know."

A hand slamming against the café door caught both of their attention. When Alex walked in, Lana initially breathed a sigh of relief. They were a half hour late, and she did wonder what had happened. Yet when she caught a look at the expression on his face, her heart sank.

"What happened now," she muttered.

"I still don't understand why you did something so dumb. You could have killed him—even the horse wrangler said that. The man was in tears, Chet. I swear we have to keep refilling the emergency kit thanks to your group's shenanigans," Alex huffed, chastising the four marketers who were walking behind him in a line with their heads hung low. Two of them had large bandages on their elbows, knees, and calves.

"Bro, we've said sorry like a hundred times already. It was a dumb joke that got out of hand, that's all."

"*Bro*, you made that cowboy cry. It's a miracle nothing worse happened," Alex replied, his tone a mix of defensiveness and sarcasm. Lana knew she had to intervene before things escalated between the two men.

She positioned herself in between Alex and their clients. "What is going on? What happened to you two? Do we need to take you to the hospital?"

"No, they are fine," Alex answered for them. "Nothing is broken, they just have a bunch of cuts and scrapes that I had to clean out and bandage up. Chet here decided it would be hilarious to slap Dave's horse on the backside. Unfortunately, the horse didn't think it was funny and slammed into Brad's horse before shooting off into the jungle with Dave still on its back. We found them later back at the ranch, with Dave hanging half off his saddle. The guide was livid—and rightfully so. Dave could have been seriously injured, or worse."

Instead of showing any sympathy, Alex's tone made clear that he thought the four marketers were complete imbeciles.

"Alex Wright! Remember what we discussed?" Lana growled.

Her boyfriend glanced over at her, but she had a feeling her words hadn't really reached him. When Alex looked to the foursome with loathing in his eyes, Lana knew she needed to step in again.

"Hitting the horse was not a smart move, Chet, I will say that. But geez, I'm just glad you are okay. What a terrible ordeal! Brad and Dave, are you certain you don't want to have a medical professional check you out?"

Dave slowly raised his head to look her in the eye. "No, we're fine. Alex got us patched up."

"I do apologize, Lana. I just thought it would be a laugh to make Dave's horse neigh. I didn't expect it to take off like that," Chet explained.

"We're just relieved that you are all okay. Can I get you something to drink?" Randy asked, as he stepped in front of his brother. From the way he kept his back to his sibling, it was clear that he was not pleased with how Alex had handled the situation.

Lana looked to her boyfriend, wondering whether he was ever going to get the hang of being a tour guide.

13

Unwanted Kickbacks

Friday—Day Six of the Wanderlust Tour, Diquís Cultural Center and Sarchí

When Lana woke up the next morning, birds were chirping in the misty canopy visible outside of her bedroom window. Instead of driving back to San Jose, the group had spent the night in one of the cloud forest's famous treehouse hotels. It was amazing, sleeping up in the high branches like this, though quite noisy with chatty animals. When her alarm beeped, Lana wanted not to rise, but instead to continue snuggling under the covers with Alex for the rest of the day.

Her boyfriend blinked his eyes open at the alarm. "Is it time to get up?"

"Yep, it's eight already. I expect a few early risers will be in the breakfast room soon."

Eight in the morning was quite late for a Wanderlust Tours guide to wake up, but considering the group hadn't gotten back until one in the morning from their night hike through the jungle, it felt early.

During their wonderful nighttime excursion, they'd seen two-toed sloths, armadillos, snakes, frogs, sleeping birds, and too many spiders for Lana's taste. Their guide had told them that most of the forest creatures were nocturnal, but she still hadn't expected to see so many moving around. Nor had she expected the noise. The forest was far more alive with chatter and calls than during their day hike.

After they'd returned to the hotel, everyone was too keyed up to go straight to bed. When Lana and Alex had finally gone up to their room at three in the morning, the rest had remained in the hotel bar, recounting their experiences over another drink. Lana was again glad to see that they could get along, under the right circumstances.

The lateness of the tour was also why they'd stayed in this treehouse-style eco-hotel, instead of returning to San Jose. Lana was glad for the change. The other one was fantastic, but it was wonderful to lodge in something so unique as this one, as well.

After they'd both showered, Alex and Lana went down to meet their guests for breakfast. Today was a busy day with visits to Xavier's site and then a cultural center in Sarchi, the town where they made the oxcarts Costa Rica was so famous for. Lana couldn't wait to see both.

When they passed by the reception desk, the manager rushed over to Lana. "You are with Wanderlust Tours, correct? Can you tell me where I can find George? I haven't seen him yet, and your group is about to check out."

Lana smiled at the man, but turned first to Alex. "Would you mind checking in with the guests? I'll be right there."

"Sure."

She shifted her gaze back to the manager. "I'm sorry, but George is not with us. He fractured his leg recently and still is in the hospital."

The man pulled a face, then held out an envelope that had "George—Wanderlust Tours" written across it. "That is unfortunate. I do not have his postal address. Could you give him his commission for me?"

Lana accepted the envelope automatically, but once his words had sunk in, her forehead creased. "Wait, his commission for what?"

"For bringing his group to my hotel." The man didn't seem embarrassed by her inquiry, rather confused that he had to explain what the money was for.

Lana opened the envelope and quickly counted the American dollars. "There's five hundred dollars in here!"

The man frowned at her. "It's ten percent of the total bill, as agreed. George didn't mention any price increases."

"Not to me, either. I'm sure it is fine," Lana stuttered.

"Good." The man half bowed before retreating to his office, effectively ending their conversation.

Lana looked again at the money in her hand. Ten percent of their group's total expenditures was being siphoned back to one of their guides? That was definitely not how Wanderlust Tours worked. Dotty's package tours were so expensive, it would be embarrassing if word got out that she favored hotels that paid her a kickback to bring them clients.

However, Lana also knew that George had worked for other tour companies in Central America before joining Wanderlust. *Maybe he is used to receiving a commission*, she thought. But Dotty should have talked to him about ending that practice, before he started working for the company.

Either way, Lana felt obligated to tell her boss about this envelope, before George recovered. But first, she wanted to talk to Alex about this. He'd traveled alongside George for two weeks during their scouting trip; maybe he knew more about it.

When she returned to the breakfast hall, she was surprised to see all of the guests were already present. Lana placed a scoop of beans and a few tortillas onto a plate, then made her way over to Randy and Alex, who were already digging in.

Maybe George had only made an arrangement with this one hotel—not all of them, she thought as she navigated her way over to the brothers.

"Something odd just happened," she whispered after taking her seat across from the pair. As soon as she had her plate down, she pulled the envelope out of her purse and laid it on the table. "The manager just gave me this, to give to George. It's his commission."

Randy's eyebrows flew up. "Commission? Dotty would never allow that. Alex, do you know anything about this?"

He shook his head, a perplexed expression on his face. "No, I didn't notice him receiving commissions during our scouting trips. But I wasn't looking for it, either. Although, come to think of it, George was constantly swapping information with potential tour operators, and I didn't get a good look at everything that exchanged hands between them."

"Maybe he was used to receiving commissions at his old job?" Lana mused, not wanting to think too poorly of George, at least not yet. "We could ask his former boss about it, I suppose. Or, rather, Dotty could."

Randy leaned forward. "Dotty needs to know about this. If anything, so she can explain that this is not alright with her. She expects us to use the best hotel and excursion operators available, not to favor the ones that bribe us to bring them guests."

Lana tapped the wad of cash on the table. "I agree, but what do we do with this envelope?"

Randy picked it up and counted the bills, whistling when he reached the last one. "That's a pretty hefty commission. How much does the hotel charge a night, anyway?"

"I say we give it back," Alex said, his tone resolute.

Lana nodded. "I agree. Randy?"

He tossed the envelope onto the table. "Absolutely. The sooner the better. Hopefully it's just a horrible miscommunication, although I suppose we'll find out soon enough, if another hotel owner or excursion operator tries to pass George's cut on to us."

Lana took in Randy's grim expression, understanding his reaction completely. If George had intentionally booked tour operators and hotel rooms based on the commissions they were offering him, Wanderlust Tours' reputation was in danger. Luckily for all of them, this was a trial run and not a real tour with paying guests.

"Don't worry, Randy. I'll take care of it."

Lana popped back over to the reception desk and asked for the manager. When she returned the envelope, adding that there must have been some sort of mix-up because Wanderlust guides were not allowed to receive a commission, the man's facial expression switched from confusion to glee in a millisecond.

As she'd walked over, Lana had wondered how many local operators expected a cut of the profits. Based on the man's delight, she'd guess most of them.

14

Casa del Mar

As soon as Lana reentered the breakfast hall, Randy's wristwatch chimed three times. He let out a long sigh as he stared at the tiny face. Lana's heart went out to him—she hated seeing her colleague and friend so stressed out. Knowing that it was his own brother that was the main source of his frustration only made things worse.

"We need to head to Xavier's site. Alex, could you let the guests know it's time to go outside and wait for the bus? I see a few stragglers still eating breakfast, but the rest should all be in the lobby by now."

The hesitation in his voice made clear that he wasn't sure how Alex would react. Lana felt the same—her boyfriend's mood seemed to swing with every minute.

"Sure."

To her relief, Alex's tone was chipper, and his smile seemed genuine. Randy seemed to sense the improvement, too, and actually grinned up at Alex, instead of scowling at him, as he'd often done during this trip.

The minivan was ready and waiting by the time all of the guests had assembled in the lobby. They filed into the vehicle, most still groggy after the last night's adventure and celebratory drinks afterward. After a few stories about their walk, the conversation petered out and most guests seemed content to look out the window, instead.

Their two-hour drive from the Monteverde Nature Reserve to Xavier's archeological dig on the Nicoya Peninsula was a wonderful mix of rainforests, agricultural fields on rolling hills, and rock formations sticking out of soil so red, it almost looked like the earth was bleeding.

They wound their way through a series of colorful villages, climbing up to the highlands before descending onto a freeway that paralleled the Pacific Ocean's coastline. Lana slid her window open a smidge and breathed in the salty air as she marveled at the endless expanse of blue water.

Too soon, Randy stood up to address the group. "We're entering El Roble, which means we are about fifteen minutes away from Xavier's dig. Please make sure you haven't left any important belongings on the bus. Our driver will stay with the vehicle, but he has to park outside of the site, so we won't have easy access to our things once we leave. Okay?"

A few clients mumbled that they'd understood as her group came to life, yawning and stretching in unison. The last few miles of the trip had been quieter than usual, but Lana hadn't realized that everyone had dozed off.

Unfortunately, soon after Randy's announcement woke everyone back up, Xavier decided to make his presence known. The archaeologist rose slowly and cleared his throat to get everyone's attention, before his booming voice echoed through the vehicle. "We are mere minutes from my dig. Would you look at that pristine forest! At only an hour out of San Jose, this site is an easy day trip from the capital. Sarchi, where the oxcart factories are located, is a short ride away, which would make the tour to the two sites a perfect combination for tourists interested in Costa Rica's culture and history. I've already begun contacting local companies to see about adding our site to their existing tours of the area."

"And how are they responding to your request?" Gregory asked.

"Most are positive, and I am already in negotiations with one. All we have to do now is agree on their commission."

Lana cringed when Xavier mentioned the payback the travel agency expected for bringing tourists to his site. It sure sounded like this was how things were done in Costa Rica.

"But your site isn't even open to the public yet," Gregory cried.

Xavier only smiled. "You'll soon see that we are almost ready to welcome visitors. Just you wait." He sat back down before Gregory could respond.

The geologist let out a cry of frustration. Lana felt his pain; Xavier seemed to have an answer for everything. "There is no getting through to that man," she heard him grumble to his wife.

"This site should be pretty incredible, considering how much money Dotty's poured into it," Alex whispered to Lana and Randy.

"Do you know how much she's contributed?" Lana asked. She hadn't dared ask her boss what the total amount was, but figured it must be significant.

Alex dipped his head further behind the seat. "Jersey left a copy of their budget on a table a few days ago, after they'd had one of their meetings, so I took it up to her room. I couldn't help but see that the total budget was almost fifty thousand dollars for one year."

Lana's face paled. "Whoa, I had no idea it was that much. No wonder Dotty wants to cut the cord."

"Slow down! The driveway's up on the right," Xavier suddenly yelled out as he pointed out the right-hand window.

The driver did as ordered, coming to a full stop in the middle of a long stretch of road so quickly, Lana and Alex's faces squished into the seat in front of them.

"Ah, there she is. Home sweet home."

At first, Lana was confused. She couldn't see any breaks in the tree line. At least, not until she leaned forward and looked through the driver's side window. From there, she spotted a long path almost hidden by palm trees.

They soon passed under a hand-painted sign straddling the wide driveway that announced they were entering "Casa del Mar."

"This is it! Welcome to my home on the sea and a soon-to-be important cultural center dedicated to the Diquís culture," Xavier declared, his face beaming.

Technically, they weren't close to the coast, but were high above it. However, Lana did catch several glimpses of the sea through the thick tree line as they slowly drove down the pothole-filled road towards his site. Luckily, their 4x4 minivan could handle the rough terrain.

Several minutes later, their driver parked close to a large, shacklike structure built on a flat spot at the top of a small hill. Tufts of rainforest rose dramatically out of the patchwork of red-brown fields surrounding the building.

As soon as they were out of the vehicle, Xavier stretched his arms up in the air and sucked in his breath. "Ah, the salty air of the Pacific. It's good to be back."

When he noticed Cecile dancing around, he added, "The restrooms are just inside the museum's entrance, on the right."

She dashed off without another word, Chet and Dave following close behind.

Xavier's eyes sparkled when he looked over to the rest of them. "Once everyone's had a bathroom break, let's walk down to the site. I can't wait to hear what you think of it. Then we'll come back up and have a look inside the museum."

"Sounds good to me," Lana replied, glad to stretch her legs after that long ride. She took a moment to take in her surroundings, noting the hand-painted sign above the entrance, declaring the building to be the "Diquís Cultural Center, Museum & Gift Shop."

It appeared that Xavier still had quite a bit of work to do on the structure. The roof was complete and the exterior walls were standing, but the windows and doors were empty holes. Through the openings, she could see that the interior walls had not yet been finished, leaving the inner beams and wiring exposed.

Lana looked to her right, past the incomplete structure, but she couldn't see much more from here. Surrounding the building was a row of banana trees, most bearing fruit, that obscured their view of the field behind it.

Before she could investigate, Xavier clapped his hands together. It appeared that the group was again complete and he wanted to get the tour started.

"Welcome to Diquís Spheres National Park and Cultural Center," Xavier said proudly as he waved his hand over the sight in front of them.

"There is so much to see and do here, or at least there will be once we get everything completed. As you can see, we've begun construction on the museum and gift shop. I expect to have the building finished and ready to open before the end of this season."

When Gregory whispered something to Cecile, making her laugh, Xavier blushed. "Let's start with the huts—those are ready to go."

Xavier led them past the building and through the row of banana plants. On the other side stood six small, round huts close together in a single row. A white picket fence, recently painted, ran around the cluster of homes. Lana stood in awe, taking in the sheer number of small and medium-sized stone spheres adorning the roofs, doorways, and even the fence.

The gate was open, and Xavier waved for them to explore the huts. Lana hesitated as she took in the heavy balls hanging over the doorway, hoping Xavier had secured them properly. *Entering a Diquís home must have been a test of faith*, she mused.

"I certainly hadn't expected to see huts still standing," Lana said as she took in the unique homes.

Sam laughed at her naiveté. "We just finished building these huts last week, to show visitors how the Diquís probably lived. Since they were wiped out in the 1500s, we don't know for certain."

It was strange to think the civilization that made these curious objects was extinct. Lana had never thought of that happening to people before—only animals.

"Sam's right. We've rebuilt the homes in the same manner that the Diquís people lived, at least, as far as can be discerned from the archeological remnants discovered in the Diquís Delta," Xavier further explained.

"Were these spheres used as decoration, or is that your own interpretation, as well?" Gregory demanded. Based on his snooty tone, he was not impressed with the huts.

"Anthropologists do believe the spheres were used to decorate their homes and gardens. But one of the more plausible theories for their creation is that the spheres were references to the people's belief in magic and their understanding of the solar system. I want to add a few more signs that explain these theories more clearly. That's also why I want to fund a research center, to see whether trained scientists can puzzle out more about the Diquís culture and the spheres' meaning."

Lana was having trouble imagining why any culture would use stone spheres as home décor, even if they were references to celestial bodies. From the expressions on the others' faces, she was not the only one.

Xavier, apparently sensing his crowd's lack of enthusiasm, added, "Some are so heavy that we had to use a crane to move them. Yet even those are perfectly round. It's quite a feat, especially for an ancient culture such as the Diquís."

"Do you know how they managed to make them so round?" Cecile asked.

"Anthropologists figure they used other stones to shape them, then sand to smooth them down."

"That's fascinating." Lana was genuinely intrigued by the ingenuity of past civilizations and how they were able to accomplish so much with so few tools. *Our generation is completely reliant on technology. I bet most of us would have trouble adapting to living in such a simple world.*

Xavier looked over to Sam and Jersey. "While I show them around, why don't you two get started on inventorying the latest arrivals. It would be good if we can get them into place next week. The mounds should be fixed by then."

"Sure thing," Jersey answered, and the pair set off for a small shacklike structure located a few hundred feet behind the cultural center.

"What's that?" Lana pointed to the relatively new-looking building made of sheet metal. It had one back wall and a roof that covered a large slab of concrete. She could see several boxes stacked up inside of the enclosure.

"That's our storage facility," Xavier answered, then pointed across the small field of grass and towards a clearly marked path leading down the hill.

"Let's head down to the main site. I can't wait to hear what you think of it."

15

Visiting the Site

The portly man rushed ahead towards the path. From the trailhead, Lana could see that it led down a steep, tree-covered slope to a vast field located a few stories below. From their high vantage point, the Pacific Ocean seemed to be playing peekaboo with them, and she could only catch glimpses of the turbulent water below through the trees, ferns, vines, and flowering hibiscus bushes.

The land was alive with color and sound. Lana walked along slowly, enjoying the soothing chorus of singing birds, buzzing insects, and crashing waves. As he led them down the red-brown path towards his site, Xavier explained how the first spheres had been found buried under the mud of the Diquís Delta in the 1930s, when land had been cleared for banana plantations.

"But this isn't the Diquís Delta, that's miles away," Gregory balked, but Xavier ignored him.

A few steps later, a large opening in the trees revealed a wide platform that had been built into the side of the hill. Xavier stopped and let everyone catch up, before declaring, "Welcome to my excavation site."

Lana stepped to the edge and took in the dig. They weren't that high above the field below, but enough that they could get a bird's-eye view of the entire site. It was larger than she'd thought, when viewed from the top of the trail. She spotted a flattened, paved area, many spheres in all sizes, and two mounds rising up in the back. A scoop and bulldozer seemed to be disassembling one, but otherwise she could see no construction going on.

"On the left, you will see the public square. It's that flat area partially paved with cobblestones, with its edges marked by those large Diquís spheres. Small ones line the pathways leading through the site and to the homes, and you can see the foundations of some of their dwellings. At the back are two artificial mounds made of cobblestones and pounded earth. They are the gateway to this village, as it were."

"The site is far more extensive than I expected it to be," Lana said as she took in the football-field-sized area of red-brown dirt with its smattering of archeological remnants.

"Thank you, we've worked hard to get it ready for visitors." Xavier bowed at her before turning to the rest, his eyes twinkling with excitement. "We still need to add information boards to better explain the site and its components, as well as provide more information about the Diquís culture. But as you can see, we are almost ready to open to the public. Once we sort out a few last-minute problems, we'll be able to do so."

He clapped his hands together and rubbed them vigorously. "So, what do you think? Would this site interest international visitors?"

When no one answered immediately, Xavier pointed to Lana. "Say, what is your honest opinion? I know you are an amateur, but it would be good to get an outsider's perspective on what I've done so far."

Lana let a snide answer roll over her tongue, but chose to be diplomatic, instead. She was supposed to be an example for Alex, not to further antagonize their guests. She leaned over and eyed the field. "I think tourists interested in archaeology would probably find it fascinating. But it is difficult to get a real feel for what you are trying to accomplish, when the site isn't complete yet."

By the way Xavier's shoulders slumped, that was not the answer he had been hoping for. "Fine, why don't I show you the cultural center? The building needs some work, but the displays are practically finished. That should give you a better idea of what we are trying to accomplish."

Lana turned her head so he couldn't see her rolling her eyes. What was it with this guy? She felt as if he wouldn't quit badgering her about his site until she proclaimed to love it. Which she did not see happening. During the course of her many tours, she'd seen some of the world's most spectacular archeological sites, and this one did not rate anywhere close to even the worst of them. Yet she had no desire to get into a tiff with Xavier about this.

"Sure, okay. You lead the way."

"What's happening over there?" Gregory asked, as he pointed to the bulldozer.

"We were almost finished last season, but due to a few faulty measurements, we had to raze part of the site and start again. It is a costly mistake, but one we must rectify. Everything must be as authentic as possible."

He glared at Jersey when speaking, but she refused to meet his eye, and instead seemed to disappear into herself.

"What do you mean by that? If you'd unearthed those mounds, why are you bulldozing them flat?" Gregory pushed.

Xavier's smiled faltered ever so slightly. "This is a recreation of the Finca 6 site in southern Costa Rica where these spheres were originally excavated. I want to ensure that my site is as exact as possible, which is why that mound has to be moved several feet to the right."

"Wait a second—are you saying that none of those spheres, cobblestones, or mounds were actually found here? Is this an excavation or a re-creation?" Cecile asked.

Xavier tittered uncomfortably, then cleared his throat. "I prefer to think of this as an orphanage for lost stones."

"Are you saying that this entire site is fake? All you did is re-create a genuine archeological excavation site, and nothing more?" Lana had trouble keeping her voice even. Xavier had conned Dotty into paying for excavation work on a site that didn't even exist. Her boss was going to be furious. *If I was her, I'd demand my money back*, Lana thought as she pulled out her phone, resolving to take photos as proof of his deceit.

Xavier puffed out his chest. "There is a backlog of spheres that have been found in farmers' fields or on construction sites that need to be moved. The Costa Rican government can't keep up with the excavation work, so it pays freelancers like me to dig them up and relocate them. Otherwise, the farmers and construction workers break them apart or blow them up, to get rid of them. The smaller spheres are also desired by smugglers and can bring in a pretty penny to the right seller. That's where sites like mine come in. We pick up the orphaned stones and place them in a safe space where tourists and locals alike can learn more about this fascinating culture. I'm proud of what I do."

Gregory turned to Cecile. "Unbelievable. This is yet another example of the Disneyfication of archeological sites. What a disappointment."

Xavier's eyes bulged out. "It's educational!"

"Why would Dotty have thought that we would have been interested in investing in this?" Cecile mused aloud.

"Once the site is finished and has been weathered a bit, I bet most tourists won't notice the difference. It's all about perception."

"But at least the Finca 6 site is an actual archeological find—this is pure fantasy! Where's the value in that?"

"Finca 6 is a five-hour drive from San Jose, but day-trippers can reach mine in an hour! I'll be able to attract far more tourists who wouldn't otherwise make the longer journey down south. It's a win for the Diquís people."

"And your pocketbook—at the expense of the genuine sites!"

Xavier shook his head. "You have no idea what you are talking about, you privileged twerp. Reconstructions are extremely common in archaeology; otherwise all you have to show visitors are piles of rocks and crumbling walls. That's what visitors want—to experience something new, not to try to imagine what the site may have looked like when it was new."

"How can you call yourself an archaeologist? This is a theme park and nothing more. Which is a shame, considering the real digs are so close by. You're trying to convince visitors who are interested in an authentic experience to visit your sham instead. I cannot believe that Dotty is funding this abysmal site, nor that she would suggest we do, too. I can only surmise that you have been lying to her, as well," Gregory pushed.

Xavier snorted. "Do you really think everything at Finca 6 is authentic?"

Gregory shook his head. "I've heard enough. You have misrepresented your project the entire time we've been here. I am certain you have been deceiving Dotty, and perhaps even your university, for the past three years. Let me be clear—I will never invest in your site or shop, not even if my life depended on it! And when we get back to the States, I am going to make certain everyone knows the truth about your supposed dig."

Before Xavier could bluster a response, Gregory was already storming back up the trail, towards the museum, with his wife in tow.

When the archaeologist noted how the rest of the group was glaring at him, most with an expression of disgust on their faces, he rushed down the steps and disappeared behind the gigantic mounds.

Lana couldn't help but roll her eyes. What had he expected—that the geologists would give him their blessing?

"What do we do now?" Chet asked.

"It looks like we have time to explore the site on our own," Randy answered.

"Great, this is so much more interesting than surfing," Chet muttered to the other three marketers.

"I feel you, bro," Dave replied. "How is it we couldn't hit the coast today, but they made time for this farce?"

"I'm glad we aren't paying for this trip," Mike added.

Lana couldn't help but blush when she heard the four bros grumbling. Their complaints only reminded her of the flaws in Dotty's master plan. At least, if she didn't take measures to ensure that only a certain type of client would be interested in booking it. Preferably ones under thirty and up for a physical challenge.

Knowing there was nothing she could do to placate the foursome at the moment, Lana instead addressed the group. "I'm going to head back up to the gift shop and grab a drink. Does anyone want to join me?"

16

Exit Through the Gift Shop

The four marketers and two guides followed Lana back up the trail towards the gift shop. No one was interested in perusing the site on their own. Granted, there was little to see at the moment, except for a few high mounds spread across a large field and flattened spaces where huts were to be reconstructed, once Xavier secured more funding.

When she reached the top of the hill, Lana could see the geologists standing outside of the gift shop's entrance. Based on Gregory's angry gestures, it appeared that the walk hadn't helped him to calm down, either.

As soon as she reached him, Gregory asked, "Can we leave now? I have no desire to spend another second in this farce of an archeological site."

"We're ready to leave, too," Chet said, clearly speaking for his group.

Xavier's booming voice rose up from behind them. "I refuse to leave until you've seen the museum and gift shop."

"I'm not going to fund your site; why can't you get that through your thick head?" Gregory whined.

The archaeologist barreled forward, ignoring the nasty looks the geologists were giving him as he disappeared into the museum.

When no one made a move to follow, Lana felt obliged to do so.

"Lana, welcome." Xavier gestured around the space. "This is our cultural center, complete with a museum and library dedicated to the Diquís people. Or it will be, once we get more funding. I hope to build another cabin at the back of the site where archaeology students can stay while they write their PhD theses about the Diquís' culture and traditions. There is still much work to be done, but I hope this gives you a better idea of what I want to accomplish." Xavier's tone had become brighter and friendlier, now that he had switched into sales mode.

Lana took a critical look at the space. Most of it was filled with Diquís spheres in a variety of sizes and grouped together on waist-high displays. On each table was a printed piece of paper describing their size, dimensions, weight, and material composition. A few of the texts recounted the story of the Diquís people, now lost, and the meaning of spheres they'd left behind.

After she'd had a few minutes to take it all in, Xavier cleared his throat as he gazed around the room, smiling with pride. "So what do you think of the museum?"

"It's fascinating," Lana managed.

His face fell.

She put more pep in her voice. "I mean, visitors interested in archaeology and pre-Columbian cultures will probably be captivated."

Xavier's ruffled feathers smoothed down, and he preened once again. "I think so, too. If I can raise another twenty thousand dollars, I should be able to build better cases, finish the exhibition hall, and pay for all of the informational boards. These texts were my first attempt, based on information I've gleaned locally and from the internet. I've already found an anthropologist willing to write up more detailed texts in English. He'll start as soon as I can pay his retainer fee."

"Isn't security a bigger issue? Sam mentioned that the smaller ones were targets for thieves."

"True, but the building needs to be complete before I can secure it."

"Where did all of your sponsors' money go?" Lana knew it wasn't her place, but the words slipped out.

Xavier snorted. "You have no idea how much equipment rentals, excavation permits, and the like cost, do you?"

"Can't you sell a few of the spheres and use the proceeds to protect the rest?"

"I did try to do that, but the government won't allow them to leave the country on account of their being national heritage."

Lana's forehead crinkled. "So they recognize the spheres' uniqueness and importance to Costa Rican culture, yet refuse to pay for their protection or care for them?"

Xavier shrugged. "I guess they figure if I am able to find sponsors for the dig, I can afford to protect their cultural heritage, too. But I don't have the kind of money necessary to protect them all."

"That's quite a conundrum," Lana said, unsure how to end this conversation without offending him. She did have to spend the rest of the week with the man.

Luckily for her, Sam walked inside before Xavier could continue and waved at his boss. "Hey, Jersey and I are finished with the inventory."

Lana saw her chance to escape and scurried towards the exit. But before she could get through the door, Gregory and Cecile bounded inside, blocking her escape.

The pair gave a cursory glance at the meager museum displays before entering the gift shop. Lana could see how Xavier tensed up when they did. After a second of hesitation, he followed them to the other side of the space.

Sensing that the group would probably butt heads, Lana trailed behind him. The gift shop was almost complete, at least in comparison to the museum, and was clearly Xavier's priority.

Most of the room was filled with display cases containing round stones of all sizes. Some stones were hanging from strings, and others were mounted onto pedestals and columns. Smaller ones had even been worked into necklaces and bracelets. Lana tried to imagine wearing one on her wrist, but figured it would not be comfortable.

Other cases were filled with the generic Costa Rican souvenirs she'd seen at most markets, including *carretas* in a variety of colors. In one corner stood a coffee nook complete with a fancy espresso machine.

The geologists ignored Xavier as they glanced over the selection of souvenirs, before Gregory picked up two small stones and slammed them into each other.

"What are you doing?" Xavier cried as flakes of rock flew off in all directions.

"Just as we thought, these are fakes. Real gabbro is much stronger and doesn't flake like that."

"Of course the spheres for sale are fakes; it is illegal to export the real ones."

When Xavier said that, Sam snorted and glared at his boss. The older man flushed briefly but otherwise ignored him.

"Then why does that sign say 'Authentic Diquís Spheres'?" Gregory asked.

"It's simply a marketing tactic. If the tourists think the sphere might be genuine, they'll be prepared to pay more for them. Though you do have a point. It would be better to remove the word 'authentic,' in case any lawyers stop by. Or maybe I can add an asterisk to it and put the fine print somewhere in the shop. I'll have to talk to my lawyers about that."

Gregory let the two cracked spheres drop to the floor before moving over to the locked display case featuring amulets, rings, and necklaces made of jade.

"Is it illegal to export jade, too?"

Xavier scurried over. "No, but these items are expensive. That's why everything is behind lock and key."

Instead of opening the case, Xavier pointed to a rack of clothing hanging on the wall behind the jewelry display.

"Did you see those T-shirts? They come in all sizes."

Instead of being distracted, Gregory and Cecile both leaned down and studied the jade for several seconds before locking eyes and chuckling. When they straightened up, Gregory said, "Is that lock part of your marketing, too? There's no need to secure these, seeing as they are all made of paste."

"Why would you say that? You haven't even gotten a good look at them," Xavier cried.

Gregory's lips pulled back over his teeth. "I don't need to get a closer look because I can tell from here that they are fakes. Don't you agree, Cecile? Real jade doesn't have mold markings. See that edge there, where the two were pressed together? You don't find that on genuine gemstones."

His wife nodded as she folded her arms over her torso.

Xavier squinted through the dirty glass. "Are you certain? You must have far better eyesight than I. They look real to me."

"You are a true charlatan, in every sense of the word. Cecile, we need to call Dotty tonight. I cannot believe that she knew what Xavier was really up to, if she suggested we invest in his project. It's time for her to learn the truth about this supposed dig."

"Of course Dotty knows what we are doing here! As one of my sponsors, she receives copies of my annual reports to the university."

"But does the university know what you are really doing?"

Gregory's challenging tone caused Xavier to back down.

"I thought so." Apparently aware that he'd won the battle, Gregory tilted his chin up and strode towards the exit, his wife following close behind.

Yet when Cecile's footsteps faltered and she mumbled, "What is that?" Gregory couldn't help but stop and look.

Cecile was standing before a strange contraption resting on a pedestal that was placed close to the exit.

"Is that a ground-penetrating radar and differential magnetometer, combined into one?" Her tone was not snide, but tinged with awe.

Xavier rushed over to answer. "You have a good eye; that's exactly what it is. She's a beauty, isn't she? I invented it myself. It's taken two years to get it right. Now I'm just waiting for the right investor to help me take my idea to the masses."

Gregory studied it critically. "It must have cost a fortune to prototype."

"It was worth it, or will be once I can start producing them *en masse*. I'm hoping the new center will help draw more Westerners in. With a little luck, one will want to partner with me."

Gregory's irritation with Xavier lost out to his curiosity. "How did you manage to combine the power sources like that?"

While the two men discussed the technical specifics, alarm bells were going off in Lana's head. Is this where the majority of Dotty's money had gone, instead of the dig? Except for a few mounds of dirt and a half-built shack, there was little to show for the thousands of dollars that Dotty had invested. Lana snuck a few photos, until Gregory's next question made her ears perk up.

"How much are you going to ask for it?"

"Twenty-five thousand per unit. It will be worth every penny to the right scientist."

Gregory whistled. "If you ask me, that's on the expensive side. Especially considering there are two other portable instruments on the market that do the same thing. And for a much lower cost, I should mention."

"The beauty of my product is that the two instruments are combined into one unit. It means there's less to carry, for one," Xavier countered, in a somewhat less boastful tone.

As if to test his statement, Gregory bent down to pick the unit up, grunting as he did. "Oy, that is heavy!"

It took him two tries before he could swing the unit onto his back. As he tugged on the shoulder straps, he added, "It's quite uncomfortable, as well. I wouldn't want to have to carry it for long. That's not going to be very useful in the field."

While he shrugged the large unit off of his back, Xavier got so red in the face, Lana was afraid he was going to explode. Gregory's smug expression wasn't helping matters.

Before the situation could escalate, Randy's voice rose from behind her. "Hey, Alex, why don't you escort Xavier outside. I think he needs a minute alone."

She hadn't even noticed that the Wright brothers were standing right behind her. Lana looked to the archaeologist with a mixture of disgust and loathing as her boyfriend ushered him out the door. Xavier had pulled the wool over Dotty's eyes for three years and showed absolutely no remorse.

The only saving grace was knowing that Xavier's attempt to get Gregory to invest in his dig had backfired. Now that the geologist knew it was a reconstruction and not an actual archeological site, as Xavier had repeatedly implied, Lana could assume that Gregory would do all he could to ensure that his sponsors would drop him like the proverbial hot potato.

17

Alone Time at the Dig

Almost as soon as Alex walked out the gift shop's exit with Xavier in tow, Jersey burst inside. "Hey, everybody. Sam and I are done with our work and ready to leave, whenever you are. Do I still have time to make a cappuccino?"

"Sure, you do. There's no rush," Lana answered.

"Great," she muttered as she tossed her backpack onto the floor, next to a case full of small spheres for sale. Unfortunately, her aim was not true, and it smacked into the base of the display. It shimmied for a moment before toppling to the ground, sending hundreds of tiny stone balls rolling every which way.

Xavier stormed back inside, presumably attracted by the noise. "What have you done now?" he roared as he took in the floor, now covered in tiny spheres.

"Jeez, Jersey, how do you do it? Careful that you don't trip over them! You probably already shattered most of them."

He slowly crossed over to the fallen case and righted it, before tossing a few balls into it. When Jersey remained standing, instead of gathering up the fallen objects, Xavier tore into her again. "Don't just stand there—clean up the mess you made!"

Jersey sprang into action, picking up two spheres with one hand.

Lana watched without another word, wondering again why this ditzy and clumsy woman had been a senior assistant on Xavier's archeological dig for the past three years. Before she could get drawn into helping clean up, she fled the space.

After taking a few cleansing, deep breaths, Lana let her eyes wander over the site, simultaneously taking in her guests' positions and the gorgeous landscape. The four marketers sat under the shade of a banana tree, chatting easily. The geologists were standing at the edge of the hill, peering down into the site. Based on their hand gestures and catty laughs, they seemed to be making fun of Xavier's efforts so far.

Figuring her guests were good where they were at, Lana crossed over to Alex and Randy. Unfortunately, the pair appeared to be midargument, from the sounds of it. She slowed her pace and let the wind bring their words to her. Randy was asking about the horseback riding incident again, and Alex was still refusing to talk about it. When he noted her approaching, her boyfriend's face turned ashen, and he shot off towards the gift shop.

Part of her wanted to run after him, yet she wasn't certain whether that would make things better or worse. Instead, she let him go and approached Randy. She lay a hand on his shoulder and squeezed. "If Alex can't see what a fool he is being, then there is nothing you or I can do to help him. If he doesn't truly want to be a guide, there is no point in trying to force him into the role." Lana knew from experience that being a tour guide was not a job you did just to pay your bills—it took someone with a passion for travel and customer service to pull it off without going crazy.

"You're right, I know. Let's just let him simmer for a while. He feels like a lost cause at this point, and I don't know what else to say that might change his mind. I was certain Alex was going to be a natural at leading a tour, but he can't seem to get his head around the concept."

Before Lana could respond, Randy threw up his hands. "You know what, I'm done talking about Alex. I think I need a little alone time before we head to Sarchi."

"And privacy to call Gloria, right?" Lana smiled.

Randy chuckled. "You got me there. Do you mind?"

"Not at all. I'm going to wander around and enjoy the views. Give her my love."

"Will do." Randy was already hotfooting it to a quiet corner in the shade.

Lana meandered down the trail towards the site, wanting to walk around some more before they got back into the minivan.

When she had almost reached the first mound, Lana heard raised voices echoing over the compacted earth. She listened a moment, confused as to who was speaking, until she finally realizing that it was the usually mellow Sam. But right now, he sounded livid.

"You can't keep ignoring me! I told you before that I refuse to lie for you. If you don't tell me what this means, then I have no choice but to show it to them."

"There is nothing illicit going on! You don't understand what you are reading because you don't have enough experience," Xavier hissed.

"Liars always try to shift the blame. If you keep me in the dark, then you leave me no choice. This is your last chance—are you going to explain it to me or not?"

When his boss didn't reply, Sam pushed again. "Know that I am not going to lie for you, not like Jersey has. An audit is serious business, and I refuse to risk my career for you."

"Your career? Give me a break!" Xavier sputtered before breaking into a laugh. "I seriously doubt you'll be able to find work in our field. I lied when I said that I'd chosen you based on your academic results. You're a mediocre student who was willing to work for peanuts this summer—that's why you got the position."

"Xavier!" Jersey yelled, her high-pitched voice easily carrying over the mound. "That's not fair. Sam does great work. You should back off, don't you think?"

"Jersey?" Something in Sam's tone changed. "Are you in on it, too? Is that why you defend him all the time?"

"Hey, wait a second, that's not fair or true. No one is lying about anything."

"Everyone knows what you did to Cindy—don't try to deny it. It's both of your faults that her career is as good as over."

Xavier's voice grew grim. "You're missing the nuances again, Sam. I've told you before that your black-and-white view of the world is going to get you into trouble one day."

Lana slowed her pace, but not fast enough to remain silent. When a few pebbles trickled down the path, Xavier's head jerked up towards the trail, causing her to freeze. The intensity of his stare made her shiver.

His eyes narrowed as he took her in, as if he was trying to gauge whether she was far enough away to have heard their conversation or not.

She looked down at him and blinked, as if surprised at seeing him, before waving.

"This is not the time or place to discuss the inventory paperwork or Cindy. We'll talk once we are back in the privacy of our hotel rooms and not before then," he growled to his assistants, before rushing up the trail and passing Lana without noting her presence.

Yet when Sam and Jersey rounded the mound to follow, both jumped in shock when they spotted her.

"What are you doing here?" Sam cried.

"I was just looking at the site," Lana said, her voice meek.

Sam gulped visibly as he looked over her shoulder. Lana let her gaze follow his line of sight and noticed that the geologists and four marketers were standing at the top of the hill and looking down. Thanks to the way sound traveled, there was a good chance they had heard the archaeologists' conversations, she realized.

By the way Sam's head dropped, he must have had the same thought.

When Sam rushed to catch up with Jersey, already halfway up the trail, Lana couldn't help but what wonder what exactly Sam was accusing Xavier of doing. She was convinced it must have something to do with Xavier's lies about the site's authenticity, or possibly his misappropriation of funds. Either would warrant a full audit, if only to give investigators a clearer idea of what Xavier had accomplished during the three years he had received university funding and support.

Speaking of which, I really need to call Dotty, Lana thought. It was going to be a painful conversation, but her boss needed to know about this farce of an excavation and get her accountant to stop any future payments to Xavier straight away.

18

Exposing Lies

Lana meandered back up the short incline towards the huts and gift shop, hoping to find a shady spot to sit in. As she approached the museum and gift shop, Lana saw Gregory and Sam arguing again. For people who supposedly didn't know each other, they sure were getting under each other's skin.

Yet before she could reach them, their verbal feud thankfully fizzled out on its own. The two men parted ways, both grumbling as they went. Lana was simply happy that she didn't need to intervene yet again. She was here to assist her clients with the tour, not play referee to their fights.

Lana slipped into one of the huts and onto a small bench in a shady corner, then pulled out her phone. She took a few minutes to select the ten most illuminating photographs that she had taken of Xavier's reconstruction of an excavation, then sent them to Dotty.

Her finger hovered over the call button, but Lana decided to give her boss a minute to study the pictures before she reached out. Her curiosity about the Diquís Delta site Xavier had mentioned drove her to look it up, instead. From the photos she found on their website, it appeared he had created an almost perfect copy of their excavation. Only the two mounds that were being flattened had been incorrectly placed.

Figuring Dotty had seen the photos she'd sent over by now, she dialed her boss's number. For a fleeting moment, Lana wondered whether the geologists had already reached out to her. She doubted it; the two were still in vacation mode and most likely enjoyed taunting Xavier with the idea of informing Dotty, more than the actual act. After all, who would want to be the bearer of such bad news?

Her boss picked up on the third ring. "What am I looking at?"

"Xavier's excavation."

"Excavation? It looks like one of those reconstructions you see at archeological theme parks. Those huts and fences look new, and that row of stones lining that curvy path couldn't have been discovered like that. What the heck is Xavier up to? Where's the dig he's been working on for the past three years?"

Lana pinched her nose. "Dotty, are you sitting down?"

She heard her boss shoo her dogs to the side on the couch. "I am now. Tell me everything."

"I think he has been lying to you about how he has been using the dig's funds and instead has used most of your money to create a prototype for a new kind of scientific instrument that he is convinced will be successful. However, the geologists have seen it and doubt that there is a market for it."

"Wait a second—are you saying that he spent my money on a prototype of a useless invention, instead of the dig he'd guilted me into funding?"

"Yep. That's what it looks like."

Dotty covered her phone's speaker with her hand to, Lana presumed, muffle the curse words she was probably using.

Poor Dotty, she thought. It was hard to see her trusting boss be so easily misled. She had taken Xavier's photos and report at face value. Yet the university had, as well, for the past three years. It wasn't just Dotty that he had been deceiving.

When her boss spoke again, her tone was all business. "I'll nail him for fraud. He took advantage of our loose family connection to sucker me into investing and then deceived me like that—and for three years, to boot! I feel like such a fool."

"You really shouldn't beat yourself up about this. He must have been lying to the university all of this time, as well. You receive the same reports that they do. But Dotty, there's one more thing you need to know about Xavier.

You and the university aren't the only ones funding his dig—he has a number of private and governmental sponsors and is actively searching for more."

"What! Every year he's come groveling to me with his hat out, claiming that no one else believes in his project enough to invest. The man is a scoundrel."

"Dotty, why didn't you ever come down to check on his progress?"

"To be honest, I never really liked Xavier, and I'm not interested in prehistoric archaeology, so there was no real reason to visit his site. Besides, he sent me a copy of the report he'd submitted to the university each year, so I didn't have any reason to doubt him. Which means he must have been deceiving them, too, because those photos you sent me look nothing like those in his reports."

"I can't believe he got away with lying to both you and the university for so long! You'd think one of his assistants would have reported the discrepancies between the reports and actuality at some point. At least now his employers will find out what Xavier's really been up to."

"What do you mean—the university will soon know about his fraud?"

"Because Xavier's dig is being audited. Now that I think of it, Sam did make some cryptic comments earlier about not wanting to lie to the auditors, and Jersey and Xavier were pressuring him to 'stick to their story.' I wonder if Jersey has been lying to the university about the dig, as well. She's the only assistant who's worked on it for all three seasons. Sam must have figured out what Xavier is up to and they were trying to pressure him to stay quiet about it."

"I sure hope he does tell the auditors about Xavier's deception. That will make things easier for my lawyers," Dotty interjected. "I'm going to contact the university's board of directors today. Can I share your pictures with them? They need to know what he's been up to, as well."

"Certainly. Let me know if you need more. I took a few hundred. But Dotty, you should know that it sounds like Xavier's burned through all of his money. I doubt he has the funds to repay you."

"I'll let my lawyers deal with that," Dotty huffed. "Lord, I hope the geologists didn't already invest in his site. I feel rotten about encouraging them to do so, and even more so for sending them on the tour with Xavier."

Lana suppressed a chuckle. "Don't worry about them. They have made it quite clear that they're not impressed with Xavier or his supposed dig. But they don't blame you. In fact, they have already said that they assume that he's been lying to you, as well as the university."

"That's a relief. Regardless, I'll have to call and apologize to them. I owe them that much. Is there anything else I need to know about this situation before I call the university?"

Lana was quiet a moment, considering the other issue she'd wanted to talk to Dotty about. She'd initially thought George's commissions weren't worth sharing now, but they were also a result of Dotty's trust being abused. Her boss deserved to know the truth about him, too.

"There is one more thing, but it has nothing to do with Xavier. We can deal with it later, if you prefer."

"Might as well spit it out now; you've got me intrigued."

"Okay. Well, did you know that George received a commission from the hotel in Monteverde?"

"I certainly did not! That's strictly forbidden—I told George that myself the day I hired him. And here I was thinking he was one of my better recent hires."

"From what Randy's told me, George does sound like a great guide, but him receiving commissions would explain the odd itinerary he's created. There are so many incredible eco-lodges dotted around the country, we could have easily built the tour as a loop and stayed at a different amazing hotel every night. Yet George claimed the one in San Jose was so luxurious, it was worth the extra drive. Now I'm thinking it was the payback he was anticipating. It is one of the most expensive hotels in Costa Rica."

"That would definitely explain that crazy itinerary. I didn't really believe using San Jose as a base was the smartest move, but I figured he had his reasons, for the good of the tour. I never suspected it was all about lining his pockets." Dotty's disappointment in George was evident in her voice.

Lana understood why her boss was feeling so low. Dotty had trusted George and Xavier, and both men had taken advantage of her. Her boss was one of those wonderful people who still took people at their word, and it saddened Lana deeply that she'd been conned.

"Lana, honey, I think I need a minute to take this all in. Will you keep me updated on any other developments?"

"Of course. Take care, Dotty!"

19

A Two-Ton Carreta

After her talk with Dotty, Lana roamed aimlessly around the site, angry for her boss. She had half a mind to confront Xavier herself, but knew that would be an incredibly dumb idea. The last thing Dotty would want was for her to tip Xavier off about a possible criminal investigation. It was far better for her lawyers to approach him in a more formal manner. Only then did her boss have a chance of recovering at least some of her investment, before he could destroy any incriminating paperwork or evidence.

Lana breathed a sigh of relief when it was finally time to round up the group and return to the minivan for their relatively short drive to Sarchi. There they would have a late lunch before visiting the *carreta*, or oxcart, factory the town was famous for. Apparently, in their city park stood the world's largest oxcart, according to the Guinness Book of World Records, a fact they were incredibly proud of and promoted frequently.

Alex was already approaching Cecile and Gregory, and Randy was pointing at the minivan as he talked to the four marketers. Lana searched the site for the three archaeologists, finding them standing to one side of the gift shop, in the shade. The two young assistants had their heads bent over notebooks filled with tiny rows of numbers, while Xavier paced back and forth in front of them, talking on the phone.

"I told you before, we're under a time constraint. If we don't complete the museum this season, I can't guarantee the spheres' safety. A solid building with a strong lock on the door and a yappy guard dog inside is the only way to protect them. We really can't proceed without your help."

He paused midstep to listen, then began to laugh heartily. "If you want to contribute enough for me to pay his salary, then I'm happy to hire a security guard. But that's a costly investment."

What the heck is going on? Is he really trying to rope even more investors into his scheme? Lana thought.

"No, the government won't contribute to the security costs, either. And those spheres fetch so much on the black market, every security company I've approached demands a fortune for their services. And I'm starting to get nervous about having so many authentic ones in the museum. With all of the local employees I've had in here working at the site, it is only a matter of time before the wrong *bandido* finds out how much they are worth and tries to steal them."

Xavier listened a moment and then burst into laughter. "True, they would have to be pretty strong to steal the larger ones. But you see my point."

Lana suppressed a chuckle. The Costa Ricans she'd met were gregarious, passionate souls who were exceedingly friendly. Yet everywhere she had traveled on this trip, businesses and even some private homes were guarded with armed security guides, mostly scary-looking men with automatic rifles strapped to their chests. She could only imagine how much it would cost to employ a private security service to guard costly cultural artifacts located out in the boondocks.

After Xavier hung up, the smile that lit up his face made clear that the sponsor had said yes.

Sam glared over at him. "You lie so naturally, it's no wonder you've gotten away with everything for so long. What would your backers say if they knew what you were really funneling the money into?"

Xavier chuckled at the caustic tone in his assistant's voice. "I told you before—your dichotomous thinking is going to get you into trouble one day, young man. Especially if you keep trying to interfere with what you do not understand."

"I understand that you have no morals or shame." Sam stormed off towards the museum before Xavier could answer, barreling past Lana as if he hadn't seen her.

When Xavier started to tear after him, Jersey sprung up and put a hand on his arm. "Leave it. He'll listen to me more than you right now."

"Fine, but you need to talk to him before he contacts the university." Xavier began to stalk away, until he noticed Lana observing them.

"What are you doing standing there, listening in on our private conversation again? Jersey was right—you are spying on us! Who do you really work for?"

Lana continued walking towards them as if she hadn't just frozen in place. "Wanderlust Tours and no one else. It's time to go to Sarchi, which is why I came over here to ask you to join us in the minivan." She intentionally added a touch of irritation to her voice before turning on her heel and setting off in the direction of the vehicle. The last thing she wanted was get sucked into a confrontation with Xavier. It seemed as if the man was constantly looking for a fight, by the way he acted.

She rushed into the museum, in search of Sam. Her target was pacing the floor and mumbling to himself.

"Hey there, it's time to leave. Can you join us at the minivan?"

"Yeah, okay." His tense reply made clear that he was still simmering with anger. Lana saw it as a chance to find out more about his disagreement with Xavier.

"What is going on between you three? It sounds like there's trouble with the project. Are you out of funds—is that why Xavier is rounding up more sponsors?"

Instead of answering, he looked at her with dull eyes. "You shouldn't be listening in on private conversations. You don't have all the details and might take the information out of context."

Lana nodded vigorously. "You are right about that. I'm sorry to have pried. You just seem so upset with the others, I thought you might need to talk it out with someone. My apologies for having overstepped."

She turned to walk away, when Sam called her back. "No, it's alright. You weren't trying to be rude. I honestly don't know what is going on, and Xavier refuses to explain it all to me, either. It's just, I don't believe him when he says that everything is on the up and up. Paperwork does not lie."

"Okay, but you seem incredibly worked up about it. Is that really all that is going on?" Lana saw her chance to find out more about the project and funding and possibly help her boss in the process.

Sam glared at her for a moment before replying, "I can't stand immoral behavior—the perpetrator never thinks of the consequences."

"That's rather heavy…"

"When my dad cheated on my mom, it destroyed her, but my dad didn't really seem to care. Lies can ruin lives. They can even kill." His voice trailed off so much so that the last sentence was almost inaudible.

Lana felt a shiver over her spine. Did his mother harm herself, as a result of his father's infidelity? She didn't dare ask. But she couldn't leave Sam like this, either.

"Is that why you refuse to lie for Xavier anymore? Do you believe that he is involved in something immoral?"

Sam flushed red. "I've said too much. You can't repeat any of this to anyone else. You don't have all the information, either. It's my battle to wage, not yours."

Lana held up her hands. "Of course. I won't say anything to anyone. But we should go join the others. Do you need a minute to compose yourself?"

Sam wiped a hand over his face. "It's okay. I'm as ready as I'll ever be."

The rest stood by the entrance gate, waiting while the driver turned the minivan around. When they reached the others, Lana noticed that the four marketers had their heads close together as if they were discussing something important. A few second later, they righted themselves and strode over to Alex. The devilish grins on their faces as they sauntered over gave her a bad feeling about how this conversation was going to go.

As she caught up to them, Lana heard Chet say, "Hey, are you Alex Wright, of Cramden Consulting? You looked so familiar, but I couldn't place you until I was scrolling through some photos of a tech conference I'd attended in Antwerp last year and found one with you in it."

Alex smiled. "One and the same."

"That was some high-level stuff. You're a great teacher—I remember because I had to write up a report for my boss. So what happened, bro?"

Alex visibly gulped. "What do you mean?"

Chet spread his arms out. "I mean, why are you leading tours in Costa Rica instead of workshops in Europe?"

Alex's nervous titter made Lana cringe. "I guess I got burned out on it, so I decided to make a change."

Chet slowly nodded before slapping Alex on his back. Even Lana could see that the man's respect for Alex was diminishing. "I hear you, bro. We've all been there. You'll find your way again soon enough."

The buddies took a few steps back, then huddled together again. Their silent stares and soft giggles as they side-eyed Alex made things so much worse. Before Lana could say anything comforting, their driver sprung out of the minivan and waved for them to get in.

"Okay, it's time to go," Lana said as loudly as she could.

Alex stepped aside to let the clients board first, before slinking in behind them. Lana groaned internally as she watched her boyfriend sink low into his seat and dip his head, as if he wanted to disappear. She silently cursed the bros, wishing fate hadn't brought them to this tour. Thanks to their caustic comments, all of her work building Alex's ego back up was for naught.

20

Building an Oxcart

The ride to Sarchi was not too long, which was a relief for both the guides and their clients. Best of all, it was along a gorgeous stretch of road, and the passengers spent their time looking outside for waterfalls and wildlife, instead of picking fights with each other.

"Isn't that a spider monkey?" Cecile cried as she tapped on the window. Yet by the time Lana turned her head, the bus had already passed it by.

"I missed it, but it could have been," Gregory replied, as he searched the trees whizzing past their window.

Less than an hour later, road signs for Sarchi came into view. They had just exited the freeway, when Sam's phone began to ring. The young man looked at the screen, but didn't answer the call.

"What's that all about?" Xavier asked.

"It's the university. They want to schedule a FaceTime chat about the site for the official audit."

"Why are they contacting you about the dig or audit? You're the second assistant!" Xavier roared.

Sam shrugged. "They're interviewing everyone who's worked on the site. Didn't you know that?"

"Of course I did. But why would they start with you? It is my project, after all," Xavier huffed.

Randy stood up in the aisle, effectively cutting off everyone's conversations.

"I apologize for interrupting, but we are about to enter Sarchi—home of the world-famous *carretas*! We are going to stop at the world's largest oxcart for a few pictures, before heading to the Eloy Alfaro Oxcart Factory for lunch and a private tour of their workshops. There, we will be able to see how they build and paint their famous creations."

Lana was glad to hear murmurs of approval coming from almost all of the guests. Only the four bros didn't seem that enthusiastic. It was going to be a challenge finding the right balance between a cultural tour and an adrenaline-filled one, Lana was starting to realize, especially given the younger age range Dotty was intending to target. Granted, Randy had said that George had only added this trip to the itinerary after the geologists asked to visit it.

Like the rest of Costa Rica, Sarchi's city center was gaily decorated in red, blue, and white, in preparation of the upcoming Independence Day celebrations. She couldn't wait to see the parades and fireworks tomorrow in San Jose. With it being the capital city, she expected they would have a spectacular display.

Soon the driver pulled off at Sarchi's city park, home to the world's largest oxcart. The group filed out, and Lana took silly photos of her guests standing next to the behemoth of a vehicle. The colorful oxcart was painted in vibrant red with elaborate floral motifs decorating the wheels and sides. A freestanding roof shielded the forty-five-foot-long, two-ton vehicle from the elements. According to an information panel, it was five times the size of a normal cart and had been built in 2006 in a successful attempt to get the name of the city into the Guinness Book of World Records.

After a brief photo stop, they filed back into the van and were quickly transported to the oxcart factory.

Close to the entrance, signs announced a special parade in celebration of Independence Day later in the afternoon, to be held in their arena. The cute photos of oxen wearing necklaces made of hibiscus flowers made her glad they would be here to witness it.

Before they could enter the center, their tour guide waved them over, then escorted them around the long line and into the workshop area via a side door.

As she walked, their guide explained the cultural and economic significance of the oxcarts.

"The traditional oxcarts, or *carretas*, date back to the mid-nineteenth century, when they were used to transport coffee beans from the central valley over the mountains to Puntarenas on the Pacific coast. The journey, over otherwise impenetrable roads and steep mountain passes and slopes, required ten to fifteen days."

"That's fascinating. I never would have guessed that those decorative oxcarts were primarily used to transport coffee," Lana replied, noting that several of her clients were also listening attentively.

She looked up at the mountain peaks towering above Sarchi's city skyline, feeling sorry for the poor beasts who had to trudge up and down those slopes with an oxcart strapped to their backs.

"Oxcarts are engrained in our culture and were even added to UNESCO's World Heritage List in 2005. If you get the chance, you should come back in March for *Dia de los Boyeros*. It's a special festival dedicated to oxcart drivers, and the parades are beautiful—much like the one the factory is holding later today."

Their guide briefly explained the construction process before leading them into an open courtyard upon which several quaint farmhouse-style buildings were located. Old oxcart parts and tools leaned against the outer walls as decoration.

"Here are the workshops where each component is constructed and built upon, as it moves through the factory."

Most of the spaces had barn-sized doors that were open to let in light and fresh air, and also provided them a glimpse inside each workshop.

In one, an older man was bending strips of steel that, according to their guide, would become the metal tires for the oxcarts. They weren't allowed into that space, probably because it was chock-full of dangerous-looking lathes, drills, and saws.

"How long does it take to build one oxcart?" Gregory asked.

"Almost one hundred hours to construct each cart, and another one hundred and twenty hours to paint them. Three carts a month is a good output for the factory," their guide answered.

When Lana considered how much work was necessary, she was impressed that they were able to make so many, and so fast.

They moved on to the woodworking area, and their guide led them inside and past several workbenches filled with lethal-looking tools. In here, each piece of the oxcart was cut out by hand, before the whole thing was assembled by workers in the adjoining space. Hanging on the walls were more tools, including many heavy mallets and thin, knifelike chisels. Considering the hardness of the wood they had to cut into, she figured they would have to be razor sharp.

Lana particularly enjoyed watching the workers pound the pieces together and seeing how the form took shape. Which was probably why she didn't see what her guests were up to, until a commotion on the other side of the space caught her attention.

When she turned to see what the problem was, Lana noticed that a security guard was asking Jersey and Cecile to step away from one of the workbenches.

Her clients were standing rather close to a table full of tools, but so were the other guests. The workshop's spaces were spacious, yet full of workers sawing and hammering on pieces of wood. There weren't many safe places to stand.

"I am going to ask you again, please do not touch the tools."

"We weren't touching anything," Jersey snapped at the security guard. "We were just looking. I don't want to actually build an oxcart with my bare hands."

"We were curious about the tools they were using, that's all," Cecile added in a gentler tone. "I promise we didn't actually touch anything."

The guard seemed to believe Cecile and, after a quick glare at Jersey, left their group alone.

Relieved the situation hadn't escalated, Lana gladly joined their guide as she led them to the following space. She could smell the strong fumes emanating from the freshly painted parts in the next workshop even before they entered the large shack-style garage. A young artisan was bent over several oddly shaped panels painted in that vibrant red the factory was famous for. The young man was adding stylized flowers in light blues and pinks, with a steady hand.

"Kevin is painting the sixteen panels that will form one wheel. This is one of the most challenging parts of an oxcart's creation because each piece needs to fit together perfectly when mounted onto the frame."

Lana took a moment to appreciate the complex task, until the strong fumes overwhelmed her and she had to step back outside.

Their tour ended in the factory's café with a simple lunch of *casado*—a medley of rice, red beans, and fish—followed by a milky slice of sponge cake topped with cherries, called *tres leches*.

When the waitress cleaned up their plates, a cowbell rang outside.

"What was that?" Randy asked.

"There's a special parade organized today, because of Independence Day." The waitress pointed to the arena accessible through the café's patio doors. "The oxen are all wearing flower garlands and special bells, especially for this parade. Try to get close to the rope so you can see the oxcarts better; otherwise it's hard to see the decorations."

"That sounds adorable," Jersey gushed. When the cowbell rang again, Jersey shot outside and pushed forward through the crowd until she was standing at the thick red rope strung around the oval courtyard that was, Lana presumed, to keep visitors from accidentally stepping out into the arena during the parade.

Lana was surprised to see that Jersey had heard what the waitress had said, let alone was so interested in seeing the oxcarts race.

Jersey waved the group over, seemingly irritated that they weren't already behind her. Yet she'd moved so quickly through the crowd, it took quite a bit of jostling to reach her.

Sam stood at the rope along with Jersey and Xavier on one side, and Gregory and Cecile on the other. The four marketers and three guides stood behind them. Lana had to stand on her tippy-toes to see it all. At first, a line of oxcarts pulled by a pair of large oxen slowly circled the oval-shaped arena. The gorgeously painted carts with the gaily decorated animals and their festively dressed riders were a delight to see.

"Aren't the oxen adorable?" Cecile gushed.

"Look at how muscular they are! I bet those adorable beasts, as you call them, could kill you with one kick and not even exert themselves," Gregory laughed.

The oxen trotted past at a moderate pace, and as they circled the arena, the carts swung out a little, coming close enough to the red rope that Lana was getting dust in her eyes.

When Jersey leaned over the rope to get a closer look at the cart cruising by, her water bottle slid out of her hands and rolled into the arena. She ducked under the rope to try to grab it before the next cart approached, but the oxen were bearing down too fast for her to reach it in time.

Sam reached under the line and grabbed her feet, pulling her back just in time from getting her head stomped in by an ox.

Cecile tugged on her shorts, helping to slide her back to where she could easily stand.

When an ox stumbled over the thick glass bottle, its hoof gliding over the slippery surface, the beast buckled his knee and snorted, jerking the driver forward and almost out of the oxcart.

"Sorry!" Jersey yelled out to the driver as she jostled into Cecile and Sam.

Lana shook her head. *What a clumsy woman*, she thought, relieved nothing worse had happened.

Yet, to her horror, Sam suddenly bent over the rope, as if he was trying to retrieve the bottle from under the oxcart.

"What are you doing? Leave it!" Lana screamed, terrified for her client. She couldn't believe he'd be so stupid to try and retrieve it.

"Watch out!" Jersey shrieked as she tried to pull Sam back by pulling on his T-shirt.

The next thing Lana knew, Sam seemed to be falling forward right into the ox's path. Before she could yell out again, it was barreling over him with the cart still in tow.

A cry of horror rose up from the crowd. The sickening crunch as the heavy cart rolled over her guest was almost too much to bear.

"Everyone, get back!" someone yelled out.

"Call an ambulance—tell them to hurry!" another screamed.

But one look at his lifeless body told Lana that there was no need for them to rush. Sam was gone.

21

A Terrible Accident

Shrieks of terror and wails of sadness echoed around the arena. The celebrations came to a screeching halt once it became clear that someone had been killed. Employees formed a human fence, attempting to block the view of Sam's body from the public.

Lana turned to her group, ready to comfort anyone in need. Though she had expected tears at Sam's demise, her own group seemed almost indifferent to his passing. Sure, Xavier and Jersey were understandably shocked, but not enough to actually cry about it. Instead, while waiting for the police, the two stood with their heads together, whispering frantically. Lana figured they were concerned about the audit or how Sam's death would affect the dig, yet was too far away from the pair to hear their conversations.

The rest milled around, chatting softly as they waited for the police to arrive, but none showed an outpouring of emotion at his demise. Perhaps it wasn't that strange that the others didn't seem to really be affected by his death, Lana considered as she watched her group. Sam had kept away from the larger group on the days that she had been present, preferring to keep Jersey company. Though she thought he was a pleasant-enough young man.

Well, he was pleasant to me, Lana thought, recalling the quarrels he'd had with other guests. He had openly argued with the geologist about his first wife's death and Gregory's possible involvement in it. Come to think of it, Sam had acted as if he knew something that Gregory didn't want to get around. Lana side-eyed the geologists. Maybe it wasn't indifference Gregory was feeling, but relief that Sam could no longer spill his secrets.

The young archaeologist had also been butting heads with his boss about the upcoming audit of their dig. What if Sam had discovered that Xavier was misusing the sponsors' money and was planning on telling the auditing committee about it? Would that give the senior archaeologist reason to kill him?

It was a motive, but Lana couldn't imagine that Sam was the only one who had puzzled that fact out already. Heck, just from overhearing parts of their conversations, she'd suspected Xavier of doing something similar. When the auditors interviewed everyone involved, surely someone else would bring up Xavier's money problems.

By the time the police arrived a half hour later, the sobbing and crying had died down, though many were still openly grieving for the young man whose life they'd seen get snuffed out. The officers quickly cordoned off one section of the arena for the interviews, before calling over those who had been standing close to Sam when the ox went wild.

Unfortunately, the police kept the rest back from the interviewees, meaning Lana couldn't listen in. When it was her turn, one officer asked to take a picture of her passport with his phone, before escorting her over to a colleague sitting on a barstool set up in the shade. The man asked about her movements before the accident, and to point out where she had been standing when Sam had fallen down. Lana did as asked, surprised that the officer then said that she was free to go.

He pointed to the other side of the show ring, where the guests who had already been interviewed were now gathered. Before she could ask any questions of him, he waved over the next interviewee.

As Lana walked away, she noted that Alex and Randy were being called over. They were the last two of their tour group to be interviewed, which gave her hope that they would be able to leave Sarchi fairly soon. She joined the others, engaged in a whispered conversation about the police's lack of enthusiasm and forensics.

"They must think it's an accident if they haven't even taken pictures of the scene," Gregory said.

"Are you certain that they didn't? I couldn't see Sam's body while I was being interviewed; maybe they took a few snaps then," Cecile said.

"Why would they think it was anything but an accident? Sam had the misfortune of being in the wrong place when that ox stumbled," Xavier said.

"That raging beast came straight for us! I think Sam must have fainted from fright just before he got sucked under the oxcart's wheel," Jersey declared.

"Is that what occurred?" Cecile asked. "It all happened so quickly, I still don't know what I saw. First Sam was standing there, cheering the oxcarts on, and then he was on the ground and that wheel was rolling over him. That poor boy." Cecile closed her eyes as her whole body shivered.

"Honestly, I'm not one hundred percent certain, but it sure seemed like the ox tripped over something before he barreled into the audience. We had to jump back to get out of the beast's path," Gregory said.

"It's Jersey's fault he's dead," Xavier declared before turning on his assistant. "You're such a klutz. If you hadn't dropped your water bottle, he wouldn't have leaned over the rope like that."

Jersey shrank at his words. "I didn't mean to drop it! And I certainly didn't ask him to pick it up."

"You never mean to do anything, but you still manage to mess up quite a bit, don't you?"

"Hey, that's not fair! I liked Sam. I never would have wanted him to get hurt, and especially not over a silly water bottle."

"Hey, guys, stop it. It doesn't matter how or why—the fact is, Sam's death was a tragic accident and certainly not intentional," Lana declared.

From everything she could see, it had to have been. Sam must have bent over the rope just as the oxcart raced past and gotten sucked under the wheel. Jersey had even tried to pull him back up after he fell forward.

Soon after her group had been interviewed, the lead officer stood before them and cleared his throat to get their attention. "We have concluded that Sam Perkins is the victim of a tragic accident. Everyone is now free to leave. We have your contact information and will be in touch if we have further questions. *Muchas gracias.*"

Randy sighed in relief. "Excellent. Let's get to the minivan and get out of here, before the police change their minds."

They were back in the van in record time. As soon as their ride had pulled out onto the main road, Randy stood up in the aisle.

"Folks, that is not how I expected our tour of Sarchi to end. Is everyone doing alright, emotionally?"

Lana pondered his question as she looked to her boyfriend, seated by her side. To her, the only consolation in this whole mess was knowing that Sam's death was an accident and not murder.

A few muttered unclear responses came, but no one seemed to be devastated or overly emotional.

"We're on our way back to San Jose now. The interviews took quite a bit of time, but we should still catch the lantern festival before dinner, and we have the Independence Day celebrations to look forward to tomorrow. That is—if you all still want to continue on with the tour."

"Of course we do. Why wouldn't we?" Gregory asked, his face creased in confusion.

"Because one of our group was just killed in a horrific accident?" Randy asked, his tone laced with disbelief.

Lana felt the same. It was clear that Sam hadn't cared for Gregory, but the geologist didn't have to be so crass about it. A human being had lost their life in a tragic way—that was worth a moment of reflection, she thought. When she looked out the window, Lana barely registered the gorgeous scenery flashing past. Her thoughts were consumed with death, instead of the natural beauty of the land.

22

Romantic Fireworks

Traffic increased significantly the closer they got to the capital. Their bus had to fight through the throngs of traffic to reach their hotel. Lana knew that tonight was the kickoff of the Independence Day celebrations, with a torch relay from Guatemala to Costa Rica, symbolizing the spread of independence across Central America. But Lana hadn't expected that the festivities would have reached San Jose already.

When they pulled up to the hotel, the driver pointed to his wristwatch. "In fifteen minutes, this place is going to go crazy."

"Crazier than this?"

He smiled widely. "Much crazier. Enjoy it!"

As they passed by the lobby, the receptionist looked up at them in astonishment before calling out, "What are you doing inside?"

"We just got back from a long day trip, and our guests want to rest for a few minutes before we head out into that crowd," Lana answered, intentionally not mentioning Sam's demise. There was need to share that tragic news with this young woman—especially not on the cusp of such an important celebration.

The receptionist sprinted around the desk and blocked their path to the elevator. "There's no time! The national anthem is about to be sung, and then the lantern parade will begin. Hurry up and get outside—otherwise you might miss it!"

Before anyone in the group could respond, the tiny woman shooed them back outside. It took Lana a minute to orient herself, thanks to the throngs of festivalgoers crowding the streets. Their hotel seemed to be in the heart of the city center, and thus the eye of the celebratory storm as it were. There was plenty to see, smell, and hear. After learning about how George had gotten injured, Lana was glad to see large pieces of plywood covering sections of sidewalk to, she presumed, conceal any dangerous holes.

Most locals were wearing festive clothing in the colors of the flag, with some singing and dancing as they waited for the national anthem to begin. The street was charged with a palpable energy that heightened Lana's sense of anticipation. At six sharp, seemingly hundreds of bands began to play simultaneously, and everyone around them belted out the country's national anthem—many with tears of pride in their eyes.

As soon as the last bar faded out, there was an explosion of applause, hoots, and cheers as the locals hugged and kissed each other with a passion Lana hadn't witnessed in a very long time. It was quite exhilarating to be in the middle of it all.

Minutes later, the streets begin to clear, giving way to a slowly moving procession of children carrying candle-lit lanterns in the form of ships, flowers, oxcarts, accordions, and traditional houses. It was a mesmerizing spectacle that seemed to illuminate the entire street, thanks to the sheer number of children.

After the lantern parade passed by, groups of musicians gathered together again and entertained the crowd as they waited for the sun to set and the fireworks show to begin. Soon, a dazzling display of color lit up the night, to the cheers of all around.

Lana took Alex's hand as they watched the fireworks explode across the sky. Maybe it was just the elation of being part of this boisterous celebration, but for the first time since she'd arrived in Costa Rica, Lana felt as if everything was going to be okay.

As she squeezed Alex's hand, she only hoped that she'd feel the same way in the morning.

23

Independence Day

Saturday—Day Seven of the Wanderlust Tour of Costa Rica

Lana woke with a start, confused as to where she was, and why a brass band was playing outside her window.

Alex rolled over and rubbed his eyes. "What the heck is that? It almost sounds like a choir of trumpets."

"It sure does," she grumbled as she rose and pulled on a bathrobe before crossing over to the window facing the street. When Lana pulled back the curtain, she was shocked to see an actual brass band merrily marching up the road in front of the hotel, to the joy of many a flag-waving Costa Rican. It was fantastic to see and hear, but quite early.

"The parade route must run past the hotel. And from the looks of things, it's already in full swing," Lana said. She took in the streamers covering the streets, and festive stalls selling foods and flags along the sidelines, excited to walk around and see more.

But first, she had to rouse her fellow guides and guests out of bed. Not that she expected that to be a problem. Based on the sheer volume of the music, she figured that they were already awake.

Lana stretched her hands over her head and yawned, still groggy from a short night's sleep. After the fireworks show, her group had stayed up late listening to the fantastic music and dancing with the locals.

She showered and dressed in record time, eager to get outside. She only hoped that their clients weren't already partied out. If the guests preferred to do something else today, then she would probably be out of luck. After all, she was here as a guide, not as a guest.

When Alex jumped into the shower, she skipped down the stairs, lost in her own thoughts, until familiar voices coming from a few floors down made her slow to a stop.

"Being closely involved with two mysterious deaths will not be good for your reputation. I wonder what the Jade Museum is going to think of this," Xavier taunted.

Lana poked her head over the staircase and looked down, spotting Xavier and Gregory two floors below her.

"Are you actually implying that I somehow harmed Sam? I wasn't even near him when he fell!" Gregory cried out.

Whatever Xavier said next was too quiet for her to hear, but she couldn't miss Gregory's reaction. "No, you're being ridiculous! No one will believe your silly stories."

"Are you willing to take that chance? Being involved in one mysterious death got so many tongues wagging that no one wanted to work with you. You managed to bury the story eventually, but now that you're involved with two mysterious deaths, are you willing to take that chance again?"

Gregory sputtered a response, but before he could enunciate his words, Xavier was already walking down the stairs, chortling as he went.

Lana sighed deeply, wondering why he couldn't just accept that Gregory wasn't interested in investing and let him be.

She waited until she couldn't hear either man's heels clicking on the tile floor, before descending the rest of the staircase.

When she got downstairs, Lana was surprised to see her guests already seated at the back of the breakfast hall, quietly enjoying the first meal of the day. *Maybe enjoying is too strong a word*, she thought after noting her guests' swollen eyelids and puffy cheeks. Xavier and Jersey were nursing cups of coffee, while the four bros sipped large glasses of orange juice. Only the married geologists were standing at the buffet, loading up their plates.

She waved at Randy before scooping up a bit of egg scrambled with chorizo and a healthy portion of black beans and rice, and then joining him.

"Where's Alex?" he asked.

"He's in the shower now. That's the downside of having two guides share one room, I guess."

"Fair enough. Say, how should we do this? Would you prefer to be out in the crowd, or do you want to hang back at the hotel?"

"I'm good, either way," she fibbed. Randy had been working the hardest of all and deserved to choose what he wanted to do today.

"Hey, guys." Alex bounded into the breakfast hall, an easy smile on his face. "That's some alarm clock."

Randy laughed. "Yeah, it's not my typical choice of music, but it does get you out of bed."

Alex slapped his hands together. "So, what is everyone up to today? Have you already asked the guests what they want to do?"

"Actually, no. Let's do that now and then see what happens."

When Randy set down his fork, Lana added, "Alex can do it. You've done enough so far."

Randy waved her comment away as he stood. "I've got this. Hey gang, as you've already noticed, the Independence Day celebrations are in full swing. There will be music and dancing most of the day and night, so do pace yourselves. Who would like to check out the parades and festivities now? And who would prefer to hang back at the hotel a while longer and go out later? Let's start with the partygoers. Who's game?"

"I'm ready to go now. I can't wait to dance the merengue again," Cecile enthused.

Gregory grabbed her hand and gently lifted it to his lips. "You are a vision when you dance."

"I'm not going anywhere until noon. It's too bad our hotel is on the parade route. Those blasted instruments are going to make it difficult to get back to sleep," Chet grumbled.

"I'm with you," Dave agreed, while the other two nodded. "The bull running doesn't start until later, anyway."

"That's going to be amazing, bro!" Mike agreed.

Lana bit her lip. "I thought bullfighting is illegal."

Mike's eyes sprung open. "No, this is something different. Trust me, I'm not down with animal cruelty, either. From what I read online, they don't kill the bull, but let people ride it or evade it. Whoever succeeds wins a prize."

"Oh." Lana smiled weakly, wondering what prize would be worth risking permanent injury for.

Randy must have had the same thought, for his forehead creased. "I'm not really up for joining in on the bull running. What about you, Alex? Could you escort them over?"

"Actually, I can accompany the geologists."

By the way Alex intentionally averted his eyes from the four marketers as he spoke told Lana that his eager tone was an attempt to disguise his real reason for not wanting to remain in the hotel. She bit her lip, not wanting to embarrass Alex in front of the others, yet she knew she had to talk to him about his attitude again. *And his relationship with his brother*, she thought as she took in how Randy was glaring at Alex.

"Oh, that's okay, we don't need a babysitter. Dave knows where it's at," Chet hastily added, as if he also sensed tension between the two brothers.

"We don't need an escort, either, but would prefer to get lost in the crowd. We'll meet you back at the hotel later," Gregory said.

"But it was nice of you to offer," Cecile added.

"Great. I hope you all have fun," Randy told them before turning to the archaeologists. "Xavier, what would you and Jersey like to do?"

Xavier looked over at his assistant. "You can go out if you want, but I would rather get some paperwork done now and join in the festivities later."

"Do you need any help?" Jersey asked.

"No, it's nothing I need your input on. It's Sam." Xavier's voice faltered. "Now that he's gone, I have quite a bit of administrative work."

Jersey's mouth pursed into a thin line at the mention of Sam's name. She began to stretch out a hand towards Xavier's shoulder, as if to comfort him, but suddenly pulled her arm back, as if she knew it was a bad idea.

"I'm not ready to go out either. I saw a spa in the basement of the hotel and am going to head down there after breakfast. Those drinks last night hit me pretty hard. You can find me down there if you have any questions."

"That means only the geologists are going out now, correct? Randy, would you prefer to stay at the hotel, in case anyone needs assistance, or would you like to go out now and enjoy the party? You have been working the hardest and deserve to enjoy the festivities—if you feel like doing so."

Alex glared at her so intently, her cheeks burst into flames. She knew he had already said that he wanted to head out now, but she held fast to her standpoint.

Randy noticed Alex's glare, too, and sighed in irritation. "To be honest, Lana, I would rather hang back at the hotel for now. I didn't sleep well last night and was up early confirming our reservations for Panama tomorrow. I could use a bit of shut-eye, at least if the guests don't need any help."

"Why don't I stay behind and be on call, so you can sleep?"

Randy's fingers glided through his hair. "No, there's no need. You and Alex go enjoy the party. I'm happy to join in later. It sounds like the rest are going to be sleeping or entertaining themselves, so it should work out just fine."

Lana studied Randy, trying to discern whether he was telling the truth or only wanted to avoid an argument with his brother.

"Great. We'll see you later." Apparently Alex didn't care, either way. He slapped his younger brother on the back before heading to the door.

Randy grabbed Lana's arm and whispered, "Can you please talk to him about his attitude? I'm so fed up with him that I'm about to ask Dotty to send him home. He can't keep ignoring the clients he doesn't like. It doesn't work like that."

Lana grimaced. She was beginning to fear that this trip was going to affect the brothers' relationship long after the tour was over. "You noticed, too? I'll do my best, but try not to worry about Alex and get some sleep, instead."

As she squeezed his arm, Randy's smile turned into a yawn. "Will do."

When Alex turned to look for Lana, she skipped up to him and hooked her arm around his. "Are you ready?"

"Yes, ma'am."

"Excellent—lead the way."

They were quickly engulfed by the jovial crowd, jostled forward along the market stalls and musical podiums dotting the streets. Lana took in the many offerings of food, handmade crafts, and souvenirs for sale, but was too captivated by the music and dancers to shop.

As they passed a side street, Lana saw a marimba band entertaining a large crowd, as a folk-dancing troupe of women, wearing red and blue dresses trimmed with white, twirled and swayed to the admiration of their public.

Everywhere she looked, women and men decorated to the nines danced to the beat of many a band, the music blending into a chaotic, yet pleasing, cacophony of sound. Lana had two left feet, but just being here in this crowd was reason enough to want to join in.

"Come on, let's try to salsa." Lana grabbed Alex's hand, and the two mimicked a pair of elderly locals dancing close to them. Despite the age difference, the seniors were far better. Luckily, they found it amusing to help the *gringos* master a few steps, and before they knew it, Alex and Lana were dancing in rhythm with the street. She'd never felt such euphoria at being part of something so much bigger than she. It was amazing and wonderful to get lost in the music.

After spending most of the afternoon dancing, Lana was wiped out. From the look of it, Alex was, too.

She pointed to a food stall. "Can I buy you an empanada?"

"Sure, they look delicious."

It took a while to get through the line, but once they'd received their beef empanadas, they maneuvered their way over to the side of a building in a less chaotic side street to eat their treat.

"This is good," Alex muttered through bites.

Lana tried to respond in kind, but her mouth was too full. The beef was so tender and seasoned with a mix she couldn't identify but found delicious. The crust was as crunchy as a taco chip, despite being much thicker. It was an incredible treat, and once it was finished, she wished she'd bought another one.

After they'd both gorged themselves, Lana decided it was time to have another heart-to-heart. She had hoped that Alex would have been able to readjust his attitude by now, but based on his actions this morning, it didn't look like that was happening.

"Say, how are you feeling about this tour so far?"

Alex grimaced. "Meh."

"Is that why you volunteered to lead the geologists, as soon as the four bros said they were going to stay in the hotel?"

He looked away, towards the main street, before answering. "Maybe."

"Talk to me, Alex. You can't ignore part of your group just because they make you feel a little uncomfortable."

"Do we have to talk about this now? Can't we just enjoy the festivities?"

"No! We're here to work, not dance and eat empanadas."

When Alex jutted his chin up, Lana felt her pent-up frustration boiling to the surface. "You know, I felt bad for you at first, when Chet recognized you, because I could see that it was a painful conversation. But the four bros have been treating you normally since then, and yet you still avoid them. What gives?"

"They clearly see being a guide as a step down." By the way Alex's jaw clenched, Lana was momentarily afraid he was going to take off and get lost in the crowd instead of answering her honestly.

"So what? It's your life, not theirs. Were you happier leading those corporate workshops?"

"No, not really. But this isn't what I was expecting, either."

"What had you expected, exactly?"

Alex leaned back on one heel, considering her question. "I had a great time with George on that research trip, until I realized that once I started leading tours, I wouldn't be able to go off my own, but would have to follow a set itinerary. Nor did I consider the ramifications of being trapped with the same small group of privileged tourists for two weeks. It's far more intense than I could have imagined."

Lana laughed. "Dealing with them is the payoff for getting to tag along on their pricey excursions. You can't have one without the other."

Alex sighed. "I suppose you're right."

"It sounds like you are ready to give up, but this is only your second tour. It was bad luck, George inviting his environmental buddies onto the Mexico trip, but nothing more than that. Maybe you need to give it more of a chance before you make a decision."

"Maybe I do. Or maybe being a guide isn't for me. That's something we both need to consider. You're right that it didn't help that the members of the first tour tried to recruit me into being an environmental activist again. The bros acting condescendingly towards me wasn't great for my ego, either."

Lana regarded her boyfriend, glad to hear he was finally opening up to her, yet distressed that he was still hung up about this supposed step down the career ladder. "A corporate job does come with a certain level of prestige that a tour guide does not have—I get that. But how important is other people's perceptions of you?"

"What do you mean?"

"I remember reading an article about a medical doctor who got so fed up with the stress of his job that he quit and retrained to become a welder. He thought he was making a better life for himself, but didn't anticipate how his neighbors would react. As their doctor, he had always been highly regarded in his community. Yet after his career switch, his neighbors acted like he'd gone crazy. But he claimed that he's never been happier. I guess you need to decide what is more important to you—being truly happy with your career choice, or the social status a job brings. You need to decide that, Alex; no one else can do that for you."

Lana rose, knowing that she'd said all she could. Now it was up to him to answer that question for himself.

24

A Painful Reminder

Lana hummed a jaunty tune as she entered the hotel, her stomach stuffed from all that great street food and her feet tired from all that walking and dancing. Yet the line of guests waiting to use the elevator was so long, she ultimately chose to trudge up the stairs, instead.

Her jovial mood was slightly dampened when she passed the second-floor restaurant and spotted Randy sitting at a table on the hotel's balcony bar, his head nodding forward and his eyes shut. *Poor guy must not have gotten any sleep*, she realized.

She crossed over to him, intending to send him up to his room. "Hey, Randy! How are you doing?"

His head jerked up at the sound of his name. "Pretty good. You can see the parade from up here. Or at least you can if you stand by the railing. That's where the four bros are."

Lana spotted her clients hooting and hollering at the parade down below. Luckily for all of them, the locals seemed to embrace their enthusiasm. One portly man even had his arm over Chet's shoulder, and they were both waving Costa Rican flags in rhythm to the music.

"I don't see any large bandages. Did any of the bros get hurt while running with the bulls?" she asked, almost afraid to hear the answer.

Randy grinned at her question. "No, apparently they had a great time and even managed not to get injured for a change. They're taking a beer break, which it sounds like they earned, before heading downstairs. It was quite intense, running from the bulls, from what they'd said."

"Fair enough. I can take over if you want to get some sleep."

Randy shrugged. "Thanks for the offer, but I doubt I could sleep even if I wanted to."

"It is pretty loud."

"Naw, it's not the music. It's Alex. Whatever I try, I can't get through to him, and now I'm getting worried about the repercussions on our relationship after this tour is over."

"Speaking of which, I did talk to him about his attitude problem, but I don't think I really got through to him either. It's so hard to tell."

"Thanks for trying. You know what, I'm going to head down and get lost in the music. I'd promised to take a few videos for Gloria. I'll see you later, okay?"

"Yeah, sure. Have fun! Alex is still out there somewhere, as are the geologists. I don't think those two will be done dancing anytime soon. We ran into them out front and saw them in action—Cecile is really good."

Lana scanned the crowded balcony but didn't spot Xavier or Jersey. "Before you go, where are the archaeologists?"

"As far as I know, Xavier is still in his room, and Jersey is in the spa. They both seem to want to be left alone, which makes it easier for us. Thanks again, Lana." He stood up, pecked her on the cheek, and disappeared before she could say another word.

Lana waved down a waiter and ordered an agua fresca with strawberries. To her delight, the sweetened juice came served with a Costa Rican flag. Lana grabbed her drink and stood close to the railing, as far away from the bros as she could get.

Soon, Alex and the geologists returned and joined her at the railing. Her boyfriend's improved mood and relaxed smile gave her hope that her words had gotten through to him, after all.

She was enjoying the parade immensely, until a dozen oxcarts rolled past. Lana felt a wave of shame roll over her when she realized that she hadn't even thought of Sam once, since waking today. By the uninterested reactions of her guests, they hadn't either. It was all rather sad. Even though Sam's death didn't seem to cast much of a shadow over the celebrations, those oxcarts were a nasty reminder that the vibrant man's life had been cut short.

"Poor Sam, he died too young," Lana murmured, wondering how the others would react. The geologists stiffened at her words, but further pretended not to hear her.

Alex squeezed her hand in response. "I'm just glad it was an accident. All we needed was a murder investigation, on top of everything else."

"You are right about that," Lana agreed and wrapped her hand in his.

25

What Sam Knew

As the afternoon sun began to wane, Lana was thrilled to see that her group was still in good spirits. However, after a wonderful day of immersing themselves in the Independence Day celebrations, they all looked pretty tired.

They'd reassembled for a late dinner at the hotel's rooftop restaurant, where they would be able to see the fireworks show set to start shortly after dark. Randy had already reserved a long table for the entire group. As soon as Lana had ordered the appetizers, their clients began to arrive, most a bit tipsy from the looks of it. Music playing from the streets echoed against the building's facades and seemed to be louder up here than down below, making it difficult to hear what the person next to you was saying.

Lana didn't mind. Their meal was a scrumptious tapas-style meal of small dishes they shared, and she was happy to focus on the food. The later it got, the softer the music became, making it easier to converse. The four bros recounted their "running from the bull" adventure in loud voices, and their funny stories had them all laughing. Soon after, the geologists talked about the styles of music they'd heard and even showed off a few of the dance passes they'd learned.

It was great to see everyone getting along. Well, almost everyone. Only the two archaeologists weren't taking part in the group's conversation. Though both Xavier and Jersey sat at the table for dinner, they'd moved to one end in order to discuss the work they needed to do in the coming weeks. With one man less, Lana figured they would have to divvy up Sam's work. She couldn't imagine that Xavier would be able to find another volunteer to fly down to San Jose on such short notice—especially one who would be satisfied with his meager compensation package.

After her group was sated, Lana sprung up to see who wanted another drink.

"A cappuccino for me, please," Gregory said.

"Me, too," his wife added.

"We're good," Chet said as he nodded to the foursome's pitcher of beer. When neither archaeologist reacted, Lana figured they couldn't hear her request over the music. They had moved even farther away, so there were several empty chairs between them and the rest.

When Lana made her way over to them, she couldn't help but overhear their conversation.

"So did he agree to drop it, or had he already blabbed?"

"I told you before—I don't know for certain." When Xavier's eyes widened, Jersey rushed to add, "I don't think he'd had the chance to. I didn't see a new message from the university or any FaceTime calls logged on his phone. Can we check his email? He might have used his laptop."

They must be talking about Sam, Lana realized. From the sound of it, Xavier was still concerned about the audit, and specifically what Sam may have already shared with them.

"I can get into his university account," Xavier said.

"That would probably be the one he'd have used. It's worth a try."

When Xavier pushed back his chair, he almost knocked Lana over. She skipped to one side so he could get up.

"You again," he growled.

"I came over to ask if you wanted another drink before they serve dessert. Or are you going back to skip it?" Lana asked, as innocently as she could.

"Er, I guess we are. We need to check something before the fireworks show begins. Is this a good time?" Xavier asked, being uncharacteristically polite.

"Sure. Can I order you another beer or coffee?"

Jersey shook her head as Xavier answered for them both. "We're good for now. We'll be back in a few minutes."

They walked off before Lana could think of another question to ask. What sins had Xavier committed that Sam could have told the university committee about? Lana was becoming convinced that it had something to do with the money. There was no way Xavier had spent one hundred and fifty thousand dollars on that site. To top it off, he was also being paid by the Costa Rican government to rescue spheres from farmers' fields and apparently had several other sponsors sending him funds.

How much had he raised during the past three years and what had he really spent it on? She couldn't imagine that he'd poured it all into his invention, but then again, she knew nothing about building prototypes like those. Could Xavier have funneled it into an offshore bank account or used it to purchase another piece of property? Anything was possible, she realized with a frown.

Whatever he'd done with it, Lana hoped to soon find out more about it from Dotty, once she'd had a chance to contact the university. Hopefully the information they shared would help to illuminate the true nature of Xavier's deceit.

26

Hiking an Active Volcano

Sunday—Day Eight of the Wanderlust Tour, Parque Nacional Volcán Arenal

Their minivan wound through the rolling countryside outside of San Jose, most of it covered in coffee plantations and colorful, ramshackle villages. The night's heavy rainstorm intensified the greens of the trees and the earth's red-brown surface.

They were on an early morning bus ride to Parque Nacional Volcán Arenal. To break up the monotony of the long journey, Alex had suggested they stop at Catarata del Toro, a waterfall located an hour outside of San Jose and on their way. The site, nicknamed the Blue Falls of Costa Rica, was easy to reach and amazingly gorgeous. The water poured out of an extinct volcano's crater that formed vibrant, creamy blue pools. They spotted several types of hummingbirds and even toucans on their walk. Lana couldn't believe that George hadn't already put it on the itinerary.

As their bus traveled closer to their destination, the villages situated near the volcano's flanks were enshrouded in mist. Lana had read that thanks to the average forty-one days of eruptions per year, the soil was exceptionally fertile and perfect for growing coffee beans. The plethora of plantations they passed in the foothills of Arenal attested to the truth of that article. As she looked out over the vast plantations, she wondered how much of the coffee that she drank at home had been grown in those rich fields. She was surprised that a visit to a coffee plantation hadn't been on the itinerary, but then again, this tour was supposed to be adrenaline-filled, not caffeine-filled.

When the clouds parted, Lana gasped in awe. Arenal was exactly the sort of volcano every child learned to draw in school. The uppermost flanks of its perfect conical shape consisted of crumbling rocks. A fringe of green ringed its mist-shrouded base. As Lana watched, a geyser of glowing red lava shot up into the sky. She held her breath as the flame crescendoed, then slowly crashed to the surface. It was Central America's most active volcano, and one of the reasons why tourists flocked to Costa Rica, yet it still seemed surreal to see actual lava spurting out of it.

Lana could hardly believe that they would soon be hiking its flanks. According to the brochure, the trail winding up through the dwarf rainforest to the crater's rim was lined with gurgling geysers, boiling pools, and steam vents. Lana's skin tingled in anticipation.

After viewing the spewing crater up close, they would then spend the afternoon at Tabacón, a hot spring famous because its many pools were fed by an underground river running close to the volcano's inner core.

After their ride pulled into a parking lot full of similar minivans, Lana and her group piled out. Their bus driver stepped out behind them before clearing his throat to get their attention, then pointed at a trailhead a few feet away.

"The main path will take you through the forest and all the way to the top of the volcano. You have four hours to hike before we drive to Tabacón Hot Springs. That should be more than enough time to see the steam vents and reach the crater."

Without waiting for questions, he got back in the bus and closed the door.

"Okay, folks, it's an easy, well-marked path to the top. Even if you don't want to go all the way up, there is plenty to see—boiling mud pits and steam vents, to name a few. And be on the lookout for birds and reptiles—lizards love it here," Randy said, his voice infused with confidence despite never having visited before.

Their clients slowly split off into smaller groups, each walking along the same trail at different paces. The three guides waited until the rest had set off, then slowly followed behind, intentionally putting distance between them and the rest. There was little for them to do because the paths were clearly marked and ropes ensured no one could fall into a vent or mud pit.

The jungle was alive with birds and primates singing and hollering. Lana kept her eyes focused up. "Hey, I think that's a sloth!"

She pointed to a high branch.

"Are you sure? It's so high up, it's hard to tell."

Lana scrunched up her eyes, trying to see it better. "I guess it could just as easily have been a monkey sleeping."

"Which is also pretty cool," Randy added.

When a flash of emerald crossed their path at lightning speed, the trio jumped back.

"Whoa—was that a lizard?"

"It sure looked like it, but man, was he fast."

"I read about those; they are basilisk lizards," Alex enthused. "And look over there, those are leaf cutter ants!"

"I'm glad we got to lead this tour. Despite all of the extra administration, it feels great to be out on the road again," Randy said with a smile.

"Costa Rica is pretty amazing, isn't it?" Alex replied softly.

The three shuffled on at a leisurely pace. The ground under her feet felt warm in places. The bubbling pools of mud and intermittently spouting geysers of steam were constant reminders that they were standing on a live volcano. Close to the top, the trees were twisty, moss-covered sculptures with orchids flowering in every crevice. It was a lovely hike on a beautiful day, and the power of nature was on full display.

They hadn't seen any of their guests, until they came across a widening in the trail where several benches had been placed. Lana spotted Gregory and Cecile on one, cuddling. A few paces away was Xavier, huffing and puffing his way in the couple's direction.

As the three guides approached the benches, Xavier reached the geologists. "I need to finish the museum building before the rainy season begins. It's the only way to protect the spheres."

Lana felt her stomach knot up. Why couldn't Xavier get the hint—that

Gregory would never invest in his site?

Yet instead of protesting, Gregory simply nodded in acknowledgment. "I can transfer the first installment into your account as soon as we're back in San Jose."

Lana felt her jaw flop open. Why on earth would he have changed his mind?

"Can't you do it on your phone?"

"No, I don't have the right apps installed. We'll be back at the hotel in a few hours. What's the rush?"

Xavier wrapped his arms over his torso. "I don't want you reneging on our deal, that's all."

"You'll get your money," Gregory growled through gritted teeth.

"Excellent. As soon as we reach the hotel, okay?" Xavier slapped him on the back, then sauntered away.

Embarrassed for having witnessed their conversation, the trio of guides shuffled past the geologists with no more than a nod of the head. Gregory and Cecile couldn't even make eye contact.

When the threesome reached a bend in the trail with benches placed to give their occupants a gorgeous view of the lush rainforest, they took a seat, enjoying the scenery and a light snack while they chatted about the animals they'd spotted. It was nice to see Randy and Alex relaxing into each other's company again, instead of feeling tense around one another.

Once they were sated, they picked up the trail again. A few minutes later, when they reached a crossroads—one path going up to the rim of the crater, and the other continuing around the middle, the two Wright brothers eyed each other.

"I'd like to climb up to the top. What about you?" Alex asked, shyly.

"Me, too," Randy mumbled. After a painfully long pause, he added, "Should we hike up together?"

"Sure, that'd be great," Alex enthused, to Lana's delight. It had been wonderful to see the two getting along today, instead of squabbling. So when Alex turned to her, she knew what she had to do.

"Do you want to join us?"

"Thanks for asking, Alex, but I would rather circle the base today. But you two enjoy yourselves. Don't forget to take pictures at the top!"

She walked off before either man could try to change her mind. It would be good for them to have some time alone, she decided.

Now that she was on her own, she slowed her pace and examined the undergrowth for wildlife. She was bent over a shrub, trying to get a closer look at a tiny spotted frog, when Xavier's voice booming up from behind her almost made her tip over.

"Are you certain you didn't find anything in Sam's backpack?"

He and Jersey must be on the trail next to me, Lana realized. She remained hunched down, hoping they wouldn't notice her under the thick foliage of the shrub she was hiding under.

"No, nothing."

"Dang it. That means we still have no idea what he'd already told them. The board is badgering me to schedule a FaceTime meeting with them, but I hate going into it without knowing what he may have shared."

"It's in my interest, too. If I find anything, I'll let you know," Jersey replied. It sounded as if her voice was farther away, Lana realized. She wanted to wait a few more seconds to give them a chance to pass her by, but a scream had her running back up to the trail.

"Hey, watch out!"

It was Cecile, and she sounded in pain. Lana picked up her pace, wondering what she'd find. As soon as she rounded the corner, Jersey came into view. She was offering her excuses to Cecile for apparently mowing into her.

"Are you okay, Cecile?"

"Yeah, I tripped over a log after Jersey rammed into me."

"I'm really sorry, I didn't see you standing there."

Cecile brushed off her knees. From where Lana stood, it didn't look as if she had any deep cuts or scrapes that had to be dealt with.

"It's okay. Don't worry about it."

"Okay, if you're certain," Jersey replied uncertainly, but Xavier pulled her down the trail before Cecile could reply.

"Hey, are you alright?" Lana asked, figuring this was her chance to find out why Gregory had changed his mind about funding Xavier's project.

"I'm fine; it's nothing, not even a scratch. Jersey just caught me off guard is all."

Lana smiled. "That can happen. Say, I couldn't help but overhear that you are funding Xavier's dig."

Cecile and Gregory exchanged glances, yet both remained tight-lipped.

"Yesterday you were calling him a pompous fraud whom you would never fund, and now you're investing in the museum. Does he have something to hold over you—perhaps something Sam also knew about?"

Gregory paled rapidly. "No, it's nothing like that. I looked over Xavier's marketing plan and the numbers again. The gift shop looks like a solid investment."

"But at the site you said—" Lana pushed, but Gregory talked over her.

"Would you look at that lizard?"

Cecile squealed when she caught sight of it. "What is that, Lana?"

"Um, I don't know. Animals are not my strong point. I have to be honest—I overheard your quarrel on the bus, too. What happened to your first wife?"

"She died of a blood infection, but we didn't know that was the cause until after the autopsy," Gregory said. "She'd been ill for quite some time, but her doctors couldn't figure out what was wrong with her. Then she slipped into a coma when we were home alone, which has led to those horrible, persistent lies about my involvement in her death. I had nothing to do with her passing, and the autopsy results proved it."

"That's terrible; I'm sorry for your loss and the personal turmoil it caused. When did she die?"

"Two years ago."

"Oh, and when did you meet Cecile?"

"I connected with Cecile several months after my wife's funeral, at the National Association of Professional Geologists' annual conference in Miami. It may sound soon to some, but Cecile was my salvation. She's helped me move on from Rowena's tragic death and create a new life. I don't know what I would have done without her." Gregory held his second wife's hand up to his lips and kissed it.

"But you did know each other before then, didn't you? You said at dinner last night that Gregory was the best PhD supervisor that a student could have."

Both blushed bright red.

"I'd hoped that you'd forgotten that slipup," Cecile said. "Yes, I was one of his PhD students, but we didn't have contact outside of the university until after I had completed my research—which was several months after Rowena died. When we reconnected at that Florida conference, the sparks flew between us, and we've been together ever since."

Gregory took her hand again and stared deeply into her eyes. "Cecile could one day be one of the most respected geologists in our fields—after me, of course—once she's published more often and made a name for herself."

Instead of rolling her eyes, as Lana would have, Cecile only smiled.

"I'm not a geologist, but might I have read about your work?" Lana asked, more to be polite than out of genuine interest.

The two glanced at each other before Cecile cleared her throat. "Neither of us has published anything since those horrible rumors began circulating. Gregory's reputation was badly tarnished, as was mine."

"Why did your reputation suffer, Cecile?"

"Guilt by association. Ever since we married, all of her submissions to scientific journals have been rejected," Gregory answered for her. "That's why this jade research project is so important to both of us. We hope it will help remind the scientific community of our worth as researchers and lead to the restoration of both of our names."

"Is that why you agreed to sponsor Xavier's dig? I don't believe that his figures impressed you, especially after you accused him of being a liar."

Gregory pinched his nose, then looked to Cecile. She sighed, then nodded. "You better tell her the truth."

"Xavier threatened to tell the press about Sam's death and my involvement in it." He spoke so softly that Lana wasn't entirely certain she'd heard him correctly.

"But you aren't involved in his death, are you?" Lana suddenly felt very exposed. If Gregory had murdered Sam, then she had made a huge mistake by confronting him on her own, instead of doing so with Randy and Alex by her side.

Luckily for her, Gregory was appalled that she would think such a thing. "No! But if Xavier were to tell the media that I was present at the scene of his death and remind them about the nasty rumors surrounding my first wife's passing, then they might choose to broadcast it, without consulting with me first. That's what happened the first time, and by the time anyone bothered to report the truth, it was too late. Joe Public would rather believe that I murdered Rowena than accept that her death was the result of a misdiagnosis by her doctors. If that happens, the Jade Museum will certainly break our partnership. This is our chance at reestablishing our reputations as scientists. That's why we can't risk it, and why I agreed to invest—so he would back down. I am rich enough that it's not worth the hassle."

Lana's eyes widened as she took in what he was saying. "Letting Xavier blackmail you for something you did not do is easier than dealing with the media?"

"Yes, without question. Those rumors have all but destroyed Gregory's career and mine," Cecile replied in earnest.

"It's just so preposterous…" Lana shook her head, trying to understand the geologist's decision, until a chilling thought took hold. She locked eyes with Cecile. "Did you harm Sam? You were standing close to him when he died, and you did say your reputation had been tarnished by association. It sounds like you have as much to lose as Gregory."

Lana studied the woman's face, searching for signs of deceit. Based on the geologist's shocked expression, she didn't think that Cecile had harmed Sam. In fact, Cecile paled so quickly, Lana was momentarily worried she might faint.

"Heavens, no! It's true that since the hubbub around Rowena's death began, all of my submissions to respectable magazines have been rejected. But that doesn't mean I have been sitting at home, feeling sorry for myself. Gregory and I have been traveling the world and made important discoveries about Mesoamerican trade routes that we could only have done because we had no deadlines to pressure us. If we'd been doing research for a specific magazine or journal, we would have had to tailor our objectives to meet their expectations, or been pressured to meet a deadline, even if the research wasn't complete. It's been heavenly, having the money to do the work without the hassle of having to sell it. So no, I would not have killed Sam in order to be able to see my byline in a few magazine articles."

Lana stared at the pair, still unsure whether to believe them. "Unbelievable. I'm going to need a minute to take this all in."

Before they could reply, Lana's phone rang. She blushed when she noted who was calling. "Oh, sorry, but I better take this."

"Where are you?" Randy cried. "You were supposed to meet us back at the minivan ten minutes ago. Get a move on."

27

Shark Teeth

Lana rushed them back to the vehicle, where the rest of the group was dutifully waiting.

After the van pulled away from the parking lot, their driver grabbed a microphone and announced, "Before we go to Tabacón Hot Springs, we will make a short stop at a local market. You will find many handcrafted souvenirs to take home: traditional embroidered wall hangings, wooden bowls, sandstone statues, *carretas*, and the like. It is quite colorful."

Lana sighed in disappointment. After that long walk, she was really looking forward to relaxing in the hot springs, not going on a shopping trip. Besides, she had already bought an embroidered wall hanging of a bird and several miniature oxen carts to pass out to friends, once she got home. She didn't need any more souvenirs.

"I don't recall that being on the itinerary," Alex said after checking his phone.

"Me, either," Randy grumbled as he strode up to the front of the bus, luckily before the driver could pull away from the curb. After they conferred for a minute, their conversation became increasingly animated. When Randy finally came back to them, his jaw was set in anger.

"What's going on?" Alex asked.

"The driver insists we go to a local market along the way because he gets a commission for bringing us there. It's part of his wages, and he refuses to take us to the hot springs unless we go shopping first."

Lana blew out her cheeks. "It sure sounds like commissions are normal around here. We'll have to let Dotty know, so she's not too hard on George."

"Good point. But for now, I guess we let him take us wherever he wants," Randy said, thankfully with a laugh, before plopping down in a window seat.

When they reached the market, the group piled out and began a slow circle through the crowded stalls, all overflowing with embroidery, clothes, leather purses, pottery, painted oxen carts, and sandstone carvings. Despite the fact that she really didn't need any more souvenirs, Lana joined the rest as they meandered past the colorful stalls and took in the handcrafted goods.

As gorgeous as it all was, she hadn't been tempted to buy anything until they passed a table full of unusual-looking necklaces. She moved closer, and her eyes were instantly drawn to a chain made of cylindrical blue shells. It was one of several inside a small glass box placed at the back of the table. She leaned over to get a better look.

Hanging off of each shell was a jagged tooth—Lana assumed at first from a dog, though they seemed to be too thin and jagged to be canine. She studied the necklace, wondering what they could be, until she realized they were probably shark's teeth.

Lana waved a little and caught the vendor's attention. The older hippie with scarves woven into his long gray ponytail smiled across at her.

"How much for that one?"

"That necklace is quite rare." He looked her up and down. "I think it would suit you. Thirty dollars."

Lana frowned. Thirty dollars seemed like a lot for shells and teeth. But what did it matter, she probably wouldn't be returning to Central America anytime soon. When she toured again, she assumed it would be in Europe. Besides, she hadn't seen a necklace like this before, which made it worth the price.

After she handed over her money, the vendor removed the necklace from the glass box and passed it to her.

When she started to put it on, his face grew ashen. "Don't wear it here or let customs find it. Put it in your bag."

"What?" Lana asked, certain she'd misunderstood him. Most Costa Ricans spoke perfect English, but the market was crowded and noisy.

"It is illegal to sell teeth from that kind of shark because they are an endangered species. Don't wear it until you get home," he said under his breath. When another group approached his stall, he motioned for them to come closer.

Lana felt herself being pushed out of the way by the group, the necklace still in her hand. Should she demand her money back, or put it on in spite of the man's warning? *Maybe he was joking*, she thought. Although his expression seemed quite serious.

She waved her hand over her head, trying to get the merchant's attention, but his eyes were now focused on something a few stalls away. Moments later, he grabbed the case of shark-teeth necklaces and placed them under his table, out of sight.

Lana looked to the left, trying to determine what had spooked him, when a group of police officers entered her view.

"I didn't want to buy anything illegal!" she cried as she held out the necklace to the man.

Yet he shrunk from her outstretched arm. "No refunds, lady! Get out of my shop!"

Lana flexed her arm to throw the necklace onto the ground, but when she noted the police looking over at her, she decided against it. Unsure as to what else to do, Lana shoved the necklace far down in her pants pocket, promising herself that she'd toss it in the garbage as soon as they arrived at the hot springs.

28

Bad News for Lana

Monday—Day Nine of the Wanderlust Tour of Costa Rica

When Lana's alarm went off, she was still worn out from their busy day at the volcano, market, and hot springs. As much as she was looking forward to traveling to Panama for a snorkeling adventure, she longed to stay in bed just a little longer. Seeing Alex snoring softly next to her, oblivious to the alarm, didn't make things easier. Yet, duty called.

After she gently woke him, they dressed quickly and headed downstairs together. They held hands for the first flight of stairs, but when they heard the voices of their guests wafting up from the lower steps, she released her grip, preferring not to get caught by Jersey again.

They had another long day in the bus, this time to Isla Colon, an island just on the other side of the border in Panama. Lana couldn't wait to snorkel in the pristine-looking waters of Bocas del Toro or dine at one of the floating lobster bars the area was famous for.

However, her spirits dampened at the sight of Randy talking with a group of police officers in the hotel lobby. Somehow she knew, before an older officer looked in her direction, that they were here in connection with Sam's death.

When Randy caught sight of her, he called out, "Lana and Alex, would you join us?"

With every footstep, the knot in her stomach tightened a smidgen more.

"These are my colleagues, Lana Hansen and Alex Wright."

The senior officer, a short and broad man in his fifties with a mustache so long its tips reached his ears, smiled up at her but did not extend a hand. "I am Detective Vargas of the San Jose Police Department. We are here to interview your group in connection with the death of Samuel Perkins."

Lana nodded, as if it was the most normal thing in the world. "Sure, okay. Most of them will be in the breakfast room by now. But why do you need to talk with us?"

"My colleagues have had time to perform the autopsy. I hate to inform you that your guest was murdered."

Lana felt herself stumble backwards. Luckily, Alex was right behind her and used the palm of his hand to steady her.

"Murder, as in someone killed him?" Alex asked, his voice unusually high.

"Yes, that is exactly what I mean."

"How can you be certain? He was trampled by an ox and run over by its cart!" Lana cried, refusing to accept that he'd been murdered.

The detective pursed his lips. "The autopsy revealed that he had been stabbed with a long and thin blade, before being trampled."

Lana gasped. "Have you found the murder weapon?"

"We did; it had been wiped clean of prints and thrown into a trash can close to the exit."

"That's horrible. Yet even if you are certain that he was murdered, why do you want to interview our group again? Do you think one of us is the killer?"

The detective's eyes narrowed at her. "A similar tool went missing from the workshop area, where your group had a private tour, just before the oxcart parade. There were plenty of sharp tools around, and it would have been easy enough for someone to have grabbed a blade from one of the workbenches and used it to stab him."

"But how? We were all standing in a crowded arena—someone would have seen the person stab Sam, wouldn't they? Especially one of us because we were standing right next to him," Randy added.

"Would you have? If everyone was watching the oxcarts, they might not have seen the killer slip the blade into Sam's side. And from the video footage we have analyzed, it is clear that only someone in your group was close enough to have harmed him. Unfortunately, it is too pixelated for us to discern which one of you stabbed him."

Lana rocked on one heel as she considered the detective's words. Sam had been standing next to the rope, sandwiched in between the archaeologists on one side, and the geologists on the other. She, Alex, Randy, and the four bros stood just behind them, creating a buffer between their group and the rest of the public.

"Can you take me to your group?"

Randy stepped forward. "Certainly. Follow me."

He led the officers into the dining area, and Lana immediately spotted most of her clients spread across a few tables at the back of the space. When it was clear that the policemen were heading their way, Lana swore she saw Gregory frantically searching around the space for another way out.

"Good morning. I am Detective Vargas of the San Jose Police Department," the officer repeated. "My officers and I are here to interview you about the night of Sam Perkins's death. Before we begin, I ask that all of you turn in your passports to that officer." He pointed to a uniformed agent on his right. "If you need to retrieve your passport from your room, one of my officers will accompany you."

Jersey held up a hand, as if she was in class, and only spoke after the detective nodded at her. "Why would we need an escort to go upstairs?"

"To ensure that none of you try to leave the hotel, once you have retrieved your passport."

"Are you saying we have to turn it in, as in you are going to keep it?" Cecile asked.

"Yes, that is exactly what I mean."

"But you can't keep our passports!" Gregory challenged.

"Of course I can."

"For how long?" Xavier cried.

He locked eyes with the archaeologist. "Until we find the killer."

29

Investigation Time

After much discussion, the group eventually turned their passports in to the police, most making abundantly clear that they were not happy to do so.

Detective Vargas seemed to grow more jovial the more they complained. By the time he was ready to start the interviews, he was grinning like a Cheshire cat. He scanned the group and then nodded at Cecile. "We will start with you. If you would accompany me to the manager's office?"

The rest were ordered to stay in the lobby, under the watchful eye of the remaining officers. As soon as their guests began to whisper among themselves, Lana waved the Wright brothers over to one corner, away from the rest.

"Here we go again," Randy grumbled.

Lana blew out her cheeks. "Exactly. I know how this works—we can wait for the police to solve this case, or we can start gathering evidence and try to work out which one of our guests killed Sam."

When Alex's jaw dropped, Lana added, "Come on, Alex, don't look so shocked. I'm not trying to be crass or insensitive, but this isn't my first international murder investigation. I really don't want the cops to point the finger at one of us, simply to close the case. They have limited access to our group, which means the chance of them figuring out who really killed Sam is pretty slim. But we're with them all day and night and can easily keep tabs on their conversations without it being obvious. Right, Randy?"

INVESTIGATION TIME

"You're right. It's not my first murder, either, and I also know from experience how easy it is for the police to misread the clues. I agree with Lana that we have a greater chance of solving this than they do."

"You do realize that you are saying that we are on tour with a murderer?" Alex whispered.

"Yep, that's exactly what we are saying. At least, that's what the police seem to think," Randy replied.

"We'll have to investigate on the sly, otherwise the guests will know what we're doing." Lana was speaking more to Alex than Randy, hoping her words would help the blood return to his rapidly paling face. When she looked over at the guests and noticed the geologists were pointing at them and whispering, Lana snapped upright.

"We should go back and sit with the others, so they don't think we're up to something."

"Fair enough. But how do we investigate our clients without them noticing?" Alex said, worry in his voice.

"Tell you what, forget about that for now. Let's just wait and see what the police ask and how the others react. Once we've all been interviewed, we can reconvene in our hotel room and hash this out. Does that sound like a plan?"

Alex nodded, though Lana noted that the tension creases around his eyes were getting deeper by the second.

30

Change of Plans

The three guides were interviewed last. By the time Alex was brought back out to the lobby, two hours had passed. Luckily the hotel was air-conditioned; otherwise, they'd have all have wilted by the time they were free to go.

Detective Vargas's expression was grave as he addressed the group. "We cannot detain you at this time, but I can restrict your travel. You are not to leave Costa Rica, in case I need to speak to you again. I also wish to receive a copy of your itinerary, so I know where you are at all times."

"Excuse me? We're headed to Isla Colon today. Our minivan has been parked outside for the past hour, waiting for you all to finish so we can leave," Randy cried.

"In Panama?"

"Yeah!"

The detective shrugged. "Not today, you are not. There are plenty of places to surf and snorkel in Costa Rica. I'm certain your guests will be sufficiently entertained."

The disdain in his voice made it obvious that this was nonnegotiable, yet Randy tried again anyway. After the detective rejected his pleas for a third time, he gave them all one more stern warning not to leave Costa Rica, then headed for the door.

"There goes our scuba trip to Bocos Del Toro. I was really looking forward to that," Chet moaned.

Before the detective could reach the door, Gregory rushed forward and blocked his path. "Wait a second, my wife and I have an important research trip to Nicaragua after this tour finishes next week. When will we be able to leave the county?"

"As I said before, once we have Sam Perkins's killer in custody. Good day, sir."

The guests' grumblings as the officers filed out made clear that no one was happy with this turn of events.

Randy stood in front of the group. "Okay, folks. You heard the detective—we are not going to Panama, as planned. Alex, Lana, and I need time to call the tour operator and hotel in Bocas Del Toros and cancel our reservations, as well as discuss other options for the next two days, seeing as we aren't allowed to cross the border. Why don't we reconvene for lunch in two hours?"

31

Suspects List

Once the guests were settled, Lana and the Wright brothers retreated to Randy's room. As soon as the door clicked closed, she asked, "Before we deal with the tour, let's talk about the murder."

"I agree," Alex said. "Who could have done it?"

"Let's start with who was standing where," Randy said.

Lana tapped her chin, trying to recall exactly where everyone had been when the oxcart went haywire. "As I recall, Jersey and Xavier were on Sam's left and the geologists were on his right."

"That's how I remember it, too. I know we stood behind the geologists, because Gregory's head partially blocked my view. The four bros were on my right, but they seemed to be paying more attention to their phones than the oxcarts," Alex added.

"Okay, now that we agree on where everyone was standing, let's start with the archaeologists," Randy said.

"Xavier should be suspect number one, as far as I'm concerned," Lana said. "If anyone had a motive to keep Sam quiet, it would be him. He is obviously concerned about the audit and was upset that Sam might tell the committee something he didn't want them to know about."

Alex's forehead crinkled. "How do you know that?"

Lana quickly caught the pair up on what she'd overheard. "Sam was going to tell them the truth about something, but I'm still not sure what. Because of what Dotty told me, my gut tells me it has something to do with the misuse of the dig's funds. However, I have no solid evidence, at least not yet. Dotty is going to contact the university and then let me know what they share with her."

Alex leaned forward, a strange glint in his eye. "What about Jersey?"

Lana puffed out her cheeks. "What about her? I know you don't like her, but I can't see her harming Sam—not even if Xavier asked her to."

"What do you mean by that?" Randy asked.

"I mean, when Xavier says jump, she says how high."

Randy frowned. "Really? From what I've seen and heard, it's as if she has a hold over him, not the other way around. Xavier is constantly badmouthing her and makes her out to be a terrible archaeologist. Yet he's brought her back for a third year, even after causing that major setback with the measurements last season."

Lana nodded slowly. "You make a good point. I mean, there must be a slew of students who would kill to be the senior assistant on an archeological excavation."

"Maybe she's a relative and he doesn't want anyone else to know. That would explain a lot," Alex offered.

"Maybe—I can look that up later online. Jersey is also noted. Who else should be on our list?" Lana looked to the brothers.

"What about Cecile and Gregory?" Randy offered.

Lana nodded enthusiastically. "The geologists and Sam also butted heads during dinner. His first wife was his mentor at university, and he implied that she'd told him something Gregory does not want Cecile to know about. Whatever it is seemed to have disgusted Sam completely, but I really don't know what it was. It could have been a motive for murder—especially since Xavier started blackmailing them into sponsoring his site after Sam's death."

"When did you find that out?" Randy asked, shock in his voice.

"During the hike around Arenal, Gregory claimed that he would rather pay Xavier to keep him quiet than deal with another media circus. His reputation still hasn't recovered from the rumors that he was somehow involved with his first wife's death."

"Gregory could have been lying to you. If they had nothing to hide, they wouldn't have agreed to pay the blackmail—right?" Alex asked.

"That question has crossed my mind several times. I'd almost decided that Gregory was too rich and arrogant to think he'd have to kill anyone to get his way. But now that we know that Sam was murdered, it puts everything they shared in a new light."

"You make a great point, Lana. They should go on our suspects list." Alex smiled.

"And the four bros?" Randy asked.

"They don't seem to have a connection to Sam or anyone else on this trip. I can't see them having done it," Lana said, keeping her tone diplomatic. She knew that neither Wright brother was a fan of the accident-prone foursome.

"Now that we have a suspect list, I'm going to check out our guests online," she continued. "When I run into any roadblocks, I'll note them down and then ask Jeremy for help." Jeremy, her old editor and now close friend, was still working in the newspaper business and could probably help her find out more about their suspects.

Randy nodded. "While you are doing that, Alex and I will work out a new itinerary for the next two days."

"It should go pretty fast; I still have all my notes from our scouting trip. There is no shortage of great excursions or hotels to choose from," Alex enthused.

Lana sighed in relief. "Great, that would be wonderful. I would rather inform Dotty about Sam's murder and the tour deviation only after we've come up with an alternative."

"Sounds good. Let us know if you need any help," Randy replied.

32

Googling the Suspects

Lana took her time looking everyone up online, preferring not to hurry through this part of the investigation. Sometimes the smallest detail could be the clue to solving a murder, and she didn't want to miss it on account of being rushed.

After a few minutes of googling, Lana was certain Gregory and Cecile were exactly who they said they were. He had hundreds of articles attributed to his name, whereas she only had a handful. But none had been published in the previous two years. Apparently the rumors had damaged both of their reputations, just as the couple had claimed.

There was also little to find online about the projects they had supposedly worked on since the academic world shunned them. Lana supposed that had to do with the fact that no respectable university or cultural institution would back their ideas. That would make the support of the Jade Museum incredibly important to both, she could imagine. Yet Lana could not see either one of them killing Sam in order to spare their reputations further damage.

Xavier's search results took more time to sift through. He was a tenured professor who taught archaeology courses for half of the year, spending the rest on a dig somewhere in Central America. During his thirty years on the job, he had spoken at several conferences and co-authored many articles about Mesoamerican and pre-Columbian archaeology.

Yet there was precious little to find online about his latest site in Costa Rica and absolutely nothing about the upcoming audit. Lana hadn't really expected to find information already available online about such a confidential process, but it would have made her life easier. Instead, she added the audit to her list of things she would have to ask Jeremy about. For all Lana knew, one of his star reporters could currently be working on an article about the audit and thus be privy to information not yet available through public sources.

Jersey, the moody archeological assistant, was more of a mystery. She had worked on Xavier's Costa Rica dig for the past three years, as she'd asserted. Yet she had failed to mention that during last year's dig, she and another assistant named Cindy had gotten into an altercation that resulted in the other student being kicked off of the project. Shortly after, Cindy then filed a complaint with the university's ethics committee, claiming Jersey had stolen her research notes and published her conclusions as her own.

The details were sparse, but it was apparent from the report that the complaint against Jersey had been dismissed, thanks to Xavier's testimony. Lana figured this was the same Cindy that Sam had been referring to, the one that Jersey had somehow messed over. She couldn't wait to see what Jeremy found out about the altercation between the two assistants, and why the ethics committee had ruled in Jersey's favor.

Last on her list were the four marketers. After a deep dive into their Instagram-worthy lives, Lana could find no connections to the other guests, or even archaeology and geology in general. They were exactly what Randy said they were—four young men hellbent on having the time of their lives, with the money to do whatever they wanted, but without enough sense to stay within their physical limitations.

After she'd completed her search, Lana checked in with Randy and Alex. They'd come up with a new, albeit rough, plan for the remaining days, thanks mostly to her boyfriend.

"If Dotty agrees to it, we can flesh out the details on the bus ride to Tortuguero. I still have all of my notes from my trip with George on my phone."

"Alex showed me that there are several stellar hotels in the region, and we even found one with enough rooms for our group, so we booked it. Once Dotty gives us her blessing, we can book the turtle and kayaking excursions, as well," Randy added.

Lana wasn't entirely certain what he meant by the turtle excursion, but liked the sound of it.

"Thanks, guys. I bet Dotty will love this. Could you send it over to her now? I want to get her up to speed, and the conversation will go more smoothly if she can look over the new itinerary as we talk."

"Sure thing," Alex beamed.

33

Fat Cat

As soon as she'd reached Dotty, Lana put the call on speaker so Alex and Randy could listen along. She quickly outlined the changes in the tour and recapped why they'd had to adjust it in the first place.

"That young man was murdered? Lana, you and Willow convinced me that you are some sort of guardian angel, not a murder magnet, so I'll try not to get too worried just yet. I sure do hope the good Lord put you on that tour to help find Sam's killer. Please do tell me if there is anything you need."

"Thanks, Dotty, I will," Lana said softly, touched by her kindness. "Until the police know more, all we can do is pray that no one on this tour is involved. But for now, we aren't able to travel to Panama, which is why we sent over that new itinerary. What do you think of it?"

"It's fantastic! Who put this together?"

"Alex and Randy," Lana replied, a smile in her voice.

"To be honest, it was mostly Alex," Randy added, pride in his.

Alex dipped his head and blushed.

"Well done, you. It's perfect. In fact, I think we should consider adding these excursions to the final itinerary. But we'll deal with that once the tour is over and we've had a chance to talk to the guests about it," Dotty enthused.

Yet as upbeat as she sounded, there was a tiredness to her voice that Lana wasn't used to hearing. It was probably the news about Sam, she thought.

Yet, she couldn't help but ask.

"Say, Dotty, are you doing alright?"

"I just have a few business decisions weighing on my mind, that's all. Everything will resolve itself in time."

"By chance, does it have anything to do with the university and the audit?" Lana gently pushed.

"I'm afraid not. They flat-out refused to talk to me, so I had my lawyers get in touch. They got a little but further, but not much. Unfortunately, they aren't able to answer our questions at the moment because Xavier is under federal investigation. All they will tell us is the audit was instigated by an outside agency and is part of a larger investigation into fraud." Dotty paused a moment before adding, "What in tarnation is going on down there?"

Lana gasped. "I can't believe it! I wish I knew. Maybe Xavier moved your money offshore into a private account—that would make it a federal investigation. I was going to ask Jeremy to check out a few guests for me anyway and will add this to the list."

"Please do. That man can wheedle just about any information out of his incredible network. I'd be willing to bet that Jeremy will figure out what's really going on before my lawyers do. But I'm not planning on waiting to confront Xavier about this much longer. It burns my britches that he thinks he can bamboozle people and get away with it—especially family," Dotty roared.

"I feel your pain," Lana sympathized.

Suddenly a series of yips coursed through the phone's speaker.

"Hold your horses, Rodney! Say, Lana, I need to take the dogs out for a walk. They are dancing around my feet like we're at a techno concert. You promise to keep me up to date?"

"Yes, ma'am. We'll get in touch as soon as we know more." Lana took Dotty off speaker and turned away from the Wright brothers. "Before you go—how is my Seymour doing?"

"Just fine. He's having a grand time swatting at Chipper and Rodney."

"Oh!"

Her boss laughed. "It's okay—my boys think it's a game. Besides, he's far too busy snoozing on my couch or eating treats to bother them much. Don't you worry about Seymour."

"Treats, eh? He does need to watch his waistline," Lana teased.

"Yeah, well, I can't resist his plaintive meows or almond eyes. He might be a little chunkier when you get back, but it suits him."

"Seymour does have the most gorgeous eyes. Thanks for pampering my fur baby."

"Anytime. Now I better run before Rodney tinkles on my floor."

"Have fun!"

34

Lana Reaches Out

"It is so nice to hear that Dotty is thrilled with the new itinerary. That means we can inform the guests and book our transportation. But before we do gather everyone together, I want to call Jeremy and get him started."

"Sure thing, Lana. Why don't Alex and I wait for you down in the lobby? That'll give you some privacy."

"I appreciate it, Randy, thanks."

After an hour of searching online, Lana hadn't found anything that would point to the killer. Her only real hope of learning more about her guests was Jeremy Tartal, her good friend and the editor of a regional newspaper, the *Snoqualmie Gazette*. In her previous murder inquiries, he had provided essential clues that helped her piece together who had killed her guests before the police could.

She had already typed the full names of each of her clients and the little intel she'd found out about them into one long text message for him. However, before she sent it off, Lana wanted to call and ask whether he had time to help her investigate their backgrounds. With three young daughters and a working wife, his life was quite busy.

Last they'd talked, he wasn't planning any vacations this month, so she kept her fingers crossed that he was behind his desk today, and not home with the kids on one of his spontaneous "daddy days."

She was in luck. "Lana Hansen, how the heck are you?" Jeremy greeted her. "Are you still in Thailand, or are you already back in the States?"

He had moved up to Snoqualmie a decade earlier, to head the local newspaper there after a lawsuit cost him and Lana their jobs with the *Seattle Times*. Despite it being a step down the career ladder, Jeremy claimed not to regret it. The slower pace of life and community-focused events that regularly took place had endeared Snoqualmie to him and his family. Lana doubted they would ever want to move back to the big city.

"I'm doing great! How about you and your girls? Is Olivia in school yet?" Lana asked, wondering when exactly his youngest would be required to go.

"Yep, she started preschool last week. I think Kitty was more nervous about it than she was."

Lana chuckled, imagining adorable little Olivia with her tiny pigtails heading off to school for the first time. She could imagine that her mother, Kitty, would have had a hard time letting her go. "Is she enjoying it so far?"

"She seems to be. When I picked her up on her third day, Olivia announced that she and another girl in her class were now best friends and could they please make a playdate for later that week?"

Lana laughed out loud. "That is great news—what a relief for both you and Kitty!"

"It really is. But I suspect you didn't call to find out how my girls were doing. What can I do for you?"

"You got me there. I'm in Costa Rica helping out on a tour."

"So soon? I thought you were going to take a few months off first."

"I was, but that's a story in and of itself. But first, I have a favor to ask. There's been a murder—"

"Not again!"

Lana sucked in her breath. "I know—that's exactly my sentiment. But one of the younger guests was stabbed, then trampled by a raging bull during an oxcart parade. Because of how we were standing, the police are convinced only someone in my tour group could have stabbed him."

"Oh, Lana, that's horrible. I'm sorry to hear that your first one back is going so wrong."

"It's okay. Technically, it's not my tour, so I refuse to let this one count."

"What do you mean?"

"Remember how I told you Alex was going to start working as a guide for Wanderlust Tours?"

"Yeah, I do. That sounded like a perfect fit for him."

"It did, but he's now working his second tour as a trainee, and things were not going well even before the death. Dotty sent me down here a few days ago to help out, but Alex isn't really open to critique. He can't seem to get the knack of dealing with all of the different personalities in one small group. But if he doesn't figure out how to lead a tour before this one is over, Dotty won't be able to hire him on."

"Yikes, that is a conundrum. From what you've told me about it, leading a tour does sound quite intense. I have to admit, I don't know if I'd have the patience for it."

"Honestly, I don't know if Alex does either."

"He's a smart guy. He'll figure it out, once his ego lets him make a rational decision."

Lana sighed. "I think you hit the nail on the head, Jeremy, but he has to see that for himself. Look, I didn't call to moan about Alex. If I sent over a list of names and the information that I've already found out about them, could you do a deeper background check on them for me? Your sources may have insider information than I wouldn't be able to find searching online."

"Sure, you know I'm happy to reach out to my network. I'm still in touch with several investigative journalists working around the Pacific Northwest, and they love to assist me with these investigations, even if they don't know why I'm inquiring."

Lana breathed a sigh of relief. "Thanks for keeping the 'why' to yourself."

"Of course. I'll read through the information you send over, but can you give me a quick rundown of the lead suspects? I'll focus my energy on them first."

"Sure. Right now my lead suspect is one man—Xavier Johns. He and the victim, Sam Perkins, had been arguing about an upcoming audit of Xavier's archeological dig because Sam was going to tell the audit committee the truth about something. Whatever it was had clearly upset Xavier and his other assistant, Jersey. But I don't know what Sam was planning on revealing to the committee."

Lana heard the sound of Jeremy's fingers working his keyboard. "Got it."

"There's more. My boss, Dotty, has been funding his dig for the past three years, and it appears that he's been lying to both her and his university about the progress he's made, which has prompted them to start that audit. When Dotty reached out to the university to ask for more information, they could only tell her that they can't share any of the details because it's a federal investigation."

"Federal! Oh, my, that does sound intriguing. I'll get right on it. Anyone else I should focus on first?"

Gregory flitted through her mind, but she'd already confronted him about his relationship with Sam. The two had butted heads, but based on his and Cecile's answers, she no longer suspected either one of killing the young archaeologist.

After Lana had caught Jeremy up on all of the guests and potential motives, he was silent for a moment. "That sounds like a pretty horrible tour. I hope you can take some time off after this one and decompress. It would be a shame for you to not go back to leading tours because of this. You're good at it and passionate about it."

Lana felt a lump in her throat. "Thanks, Jeremy. That means a lot."

"About your suspect list, I'll do what I can. The geologists' names do sound familiar, but I don't know why. I'll ask my network whether they know anything more. If I find out something worth sharing, should I text you the information or email it? I know you're usually too busy to answer the phone when you're leading a tour."

"A text message is the easiest. You're a lifesaver, Jeremy. Thank you."

35

A Sore Backside

After Lana's call with Jeremy, the three guides gathered the guests together in the lobby and informed them of the new plan.

"Instead of driving to Panama to go snorkeling, we are heading to the famous Tortuguero National Park where we will hopefully see sea turtles lay their eggs under the moonlight tonight."

"That sounds amazing!" Cecile cried out.

"I'm glad to hear you say that." Randy smiled at her, before continuing, "We'll arrive in the afternoon, and you'll have time to explore the town before we meet up again for a late dinner. Our guides will pick us up afterwards and take us over to the beach. Tomorrow, we are going kayaking through a mangrove forest along the coast, before heading back to San Jose."

Xavier groaned. "Tortuguero is on the Caribbean Sea, isn't it? How long is this bus ride?"

"Around three hours, plus our lunch stop," Randy replied.

"That's ridiculous! It feels like we've been driving more than sightseeing," Xavier pouted.

"It was always going to be a long drive, and in fact this one to Tortuguero is shorter than the trip to Isla Colon that was planned for today," Randy explained in a patient voice.

"I didn't look up the times on the itinerary, but Xavier is right. It sure seems like we are in the bus a lot," Chet added.

"Luckily for you, everything is free," Alex muttered, not even trying to hide the disgust in his voice.

"Alex Wright," Lana growled under her breath.

Xavier smirked at Alex. "True, it is free because Dotty wanted feedback. Well, here's mine: my backside is sore from all this sitting. I had expected to be taking part in more pulse-pounding excursions, considering Dotty is going to market this as an adventure tour."

"I hate to say it, but I agree with Xavier on this one," Gregory said in a snide tone. "I would be pretty disappointed if I had paid for this trip. Especially since there are so many incredible places to stay in Costa Rica. The hotel in San Jose is lovely, but not enough to justify driving back to it every night."

"Thanks, everyone. This is great feedback we can use to adjust this tour before offering it again. It is exactly the kind of information Dotty wants, instead of money," Randy said, in a clear attempt to change the subject. "But there is nothing we can do about the drive today, unless you would rather stay in San Jose."

"I would really like to see the turtles, no matter how long the drive. It sounds like an incredible opportunity. I'm so glad we're here at the right time of year to witness it," Cecile pushed.

"The kayaking trip does sound pretty cool," Dave added and the other three bros nodded.

When Randy looked to Xavier, the archaeologist shrugged his shoulders. "Fine. I'll stick with the group, but I am glad to have registered my complaint."

Randy's face lit up. "Great, it's settled. If everyone is packed up, we can head out. The minivan is waiting outside."

36

Alex the Planner

After they'd gotten everyone settled into the minivan for the long journey to Tortuguero, the three guides took the seats closest to the front so they were well away from the rest.

"The guests are right; this tour is a disaster. Tourists who pay thousands to take this trip will not be pleased with all of the unnecessary driving. We need to hammer out a better basis for this tour—one worthy of Wanderlust Tours. And now that we know George had an ulterior motive for booking certain hotels and tour operators, we should set his aside and make a new one for the entire fourteen days." Randy turned to his brother. "Alex, we could really use your expertise to flesh this out. What do you say?"

Lana could see Alex swell with pride. Finally, he felt as if he could contribute. "Sure thing. Give me a few minutes to look through my notes, and then I'll sketch out a few ideas for you."

"Take your time. We've got a long ride ahead of us," his brother replied.

Randy and Lana exchanged a smile as Alex began to scroll through his phone. The pair looked out the window instead of conversing, to give Alex the mental space to plan without disruption. Not that it was a bother to do so. The sights along the way were stunning, making it easy to enjoy the long ride.

Forty minutes later, Alex looked up and smiled over at them. "Hey guys, I think I have something. I'll send it over now."

When her phone pinged, Lana looked over the itinerary that her boyfriend had just put together. He had created a ten-day tour that looped through the country, taking in the most important tourist attractions for an adventure-loving visitor. He'd even taken the best times of day to do certain excursions into consideration, as well as including a map with dots signifying where the hotels were located.

"This is great, Alex. Well done."

Her boyfriend blushed at her words.

"I'm not just saying that to stroke your ego. This itinerary looks better than the one George put together. Most importantly, it's a loop, and the tourists aren't in a bus every day. I think Dotty is going to love this."

Alex may not be a great tour guide, but he is a natural planner and has a great feel for what a typical tourist would enjoy, Lana realized.

"Planning and organizing are really your thing, honey," she added with a smile.

"Yeah, it's only too bad I can't figure out a way to do this job without having to deal with the guests," he said, souring the conversation again.

Part of her wanted to ignore Alex's negative comment and instead get lost in the scenery. Yet his comment sparked an idea, one she had to share with him.

"You know, you're really good at this sort of planning. Maybe you'd be better suited to working the back end—you know, organizing the details of the tour instead of leading it? I know that kind of thing consumes a lot of Dotty's time. She loves to micromanage everything and might be happy to have someone to assist her with it all."

A glimmer of hope shone in Alex's eye. "That's a great idea; thanks, Lana. I'll have to think it over."

He ducked his head down below the seat so that he could kiss her on the neck without the guests seeing. "Thanks for believing in me, hon."

She chuckled and kissed her fingertip before bringing it to his lips. "I love you, too."

37

Tarnished Reputation

They were an hour out of Tortuguero when the driver pulled into a restaurant along the side of the road. The colorful café looked fairly run-down, but Lana figured he knew better than she as to where to stop for a good meal.

As they pulled into the parking lot, Lana's phone beeped, alerting her to a new message. She opened the text from Jeremy, eager to know what he'd found out.

"Hey Lana, the situation with Jersey and Cindy was easy enough to solve. Here's a link to an article in a local university's newspaper about it. A crime reporter I know is working on an article about Xavier and the spheres, but won't share any information over the phone. I'll message you after I meet with him later tonight, okay?"

Lana quickly thanked Jeremy, then opened the link and skimmed it. It seems that Cindy and Jersey had worked on Xavier's site last year, and after the dig concluded, both women had accused each other of plagiarism. First, Cindy lodged a complaint after a renowned archeological journal published an article authored by Jersey and Xavier, claiming that she had done the research used in it, not Jersey. In response, Jersey lodged a countercomplaint, claiming Cindy was lying about who had done what in an effort to discredit her. Her claim was backed up by Xavier, who testified before the committee that it was Jersey, not Cindy, who had provided the research necessary to complete the article.

Something about the story stuck in Lana's craw. Could Xavier have lied to protect Jersey? Randy had made a great point earlier about how Jersey seemed to have a hold over the archaeologist. Not for the first time, Lana wondered what that could be. But for now, all she could do was take this article at face value. The ethics committee had clearly ruled in Jersey's favor, and according to this article, Cindy had stopped with her study shortly after. That must have been what Sam had meant, when he'd said that Xavier and Jersey had ruined her chances at a career.

It was murky as to who was really in the wrong in that situation, but Lana didn't think it had much, or anything, to do with Sam's death. As far as she could tell, he wasn't involved in the disagreement and had not participated in last year's dig.

When the bus doors opened with a hiss, Lana pocketed her phone and switched back into guide mode. Because they only had a half hour to eat, the guests were thankfully focused on their meals and not baiting or degrading each other. It was a pleasant change of pace.

The only minor irritation was Xavier's phone, which seemed to beep every few minutes, alerting its owner about a new message.

"Would you answer your phone already?" Gregory finally asked, in his direct manner.

Not in the mood to let this meal turn into another round of insults, Lana held up one of the large platters of food they were sharing and nodded at the geologist.

"Have you tried these yet? They must be the best black beans I have ever tasted. I wonder what seasonings they use. Do you know? It is scrumptious."

"No, I do not know how they are prepared. But I agree, these are particularly delicious. I'll take another spoonful, if you don't mind."

"Certainly not." She served Gregory and looked to the rest. "Any other takers?"

Chet held up his plate. "Thanks, Lana."

She was more than happy to oblige. Once she'd put the now empty platter back down onto the table, the group was once again focused on their meal, instead of irritating each other.

Yet when Xavier's phone began to ring and was yet again ignored by its owner, Gregory lost it. "Why won't you answer, instead of letting it go to voicemail?"

Xavier glared over at him. "I don't want to talk to the caller, that's why."

"Then could you set it to silent? The constant ringing is getting a little annoying," Lana asked.

Xavier narrowed his eyes at her.

"Unless you want to explain to us why you don't want to answer their call. Who is it, anyway? Does it have anything to do with your dig?" Lana batted her eyelashes as she conjured up her most innocent tone.

Instead of answering her directly, he held his phone up in the air and made a point of showing everyone how he turned the ringer off. "Happy now?"

"Yes, thanks." Gregory's catty reply got a chuckle out of his wife.

"Is it the university? Why won't you answer them? They have been messaging me, too, you know," Jersey grumbled.

"I refuse to discuss this with them while I am eating. They can wait."

"You'd better not wait too much longer, or they might think you are avoiding them, which will only make matters worse."

"I'll call them when I'm good and ready." Xavier shoved a spoonful of rice into his mouth, making it apparent that he was done with this conversation.

After they'd finished eating, the driver was still busy checking the oil and water levels, leaving them another five minutes to stretch before they embarked on the last leg of their journey.

Most sat down in the shade to wait patiently. Xavier, however, was apparently too restless and instead circled the parking lot, with Jersey trailing after him.

When his phone began to ring again, she cried out, "Will you please answer the call? Based on what they ask you, we might be able to figure out what Sam's already told them."

Her pleading tone spoke volumes, as did his nonchalant response. "If it means you will stop pestering me, then yes, I will."

Xavier turned away before barking into the phone, "Jason, it's Xavier. What is the meaning of all of your messages? The committee can't seriously believe—"

Whatever Jason said shut Xavier up fast. His face grew pale as he listened.

"Who's Jason?" Lana whispered, hoping Jersey would reply.

"The director of the university," she whispered back.

A few seconds later, Xavier exploded again. "How dare you! I'm a tenured professor of archaeology—be careful what you accuse me of!"

Neither Lana nor the rest of the group had trouble listening in, at least to Xavier's side of the heated conversation. The tension in the air seemed to grow the longer the conversation continued. When Xavier finally yelled out, "Enough! I refuse to listen to your lies any longer. We will discuss this in person later this week. The committee shouldn't draw any conclusions until I've had a chance to share my side of the story. I'll contact you as soon as I've arranged a flight back."

When Xavier hung up, Jersey grabbed his arm. "And?"

"This audit is turning into a witch hunt! The university is bleeding money, and Jason has decided I will take the fall for the board's incompetence. I seriously doubt they will give me a fair trial. From what he says, they are talking about prison sentences."

Xavier shivered as Lana covered her gasp with her hand. *Prison! What exactly has Xavier been up to all these years?* she wondered.

"What exactly did he say?" Jersey pressed.

Xavier stuck out his chin. "All sorts of discrepancies are coming to light that they are trying to pin on me."

When he tried to shake off her arm, Jersey only tightened her grip. "What is that supposed to mean?"

He glared at his assistant. "That means, with the upcoming audit, our deal is off."

"No way!" Jersey's shriek echoed across the parking lot.

"Yes, way. If they compare the originals with the backups, they are bound to figure everything out, even without Sam's testimony. Which means I am not going back to the States. If I do, they can imprison me. Down here, I'm free from extradition. You are on your own, Jersey."

She fell to her knees. "After all I did for you? You promised to help me secure my first position."

Instead of showing any form of sympathy, Xavier began to laugh. "I have no regrets about that. You are a terrible archaeologist, and it pained me to have to recommend you for any assignment these past three years. I still can't believe you talked me into shafting Cindy. She actually has a future in archaeology. Or had one, until you destroyed it. Gosh, it feels freeing to finally say that aloud."

"Oh, you will regret this decision—I'll make certain of it!" Jersey yelled before turning to search the parking lot.

When she spotted Gregory and Cecile, she stormed over to them. "I hope you haven't given Xavier any money."

The geologists looked at her with puzzled expressions on their faces. "Why would you say that?"

"Xavier is cutting his ties with the university, which means he will have no access to funds or their network, and will most likely be out of a job. I thought you should know before you invest in his project."

The senior archaeologist barreled over. "Don't listen to her! She doesn't know what she's saying. Of course I'm going to continue with the site. It's almost finished—why would I abandon it now?"

Gregory's eyebrows shot up. "Surely you cannot continue if you are breaking your association with the university. It is their land you are digging on."

"It is my land, not the university's, and I have a temporary residence permit that is valid for eight more months," Xavier reassured the geologist. "Now I'm even more reliant on the gift shop, so I'll do my darndest to promote it. It'll be a good investment for you."

Lana paled. That was not what he had told Dotty; she was certain of it. "How can that be? Dotty told me you'd used part of her money to buy the land in the university's name—not your own."

"She was wrong about that, as well. Gosh, the old girl really is getting up there in age, isn't she?"

Lana's blood boiled, hearing him denigrate Dotty like that.

Yet before she could retort, he turned back to Gregory. "I need that money you promised me. Jersey is right in that I am about to lose access to the university funds. And now that Sam has been murdered, there'll be even more media scrutiny surrounding his final days."

Instead of trembling, Gregory folded his arms over his torso and smiled smugly. "No way—we want out. Sam was your assistant, not mine. We had nothing to do with his death."

"Are you sure? It would be too bad if the wrong version of events got leaked to the media. Besides, you can't back out now; you've already signed a contract."

"We aren't paying you one cent," Gregory declared.

"I'll send my lawyers after you!" Xavier screamed. "And the media."

"Good luck with that and getting back into the States without being arrested," Cecile laughed.

The geologist made a great point. If Xavier was no longer able to return to the United States, he would be the one to have his reputation ruined by the media exposure. Even if he tried to disparage Gregory in the media, he himself was about to become the laughingstock of the archaeology world. Lana doubted many media organizations would take him seriously, once news about the audit surfaced.

Lana glanced over at Jersey, who looked as satisfied as a well-fed cat. She'd gotten her revenge, and quite quickly. Without access to his sponsors' money or Gregory's new capital injection, Xavier probably had a serious cash-flow problem.

When the couple sauntered off, openly laughing at the archaeologist, Xavier turned to Jersey. "You spiteful wench! You want to be open and honest about everything, do you? Shall I do the same and confess everything to the university, Jersey? Would that make you truly happy? If so, I'll share what I've done for you over the years, including that incident with Cindy."

Her smug expression turned to fear. "You wouldn't—your reputation will suffer even more if the truth came out."

Xavier laughed heartily. "What reputation? After the audit, there will be a warrant out for my arrest. I have nothing to lose. What about you, Jersey?"

38

Confronting Xavier

The last leg of the bus ride to Tortuguero was relatively quiet in comparison to the first part of the journey. The guests seemed to be ignoring each other again, which was probably for the best.

After driving past several banana plantations, they stepped into a boat that brought them to their lodge. According to the hotel receptionist, the waterways surrounding the village often flooded to the point where it was only accessible by boat.

When they docked in town, Lana's phone beeped with a new message from Dotty, asking her to pull Xavier aside so they could have a FaceTime chat. Lana looked over at the archaeologist, staring out at the milky blue water in an attempt to ignore Jersey. The young assistant sat in the row behind him, glaring at the older man with such disdain, Lana wondered how they were going to get through the rest of the tour.

The plantation-style hotel Alex had booked them into was basic, yet fancy at the same time. The outer walls and railings were painted in a mishmash of bright reds, blues, and yellows. The pool and terrace built out over the river looked quite inviting, as did the thatch-roofed bar. Palm trees and flowering banana plants towered over the hotel and pool. A thin strip of mangrove forest shielded the buildings from the sea, but they were close enough that Lana could hear the waves crashing against the shoreline.

The guests had three hours to unwind before they were to meet up in the hotel lobby for dinner. After they had checked everyone in, Lana knocked on Xavier's door. "Dotty needs to speak with you. Can we call her now, while we have a break from the tour?"

Xavier tried to push it shut, but Alex and Randy barged in before he could.

"We can do this the easy way or the hard way," Alex growled as he walked into Xavier's room, forcing the older man to back up. When he was inside, Lana and Randy joined him before slamming the door shut.

"What is the meaning of this?" the archaeologist cried, but not with much conviction.

She had convinced herself that Xavier had harmed Sam, which was why she insisted that the Wright brothers accompany her to his room. He was strong enough that he could have stabbed Sam and pushed him under the ox. It wouldn't have taken much power to knock the younger man off balance, especially if he was already injured and bent over. With a lot of luck, Xavier would soon confess his crime to Dotty, they would call the police, and this nightmare would be over.

"You know exactly why we are here. You've been lying to Dotty and the university about the state of your dig for three years and counting. She wants answers, and the university isn't being too forthcoming, so that means she wants to have a chat with you."

Xavier began to retort, but Lana dialed anyway. Seconds later, her boss's upper body filled the screen. Dotty leaned into the camera and glared at the archaeologist. "Xavier Johns, you have some explaining to do."

"Dotty, darling."

"Don't 'darling' me. Lana's told me all about what you've been up to and sent enough pictures of both the site and your fancy invention that I have a pretty good idea of where my money went. Those funds were for the excavation and development of an archeological site, not a Disneyfied-version of history—especially not when a real site is located so close by. And certainly not for an invention no one wanted to fund. Have you no shame?"

"Are you accusing me of committing fraud? I have invoices to justify all of my expenditures at the site. That invention was a side project, and I funded its development through private sources."

"Are you certain about that? You better tell me the truth about how you spent my money, or I'm going to sic my lawyers on you. I'll also do all I can to convince the local police that you killed Sam!"

"I didn't kill anyone! Yes, he was going to tell the auditors the truth about my finances, but killing him wouldn't have helped matters. If slacker Sam was able to find discrepancies in the paperwork, then the professional auditors are bound to, as well."

"I've gifted you one hundred and fifty thousand dollars over the past three years. Lana's shown me the photos—if you didn't use it to make your prototype, then where did my money go? I can't imagine you invested it all in that poor excuse of an archeological dig. You abused our family ties to get me to invest. Now I'm asking you, as kinfolk, to tell me God's honest truth. What did you spend my money on?"

Xavier hung his head. "Alright, fine. We are family, after all. I did use most of the money I'd received from you to pay for the development of my invention. But I can't get it to work as I'd hoped, which means the chances of someone swooping in to mass-produce it are pretty much null. But when I got wind the university may be auditing me soon, I knew I had a problem because I'd spent most of it on research and development instead of the dig. That was why I was reaching out to other sponsors for more money, so I could use it to cover my tracks. That was my only hope of the auditors not discovering my deceit. But I wasn't able to raise enough to cover what I'd already spent."

"You are a despicable man, Xavier Johns."

He sighed and looked away. "I know, Dotty. I know."

"How does Jersey fit into all of this? It sounds like she's a terrible archaeologist. So why has she been your senior assistant for the past three years?" Lana pushed.

"Quid pro quo. She discovered that I'd been misusing funds during that first summer and offered to turn a blind eye, as long as I helped her advance in our field. That's why I hired her back, despite her meager abilities, and kept supervising her PhD research. Yet after I lied to help get her out of that nasty situation with Cindy, she demanded I help her find a job, too. It was almost too much to bear, but Jersey knew what I was doing. I couldn't say no, and she knew it. One word to the wrong person and I would lose my job."

"You destroyed Cindy's career to help Jersey?" Lana gasped.

"I still deeply regret doing that, but at least I'm done with her now. It would have pained me to have to recommend her for any job. She is an atrocious archaeologist, and I would hate for any colleague of mine to be saddled with her. It's freeing to know that I no longer have to recommend her for a position and never will."

He looked to Lana and then Dotty. "I have been upfront with both of you. I had no reason to harm Sam. All I wanted to do was delay him from contacting the audit committee for as long as possible. But it didn't matter. The head of the university told me that their auditors have already discovered my deceit."

Lana didn't know what to think. Xavier was such a callous and unforgiving person that she would have loved to have pinned this crime on him. Yet his reasoning made sense, and her inability to accept that he could be innocent made her feel as if she was searching for a reason to accuse him of murder.

And yet, a federal bureau was investigating him. For what, neither she or Dotty knew. As much as she wanted to ask him about it, she figured that would be akin to interfering with a police investigation. She only hoped that whoever was investigating him could still get to him while he was down here in Costa Rica. It would be a shame if he was able to skate out of a prison sentence, after all.

39

Hanging with Sea Turtles

Most of her guests chose the optional boat ride through the jungle, and Lana was more than happy to tag along. Tortuguero National Park was a spiderweb of small canals and streams that they floated through in flat-bottomed, canoelike boats.

Thanks to their guide's keen eye, they spotted leopards sleeping high up in tree branches and crocodiles warming themselves on the sunny sandbanks. Everywhere they went, they heard birds calling out and monkeys hollering. They sure did make a lot of noise as they swung from tree to tree, as they checked the tourists out. Lana couldn't help but laugh as one group of primates seemed to study them intently, before chattering amongst themselves about what they saw, as if the humans were the exotic creatures on display.

The trees' canopies had grown so close together, they formed a glorious green arch over most waterways that helped enhance the feeling that they were on an adventure, despite the busyness of the waterways. There were quite a few boats out, to the point where their group sometimes had to wait for one to pass before they could move forward. Lana didn't mind, nor did her tour group. It gave them more time to study the gloriously curious and colorful wildlife that crossed their path.

After the boat ride, her group had chosen to spend their remaining free time exploring the area on their own. During a wonderful seafood meal, they chatted easily about what they'd seen on their brief walk around the city center and coastline, and the turtles they hoped to see on tonight's moonlit walk along the beach.

Only Xavier was not interested in joining them, preferring to stay behind and relax with a beer. Lana didn't mind, nor did the geologists based on their smiles at his announcement. Shortly after dinner, two naturalists arrived, each to escort half of the group along Tortuguero's beach, in search of nesting turtles.

Alex and Lana escorted Jersey and the geologists, while Randy got stuck with the four bros again. Their guides used a soft, almost invisible flashlight to lead them down the beach. One guide had warned them before leaving the minivan that the turtles used the bright moon to navigate their way up and down the beach, which was why they wanted to avoid shining any bright light sources, for fear of confusing them.

The guide pointed to several small mounds of sand high up on the beach, just above the tideline. "Those are turtle nests. Come, I see another guide signaling that she has spotted one about to lay eggs a few feet in front of us."

The moon was full, making it easy to see the turtle's massive shell as she slowly worked her way up the dunes. In the blue light, Lana could see the exertion on her face as she opened and closed her mouth, while swiping her front flippers across the earth to propel herself forward.

It felt like it had taken the turtle hours to reach the tideline, but once she did, the turtle turned itself around and then began digging a hole in the sand with her back flippers.

The guide motioned for them to step away, before pointing to the turtle. "Do you see the long fingernails growing off of her back flippers? That's what she uses to dig a deep hole. When she senses it is big enough for all of her eggs, she will back up into it and use a long birthing canal to drop the eggs into the hole."

It took quite a long time to lay her eggs, with soft peeps and grunts as she went to work. Seeing how many seemingly hundreds of eggs she'd been holding inside of her was amazing and almost unbelievable. *What a relief it must be to release them all*, Lana thought.

After the bucket-sized hole was filled with her future offspring, the turtle slowly covered the top and sides so that there was nothing more than a slight mound to show for all her work.

After it was all over, she seemed to stop and rest a bit, before suddenly pushing herself slowly across the sand and back into the sea.

Lana watched the beast in awe, amazed again by the wonders of the natural world. Costa Rica truly was a paradise for nature lovers.

40

Not an Accident

Tuesday—Day Ten of the Wanderlust Tour of Costa Rica

A sharp yelp woke Lana with a start. Groggy, she swatted at her clock, thinking it had gone off. It took her a minute to understand that the noise was human, not her alarm.

"Is that someone screaming?" Alex mumbled from under the covers.

His words caused Lana to bolt upright. "Oh, no! It might be."

She sprung out of bed and pulled on her bathrobe, knotting the cord while she pushed her feet into her slippers. When she opened the door, she was shocked to see the hallway filled with confused guests and the hotel manager holding one of the cleaning ladies in his arms. The poor woman was wailing loudly, and her face was a mess of tears.

"What's going on?" Lana asked, of no one in particular, just as Gregory stepped out into the hallway.

When he spotted the weeping maid, he asked her something in rapid-fire Spanish.

After she replied in a quivering voice, he turned to Lana, his face a mask of confusion. "It's Xavier. He's dead."

"Oh, Lana, not another one," Randy cried.

"Dead? What do you mean, dead?" Lana bolted over to the open door, her mind unable to accept Gregory's words. Yet her eyes could not deceive her—Xavier was sprawled out on his bed, and his chest wasn't moving.

Sam's death may have initially been deemed an accident, but there was no question that this was murder. Blood had poured out of Xavier's head and flowed like a river over his chest and was now congealing in a crimson pool on his bedsheets. Resting on the pillow next to him was a small Diquís sphere, partially covered in blood.

When Randy and Alex joined her at the open door, Lana murmured, "We'd better get downstairs. I'm certain the police will want to question us all, as soon as they arrive."

Yet as horrible as the scene was, Lana had trouble taking her eyes off of it. However, experience told her that they were about to undergo another police interrogation, and she wanted to properly dress before the cops arrived.

"You're right," Randy replied, before turning back towards his room. Alex was also quiet as they dressed. Lana understood completely. It was not the first time she'd seen a dead body, but it didn't make it any easier. Seeing another life extinguished like that was such a disturbing experience, that it really made you question your own mortality.

Just as they finished dressing, a knock on the door signaled the arrival of the local police. They were busy cordoning off the hallway and ushering the guests on that floor downstairs, so they could be interviewed.

"So much for sleeping in," Dave grumbled.

"I bet this will make us late for the kayaking trip, too," Chet added.

"Between the bus rides and delays, it's not really an adventure-filled adventure, is it?" Dave complained.

Lana was shocked by their incredibly callous reaction to a death, even if it was someone as unlikable as Xavier. "This is not ideal, I will give you that. But another man is dead. We should all do what we can to help the police find his killer, right?"

"I suppose. It's not like the world will miss Xavier. He was a horrible man," Gregory snapped.

Lana leaned in towards him. "I know you had your differences, but you may want to watch what you say around the police. They are looking for those with a motive to kill him, after all."

Gregory blushed. "Sure, okay."

"And if you had signed a contract with Xavier, it's better to tell the police about it now. If they find out later, they'll assume you were trying to hide that information from them."

By the way he paled and dipped his chin, she could tell that he had, indeed, been planning on lying. Lana shook her head in disappointment.

41

Robbery Gone Wrong

It took the police a few minutes to get organized. Once the officers began calling her clients over to be interviewed, Lana demanded to speak to the lead agent.

A middle-aged officer crossed over to her, bowing slightly instead of offering a hand. "Detective Rodriguez. May I be of service?"

"Hi, hello, sir. My name is Lana Hansen. I'm a guide for Wanderlust Tours and here with eight guests and two more guides. We have a kayaking trip that starts in one hour. Do you think we are going to make it?"

"Wanderlust Tours, you say? The victim, Xavier Johns, was one of your clients, correct?"

"Yes, he was."

The detective chuckled. "I am afraid your trip will be delayed because I wish to speak to the rest of your group. I'm sorry that your client's death has inconvenienced the others."

Lana blushed, understanding what he was implying. "I'm sorry, that did sound crass. We'd already had to rearrange an earlier excursion because of another death…" As soon as the words were out of her mouth, she knew they were in for a long morning.

The detective's jaw clenched slightly as he regarded her again. "Are you saying that Xavier Johns is the second client of yours to die during your tour of Costa Rica? I think we have much to discuss. Please, join me."

He waved her over to a pair of wingback chairs where she told him everything she knew about Sam's death, his relationship with Xavier, and the few clues she had gathered so far.

"To be perfectly honest, I was starting to think that Xavier had murdered Sam. He had the most to lose, if Sam had lived to tell the university audit committee whatever it is that he knew. I don't know if they could have forced Xavier to repay the money he'd stolen, but he would most certainly have lost his job."

"Have you shared your theory about Xavier's involvement in Sam's murder with the San Jose police department yet?"

"No, I have not." Lana shifted uncomfortably in her chair. "I don't have any real proof, just a lot of circumstantial evidence and a strong feeling that Xavier stabbed Sam to shut him up. But I figured the detective would not appreciate hearing my unsubstantiated theory."

The officer sensed the hesitation in her voice. "And now that Xavier is dead?"

When he looked over at her expectantly, Lana sighed. "Now I don't know what to think. Xavier was an abrasive guy who rubbed everyone the wrong way. He'd lied to his investors and his employer and showed absolutely no remorse when he got caught. And he picked fights with almost everyone on this tour. He won't be missed by anyone but Jersey, I'm afraid. But I have no idea which one would have been mad enough to have killed him."

When the detective smiled mischievously, Lana suspected he already had someone in mind. "I probably shouldn't be telling you this, but seeing as how forthcoming you were…" He leaned in even closer. "I believe that Xavier was killed during a robbery gone wrong."

"Excuse me—why would you think that?"

"The evidence found at the scene. There were signs of a struggle, his wallet had been removed from his pants pocket and stripped of cash, and we found this."

He pulled out his phone and turned it towards her. The screen was filled with the small sphere she'd seen on Xavier's bed, still covered in blood when this photo had been taken. "This stone is what killed Xavier. Do you recognize it?"

Lana gulped. "Yes, it's a Diquís sphere. He is, or was, an archaeologist, and his site is full of them."

"That may be, but this is still an object protected by UNESCO and our cultural heritage laws. It should not have left the site and certainly should not have been in his hotel room."

The detective smiled down at the image, as if it held the key to solving this crime. "The presence of this sphere changes everything. Him having this in his possession raises the question of why he had it in his hotel room. Was he intending on selling it to someone?"

"You mean—illegally?"

The man smiled. "Yes, that's exactly what I mean. He could have been meeting with a buyer; they argued and fought; and the person killed Xavier. The buyer must have taken the rest of the stones with him."

"What other stones?"

The detective smiled gently at her. "If Xavier had taken one from the site, he could have easily removed more. Do you know who he could have been selling them to? Who else could have known that he had these spheres in his possession?"

Lana blinked in confusion, until his words registered. Then she felt a faint glimmer of hope. "Oh, you think an outsider did this, not someone in our group? I wish I could help you, but I only met him a few days ago when I joined this tour. He's traveling with his assistant, a young woman named Jersey. She should be able to help you. I can say that it was pretty obvious that he had money troubles because he was constantly on the phone, trying to rustle up more sponsors. And last night he decided at the last minute not to join us for the turtle excursion. If he'd arranged to meet with a buyer, that could explain why."

Lana let her mind wander, wondering whether she was forgetting anything else of importance, when another thought popped into her brain. "Wait a second, there may be another explanation for this sphere's presence in his room. Xavier made a remark about how he always traveled with one because it was the easiest way to show an amateur why they were valuable."

"That does not mean that Xavier did not have more spheres in his possession. In fact, it proves he had no regard for our laws." Based on the detective's defensive tone, he was already convinced he knew what had happened that night.

Lana didn't mind. In fact, she was thrilled to know that no one in her group would fall under suspicion, if the detective assumed a rogue buyer murdered Xavier. She bit her lip, thinking the situation through. "There was one more thing you should know. In his gift shop, he was trying to pass fake spheres off as authentic. You may want to have that sphere tested, to ensure it is genuine."

The detective's smile faded slightly. "Thank you for letting me know. Yet even if this is a fake, the buyer may not have known that."

Wow, he is ready to close the case, Lana thought. A robbery gone wrong was a plausible explanation, especially when her suggestion that Xavier had killed Sam to hush him up seemed to strengthen his case. It did make for a neat solution, one that would satisfy both the local population and tourist organizations, she realized. She could imagine the entire Costa Rican police force would be thrilled to have these tourists' murders solved quickly and quietly.

After a few more routine questions, the detective excused her and waved Jersey over. As the two women crossed paths, Lana was shocked to see how pale the young archaeologist looked, and how dark the circles under her eyes were. Lana could imagine the shock of having her fellow assistant and boss killed within the span of a few days would mess with a person emotionally—even someone as cold as Jersey.

As much as the young woman irritated her, Lana's heart went out to her. She had a lot to deal with, and she was now the only one left who knew the ins and outs of Xavier's expansive project. With the upcoming audit, that would put a lot of additional pressure on her. Lana did wonder whether Jersey was up for the task, based on her behavior so far. So far, the young lady had not proven to be very reliable or detail-oriented.

42

A Neat Solution

After everyone had been interviewed, the police thanked her group for cooperating with them, then allowed them to leave. Lana was thrilled to hear that none of her clients were suspects for a change, because the detective remained convinced that Xavier's death was a robbery gone wrong. Based on how some of her previous tours had gone, she'd almost been expecting one of them to be led away in handcuffs.

"I hope that means we'll be able to travel to Nicaragua next week," Cecile said.

"I don't see why not. None of us are under suspicion," Gregory added.

Lana wished she could share their confidence. Sure, the local detective had let them leave without further restricting their travel, yet until Detective Vargas returned their passports, she felt as if anything could still happen.

The detective's theory—that Xavier murdered Sam and later a rogue buyer killed him—sounded good. She only hoped he was correct, otherwise there was still a killer hiding among her clients. Lana tried to push that horrible thought aside and to instead think about her group's current needs.

"Did we miss the kayaking tour?" Chet asked.

The four bros were right earlier in that they would be late for their scheduled kayaking trip. Thankfully the operator was quite laid-back and offered to delay the tour for as long as necessary.

"No, the owner is waiting for us to show up. He sounds like a pretty relaxed guy, but if everyone is ready to go, I would like to head out to the minivan. Does everyone still want to join in?"

"I would rather stay behind. There's a lot of paperwork to deal with, now that Xavier and Sam are gone," Jersey replied.

"That's brave of you. But no one should expect you to tackle it all on your own."

Jersey shrugged. "I'm the one who knows the project the best. It will be easier for me to tie up the loose ends than it would be for someone else."

Lana nodded. "Okay. Let us know if we can be of assistance. Are the rest of you ready to go?"

"I would prefer to change into something lighter and less constricting than this," Gregory said, gesturing to his neatly pressed polo shirt and tailored shorts. "Cecile and I bought some beach clothes specifically for this kind of excursion."

"That's a good idea. Kayaking is much easier if you can freely move your shoulders. Tell you what, why don't we meet back down in the lobby in fifteen minutes? Does that give everyone enough time to get ready?"

A chorus of nods was their reply.

"Great! See you then."

Lana turned to her fellow guides and asked in a soft voice. "We still need to figure out who is going to do what today. I also have a question I'd like to ask you two, in private. Can we go up to our room?"

"Sure," Randy replied.

As soon as the hotel door was closed, Lana turned to the brothers. "Do you really think a rogue buyer killed Xavier and then stole a bunch of Diquís spheres from his room?"

Randy regarded her for a second before answering. "That is what the police seem to think and is based on the evidence found at the scene. The detective's theory also solves both murders, which is a relief. But you don't seem to buy it, do you, Lana?"

"I don't know what to think. Xavier was up to so many shady schemes, I wouldn't be surprised if he was selling spheres illegally. I guess I had expected us to have noticed that he was meeting with an outsider. But then again, he must have been killed while we were on the beach looking at the turtles."

Having a stranger be the killer would be a dream come true. Yet when she considered the evidence, she did wonder whether that was the only possibility. It wasn't simply a mental exercise. Lana had to assume that if one of her remaining guests was a murderer, they would do anything to ensure that their true identity was not revealed—even if that meant killing again to keep their secret safe.

They did have four more days to get through, and Lana wanted to do all she could to ensure that she and the Wright brothers would survive this tour.

"Did the detective say that Xavier was killed while we were out? If that's the case, then we are in the free and clear," Randy pointed out. "We were all together on the beach for the entire excursion. And I assume that the guides who drove us out there kept the car keys on them. It would have been impossible for any of us to have stolen their Jeep, raced back to the hotel, and then gone back to the beach, without someone noticing."

Lana thought back on her conversation with the detective. "I honestly don't recall him saying when Xavier was killed specifically. But it would explain why the detective isn't interested in our group."

"I, for one, hope the police are right. It would be wonderful to not have to worry about having a murderer on the tour," Alex said, conviction in his tone.

Lana took his hand and brought it up to her lips. "Me, too, babe. Me, too."

43

A Monochrome View

After her chat with the Wright brothers, Lana was feeling pretty good about the Xavier situation. All they had to do was wait for the local detective to get in touch with the San Jose police force, and they would have their passports back in no time.

"The guests should be heading back to the lobby by now. What do you say we head down, as well?" Alex asked.

"Fine by me."

He'd just opened the door when Lana's phone pinged. She looked at the screen. "Do you have a minute to talk?" was all Jeremy had written.

"It looks like Jeremy's found out something. Let me call him back before we go down."

Lana dialed her friend's number, and he picked up on the first ring. "Hey, Lana, I hope this is a good time to talk. I've discovered an interesting tidbit that was easier to share on the phone than via a message."

"Great—I'm all ears."

"It looks Gregory and Cecile may have lied to you about how they met."

"Really? Do tell."

"Gregory's first wife, Rowena, died ten months after the Miami conference took place, not before. It was held in Boston the year after her death. So if they met in Miami, then they were having an affair."

"Holy guacamole—that means Gregory was cheating on Rowena!"

"I guess it does. But Lana, the reason why I called instead of sending this over is that if they lied about when they met, that means they could have plotted to get rid of the wife. Let me be clear, the autopsy showed that Rowena succumbed to an infection, but they could have helped to speed up the process. And if Sam had some sort of proof…"

Lana's head spun with the possibilities, each one more murderous than the next.

"Yikes! Thanks, Jeremy. I'm going to go have another chat with Gregory."

"Be sure to take someone with you. It sounds like he could be dangerous, if he killed two of your clients."

"True. I promise to be careful."

She hung up and looked over at the Wright brothers. "You are not going to believe this!"

After catching Randy and Alex up, the trio headed down to the lobby to find the geologists. It wasn't hard, considering the pair were loudly celebrating Xavier's death in the hotel's lobby bar.

Seeing them laughing and having a great time made her blood boil. Jeremy proved that they were cheats and liars—were they murderers, as well?

Cecile raised her drink. "To Xavier's killer, whoever that delightful person may be."

Gregory laughed as he clinked his glass to hers.

Lana's eyes narrowed as she studied him. Could Gregory have harmed Sam and Xavier? Part of her knew that it really didn't matter because the police would certainly blame Sam's murder on the archaeologist, and Xavier's demise on a rogue buyer who would most likely never be caught.

Still, Lana felt angry and frustrated, but most of all played by the couple. She had believed them when they told her that they had nothing to do with Sam's death. But they had fibbed about how and when they had met.

"You lied to me, and I want to know why."

Gregory looked over at Lana in confusion. "What are you talking about?"

"The conference in Miami took place a year before your first wife died, not after."

His shoulders slumped as Cecile grabbed onto his hand. "I knew it would come out one day, but I hadn't expected a mere tour guide to figure it out. Or did Sam tell you?"

Lana bit her lip at the insult, not wanting to reveal her source. "No, I looked up the conference you'd mentioned and noted the date. It wasn't that difficult."

Gregory held his head up high. "It is true that we didn't come out as a couple until several months after my wife passed. We lied about when we started dating because Cecile was still one of my PhD students at the time. Dating a student was a fireable offense, made worse by the fact that I was still married—and to another staff member, no less. The university's director and board were all quite conservative and moralistic. I would have lost my position, despite my tenure, and been further disgraced. So after Rowena died, we lied about when we started dating."

"Is that why you killed Sam—to keep your secret safe?"

"Don't be absurd! You're right in that Sam knew that we were already romantically involved while I was still married to my first wife. Sam's dad had cheated on his mother, and it had ruined her and scarred him. Sam was certain that my first wife had died of a broken heart after learning about our affair. He even threatened to tell the Jade Museum about my infidelity, as a way of getting back at me for hurting Rowena. But I don't think the Jade Museum's director would have cared enough to drop the project. It was embarrassing, but not a reason to kill anyone."

"I still think the police should know that you lied."

"Why—what good would it do? Xavier killing Sam to keep him quiet about the audit makes perfect sense. I had no reason to harm him. If he'd kept pestering me about it, I would have had my lawyers deal with him. I'm certain if I'd offered him enough money, he would have kept his mouth shut."

"I don't know, Sam saw the world in black and white. He may have told the Jade Museum's director about your infidelity, just to spite you."

Gregory waved her remark away. "Everyone has a price."

Lana considered his words. Sam strongly believed people should not lie. His black-and-white view of the world may just have gotten him killed. But after talking with Gregory, she was no longer convinced that the geologist was his killer. Nor could she see him killing Xavier. The geologist was far too rich and full of himself to have killed either man.

44

Going Kayaking

The rest of her clients had gathered in the lobby by the time she'd finished interrogating the geologists. Gregory and Cecile joined the group last, quieter than they had been.

"Are we certain Jersey doesn't want to join us?" Randy asked.

"She wants to work, not kayak. Not that I can blame her; she must have a lot to deal with," Lana replied.

Alex sniggered. "That's probably for the best; she is so uncoordinated, she'd probably tip over the first time she tried to turn."

Lana couldn't help but chuckle. "Indeed. It is a wonder that she's chosen archaeology as her profession, considering how meticulous they are expected to be."

"I think Xavier agreed—he didn't seem to respect her much," Randy said.

"And yet he kept her on, for three years in a row," Alex added.

"Because she was blackmailing him." Lana quickly filled them in on Xavier's confessional conversation with Dotty.

Alex's eyes grew wider the longer Lana spoke. "Wow, Jersey is far more devious than I realized."

Before Lana could respond, Randy's phone pinged with another reminder. He looked at the screen, then up at his fellow guides. "Guys, give me one second to make a call, then we can leave."

When he stepped aside, Lana looked to her group, glad to see that everyone was present and dressed in loose-fitting shorts and T-shirts. She was just about to lead them to the minivan, when she caught sight of Randy's face. His somber expression made her cross over to him first.

"What's going on?"

Randy ran a hand through his hair. "I'm having trouble reaching the hot air balloon company. The departure time is weather-dependent, and I promised the four bros I'd check back with the operator for them. I better stay here and deal with it. You two can handle the kayak trip without me. There's a local guide, and the sea is supposed to be calm today."

Lana regarded Randy's face, noting the dark circles under his eyes and stubble on his chin. He'd been dealing with his brother's bad attitude, as well as pretty much everything tour-related, since George's injury, while she and Alex had enjoyed the excursions alongside the guests.

"You know what, why don't you go kayaking and let me deal with the balloon operator. Someone should stay at the hotel with Jersey, anyway, in case she has a question or complaint."

Randy's face lit up in a smile. "Are you certain? I know how much you love to kayak."

"That's true, I do. But we're a team, and you shouldn't have to deal with all of the administration. Let me take my turn, okay?"

He slapped her on the back. "Then I'm more than happy to hand the dossiers over to you, Lana. Thanks. I was looking forward to seeing the bays and try riding the waves today."

"Excellent. I hope you and Alex enjoy it! I'll see you back here in a few hours." She looked over to her group and noticed no one was paying attention to the guides. Lana quickly pecked Alex on the cheek. "Have fun today."

He squeezed her elbow and flashed her a thousand-watt smile. "Thanks, babe. See you soon."

45

Jeremy Calls Back

It took Lana a half hour to reach the hot balloon operator and confirm the four bros' departure time. After she'd completed that and a few other tasks, Lana was debating whether to call Jeremy and tell him about Xavier's death and the police's theory as to his killer, when her phone rang.

"Jeremy! I was just thinking about you! Xavier was killed last night."

"I know."

Lana leaned back against her bed's headboard. "You do?"

"Yes. I'm sorry to interrupt, but I've discovered something important you need to know about—Xavier's dig is being investigated by the FBI."

"What! The FBI, as in the Federal Bureau of Investigation?"

"Yep, one and the same."

"Oh my, that is big. What can you tell me about their investigation?"

"Quite a bit, actually, but this has to remain between us, okay?"

"Oh, it sounds serious."

"It is. One of my former reporters is now a star investigative journalist for a regional magazine that shall remain unnamed and is about to publish an exposé on Xavier. She shared part of her research with me, under the strict requirement that we not share this with anyone else—not even the police. She's gotten full cooperation from the FBI so far and doesn't want to ruin that access."

"Certainly; you know I won't blab."

"Yes I do, otherwise I wouldn't have even mentioned it. So it seems that the FBI suspects Xavier of smuggling Costa Rican cultural heritage out of the country. They'd set up a sting operation, but apparently he was killed before it could take place."

Lana bit her lip, fearing the worst. "You are certain? He was bludgeoned to death with one of those Diquís spheres he'd been excavating. The local police think he had been meeting with a buyer, they argued, and the buyer killed him with one stone before escaping with the rest."

"And you wonder if the buyers were really FBI agents?"

"It did just cross my mind."

"I see why, considering the timing, but my reporter tells me that the feds had not yet acted, and I believe her. But if he had been killed by a disgruntled buyer, that would fit right in with the FBI's suspicions, I suppose. Although her investigation is focused on another aspect—that he was smuggling spheres into the United States, not selling them in Costa Rica."

"Does she know how he was supposedly doing that?"

"Apparently Sam Perkins, the assistant you'd mentioned, had been in contact with the committee that was auditing Xavier's dig. He'd already found transportation slips and invoices that proved the number of spheres Xavier was sending back didn't match with what the university received."

"Oh, I thought that it was illegal to export the spheres because they are protected cultural heritage."

"It is illegal for private citizens to take them out of the country, but Xavier's university had obtained permission to export a small number each year so they could be displayed in their museum. That's one of the only exceptions to the export ban."

"And the FBI suspects that Xavier or one of his cohorts was intercepting the crates, removing the extra spheres, and selling them off for a profit?"

"Bingo. Someone gets a gold star," Jeremy laughed. "Apparently the FBI had raided an art collector's home last year and discovered several illegally acquired objects of cultural significance—including three of the Diquís spheres. In exchange for a reduced sentence, the collector told the feds about Xavier, and that's why they started investigating him. They even instigated the university's audit of his archeological dig. But from what my reporter friend shared, they haven't yet figured out how Xavier is removing the extra stones, before they reach the university. That's where they are focusing their investigation on now."

"That is big news; thanks for calling to let me know about this," Lana said, as another thought popped into her head.

"No problem. But why don't you sound ecstatic? This is great news, isn't it?"

"It sure is. It's just that now that Xavier is dead, we may never know for certain if he killed Sam or why. But if he knew that Sam had already discovered he was smuggling spheres into the States, that would give Xavier a strong motive to kill him before he could talk with the university."

"Indeed. But it sounds like he was too late, which means he hadn't known that Sam had already made the university aware of his illegal activities."

"I do wonder whether Jersey knew about the smuggling, as well as Xavier's misappropriation of funds. Sam had apparently figured it out quite quickly, and she had worked on the dig for three years."

"You'd think she would have. Unless she is incredibly obtuse and Sam was incredibly perceptive."

"I wouldn't call her obtuse, but Sam wasn't that brilliant, either," Lana laughed. "It really doesn't matter either way, I know. It's just a relief to know the police have solved this one without my help, or without having any of our guests led away in handcuffs."

"That does sound like a relief," Jeremy chuckled. "I can share Jersey's name with my contact, if you think she would be open to talking to a reporter."

Lana snorted. "I doubt Jersey would say anything disparaging about Xavier, but your contact can always try. Here's her number."

"Great, thanks, I've got it noted. I've got to get to a meeting. Talk later?"

"You bet. Hey, thanks again for sending that information over. I owe you a dinner when I get back."

Her friend laughed. "I'm holding you to it."

46

Going For A Swim

After Jeremy's call, Lana still had an hour to kill before the rest returned from the kayaking trip. Instead of hanging out in her room, she decided to go for a swim. The outdoor pool looked so inviting, especially since the sun was really bearing down today.

Not only would a dip in the pool be a great way to unwind, it would also give her a chance to come to terms with both deaths and put them into perspective.

During their time together in Iceland, her best friend, Willow, had convinced her that she was put in these situations so she could help those wrongly accused of a crime. Her boss, on the other hand, thought the suspicious number of deaths on Lana's previous tours made her an angel of death.

She supposed time would tell. But right now, she felt as if she was neither. More than anything, Lana felt like someone who had the knack for being in the wrong place at the wrong time.

At least during this tour, she didn't have to do much to prove either woman right. The Costa Rican police would surely blame Xavier for Sam's death, and the unknown assailants for his own. That pat solution was vastly preferable to having to deal with the international media descending in droves, demanding to know whodunit.

Lana hoped the police had come to the correct conclusion. It did make sense, Xavier killing Sam to keep him quiet about all of his wrongdoings. He couldn't have known that Sam had already alerted the university or that the feds were closing in on him.

The idea that a disgruntled buyer had taken Xavier's life was somewhat fitting. She could imagine that the buyer would have left the blood-soaked sphere behind and taken any others that Xavier had brought to the hotel room. For all intents and purposes, it seemed as if the Costa Rican police had solved the case in record time.

As reassuring as that thought should have been, it didn't bring her much peace. Two people were still dead.

However, it did mean that Dotty wouldn't try to stop her from touring again. As badly as this one had gone, it did feel good to be on the road again. She really couldn't see herself doing anything else, career wise, besides leading tours.

Alex's attitude was still a problem, but it was his to solve. All she could do was be there for him when he needed her.

Her problems seemed to solve themselves with every kick of her legs. When she pushed off of the side one last time, Lana was happy to accept the police's conclusions as correct and move on with her life.

By the time she stepped out of the pool, she felt more at peace than she had in months. It was an empowering feeling, one she'd missed.

47

Case Closed

After her swim, Lana was at peace with the arrests, or lack thereof. A voicemail from Detective Vargas, announcing that they had officially closed the cases and he would return their passports as soon as possible, was the icing on the cake.

After listening to his message a second time, she sought her boyfriend and his brother.

"Did you hear? The police have officially closed both murder cases. We are now free to leave the country!"

"What a relief. We should inform the others. Gregory is particularly anxious to get his passport back," Randy said.

"It's almost time for lunch, anyway. Why don't we share the great news over an aperitif?" Alex suggested.

"Sounds great. I know the four bros were heading to the pool. I'll let them know."

Lana's brow furrowed at Randy's comment. "Oh, shoot. I forgot to check on Jersey while you were gone. I'll head up there now and let her know we're planning on meeting for lunch."

As she climbed the stairs to the fifth floor, Lana thought only of the future. Now that the murders were wrapped up, it was time to focus on the tour. They were booked into a traditional restaurant tonight with more live music and dancing. Tomorrow they would have a chance to try surfing, before visiting a park known for its abundance of sloths. After that, they only had one more day of sightseeing in San Jose before the tour officially ended.

The last few days were going to fly by, and then she and Alex could take a little time off to be together. At least, if he was interested. The way he had been acting, Lana didn't know where his head was at.

She'd just reached the correct floor and had stepped into the hallway, when Lana suddenly heard Jersey say quite clearly, "Yes, hi, thanks for calling me back."

Why is Jersey's voice so loud? she wondered, until she reached the younger woman's door and saw that it was still open. *She must have run back inside to take a call and not closed it properly*, Lana realized as she started to turn around. Jersey had accused her of eavesdropping several times during this tour, and she didn't want to get caught again.

Yet something in Jersey's unusually friendly tone caught her attention more than her words, and her feet remained rooted in place.

"Did you receive Xavier's reference letter?' Jersey asked sweetly.

Lana's eyes bulged out. After everything he said, Xavier wrote a reference letter for her? He obviously hadn't thought she was qualified and had even told Dotty so himself.

"Yes, I know that technically I'm not allowed to even know he sent one to you, but he was my mentor, and now he's dead. It was so important to Xavier that I be selected for this position—he told me so himself. That's why I felt compelled to call, because he no longer can. If you could confirm for me that it reached you in time, I would appreciate it. According to his email, he sent it over last night. The timestamp says 11:47 p.m.—he was killed shortly after," Jersey added, Lana presumed for dramatic effect.

Apparently it worked.

"Excellent, thanks for checking on that. I'm thrilled you think I have a shot at the position. You're right, me being chosen for this position would be the perfect way to honor Xavier's memory. I hope the others agree with you. I look forward to talking with you again quite soon." From the relief in her voice, Jersey was overjoyed with the person's response.

Not only had Xavier sent over a job recommendation for Jersey, but also it was apparently so good that the person on the phone was already convinced she would be a qualified, viable candidate. No matter how Lana twisted it in her mind, she could not make sense of that conversation. There was no way on God's green earth that Xavier had willingly recommended Jersey for anything—especially not a job.

As if a bolt of lightning had struck her down, suddenly Lana knew who had killed Sam and Xavier. And it sure wasn't because of a robbery gone wrong. Feeling emboldened by the truth, Lana knocked on Jersey's door once before entering.

"Hey! What are you doing, barging into my room?"

Lana closed the door and leaned against it. "Just before his death, Xavier, Dotty Thompson, and I had a heart-to-heart about his dig. During that conversation, he made quite clear to both of us that it would have pained him to have to recommend you for any job. I believe his exact words were that you are 'an atrocious archaeologist and I would hate for any colleague of mine to be saddled with you.' You wrote that recommendation letter and sent it via his email last night—didn't you?"

"How dare you speak to me like that? Were you listening in on my conversation again? What is it with you and eavesdropping, lady?"

"You left your door open—anyone walking down the hallway could have heard you. Xavier helped you with the ethics committee when Cindy accused you of fraud. But I would bet money that you were in the wrong. Am I correct?'"

Jersey paled. "I did that research—Cindy tried to take credit for my work, not the other way around!"

"Really? Why don't I believe you, Jersey? Xavier told me and Dotty that you'd discovered he was misusing funds, and used that to blackmail him into helping you further your career. I bet you knew about him smuggling spheres out of the country, as well. But it wouldn't make sense to kill him, if he was helping you to seek employment…"

Lana stared at the young woman, who was defiantly glaring back at her, when the solution popped into her brain. "Of course! I thought you were ruthless for messing over Cindy like you did, but I didn't realize that you'd actually kill to get a job in the field!"

Jersey pushed out her chin. "I don't know what you are talking about—I didn't kill anyone! And I wasn't blackmailing Xavier, either. We worked well together, that's all."

"Sure you did. Until he lost his job and had no reason to continue helping you. That's why you snuck into his room after the turtle tour and smashed his brains in with the sphere he always carried in his luggage. You had to kill him, before he could badmouth you to his colleagues. Without his support, you would never find a job on your own."

Jersey's eyes widened. "No, that's not what happened. His room was on the ground floor; anyone could have done it."

But Lana was on a roll and not in the mood for more of Jersey's lies. "If you figured out what Xavier was doing, Sam must have, also." Lana jerked her head up. "You killed them both, didn't you?"

"What's with you? I liked Sam. Why would I have harmed him?"

"Because he was going to ruin everything. I kept thinking you had no reason to kill Sam, that only Xavier did. But Sam was determined to tell the university everything about Xavier's deceit, and he made that clear to anyone who would listen. And you listened, didn't you? If Sam's testimony had cost Xavier his job, he wouldn't have been able to continue helping you further your career. It was clear that Sam was above blackmail or bribery, so you had no other choice but to silence him. You couldn't have known that Sam had already told the university about his suspicions. A reporter friend of mine confirmed it—the university knows all about Xavier's deceit. And, I assume, yours as well."

Jersey's eyes narrowed to slits as she muttered something nasty. "I should have known that Goody Two-shoes had already told the university about Xavier's side projects. Sam's morals got him killed. He hated liars and cheats, because of the way his dad treated his mom, and there was nothing I could say to change his mind. When Sam told me that he was going to tell the audit committee about Xavier's smuggling operation, I knew I had to act fast."

"And that was why you killed Sam."

Jersey hung her head. "Yes."

Lana looked at Jersey with new eyes. "How did you kill Sam? Did you push the blade into his side when he bent over? I thought you were trying to help him back up, but it was the opposite, wasn't it?"

"Yes." Jersey's lip began to tremble as she moved a step closer. "What are you going to do now?"

Lana regarded the young woman, now a confessed double-murderer. "What do you think I'm going to do? Call Detective Vargas. I would like to have my passport back, especially since I didn't do anything wrong."

"Oh, okay," Jersey said, then suddenly swung her purse wide, smacking Lana in the face.

"What the?" Lana stumbled backwards, into the bed. Before she could regain her balance, the younger woman was already out the door and tearing down the hallway.

Lana raced to catch up, screaming as she went. "Don't let Jersey get away—she murdered Xavier and Sam!"

48

The Tour Must Go On

"How are you holding up?" Dotty asked. The concern on her face was evident, even through the tiny screen on Lana's phone.

She and Randy had requested the call so they could catch their boss up on Jersey's arrest. Dotty had listened silently while they relayed the news, her expression growing sadder with every word.

It was a relief to all that Jersey was behind bars, awaiting trial for murdering both Sam and Xavier. After whapping Lana with her purse, Jersey had torn down the stairs. Yet as soon as she had run into the lobby, she'd slammed right into the four bros. When they heard Lana screaming about Jersey being a murderer, they had kept the young archaeologist pinned down until the police arrived.

Shortly after Jersey was taken into custody, Detective Vargas drove up from San Jose to personally deliver their passports and his thanks.

"I think I speak for both of us when I say we're doing fine," Lana finally replied. "It's just strange to think that Jersey was the killer all along. I'd never really suspected her, not until it was almost too late. If I hadn't overheard her conversation about Xavier's recommendation letter, she would have gotten away with it."

"I for one am thrilled you were able to work out the killer's true identity again, Lana! You might want to consider a job in law enforcement."

Lana laughed, pleased to hear her boss say this, instead of calling her a murder magnet again.

"Not to put a damper on the conversation, but I do want to hear what you think of Alex's performance. Please be candid, I don't want to hire him on unless he's really up for the job."

Lana looked to Randy, unsure of what to say.

Before either could speak, Dotty shook her head sadly. "You don't have to say a word—I see it in your faces. He's not the right man for the job, is he?"

"We don't need to rehash all of the details, but no, leading tours is not for him. And I think Alex knows it," Randy said, as diplomatically as possible.

"Will you two let me break the bad news?" Lana pleaded.

"Be my guest," Randy said, a little too quickly for Lana's taste. Alex was his brother, after all.

"Are you certain? Technically, I should do it. It is my company." But Dotty wasn't convincing. Lana suspected that she really didn't want that responsibility and, just like Randy, was more than happy to hand the task over to her.

"I wouldn't worry too much about how Alex is going to react. I agree with Randy in that I think Alex knows he's not cut out to lead tours. But before you give up on him completely, Alex is good with planning. He redid the Costa Rica tour in a less than an hour, and even you said it seems to be a more solid itinerary than George's version. Hiring him on may be something to consider, but that's for you two to talk through, if you are even interested," Lana rushed to add. The last thing she wanted to do was make her boss feel as if she had to hire Alex in some capacity.

She need not have worried. Based on the older lady's reaction, Dotty was thrilled to hear about Alex's recently discovered skill set. "That's great to know. Lately, I've been thinking of ways I can step back and am drawing up a list of tasks I'd like to hand over to others. This may be worth talking to Alex about. Let me have a think before I get in touch with him, okay?"

"You got it."

"What about you two—did you enjoy leading this tour?"

"More than I had expected," Randy enthused.

"I did, too, for the most part. There's no reason to wait any longer. You can schedule me in on a European tour, whenever you need me."

Dotty's relief was evident even through the tiny screen. "That's music to my ears, Lana. Margie just broke her ankle, thankfully on the last day of her Scotland tour. But that leaves me a guide short, and she was scheduled to lead a tour around Zurich in two weeks. That would still give you a few days in Seattle to decompress before you have to fly over. Are you game?"

Her eyes widened at the thought. She'd just told Dotty that she was ready, but two weeks seemed sudden. Yet if she was ready, why wait any longer? "Yes, I am. In fact, that sounds incredible. I've not yet been to Switzerland."

"It's so pretty this time of year, and the tour includes a trip to the Alps. I think you'll enjoy it, Lana. I'll talk to you both soon."

As soon as Dotty hung up, Lana turned to Randy. "So you enjoyed it, too? Honestly, I thought you were pretty stressed out about the itinerary details."

"It was Alex, not the tour, that was stressing me out these past few days. In fact, it's been a nice change of pace dealing with tour operators again, instead of processing room cancellations and fixing broken lamps. More than I expected, really. I didn't mind work at the bed and breakfast until I flew down here. But leading this group has reminded me of how much I missed traveling." Randy's voice trailed off as he gazed off into the distance.

Lana studied her friend, surprised by his reaction. She knew he had only stopped leading European tours so that he and his new bride could build up a life together in Seattle. But he'd never openly complained about working at the bed and breakfast before. "Do you miss it enough to want to lead tours again?"

Randy laughed. "I don't know about that. I love sleeping in the same bed as my wife every night, even more."

He tipped his beer at her. "But you slipped right back into guide mode. After what happened in Iceland, I wasn't sure where your head would be at. But you did great and seem completely ready to go back to work."

Lana beamed. "Thanks. I can't think of anything else I would rather be doing. I guess we'll see what Alex decides to do next. If he finds a job back in Seattle, I may have to rethink my career choice again. But for now, this suits me."

49

Home is Where You Are

Lana knocked softly on the hotel door before entering. Alex sat on the end of the bed, his hand wrung together as if he was awaiting news of a prison sentence.

"What's the verdict?"

She sat down next to him and took his hands in hers. "Before I tell you what Dotty said, I would like to know what you think of your performance."

Lana was taking a gamble by asking him to rate himself first. They both knew that Dotty had already made her decision. She just hoped Alex had already come to the same conclusion—that he wasn't fit to lead tours. She'd much rather see him to choose to quit than to have Dotty fire him.

"Sure. I am a terrible tour guide and know that I will never be a good one. I just don't have the same *je ne sais quoi* that you and Randy do. Somehow you can make any guest feel at ease and simultaneously important, even when they are complaining about something frivolous. I just don't have it in me."

Lana breathed a sigh of relief, not unnoticed by Alex. "Dotty had already decided not to hire me, didn't she?"

She bowed her head and nodded yes. "Not as a guide, no. It wasn't an easy decision, but as you said, she's looking for employees who truly love working with high-end clients. I see the same irritating, privileged behavior that you do, but I choose to handle my annoyance differently than you. That's all. It doesn't make me a better person."

"Oh, honey, I know that. I'm not upset with you for being good at something you love. In fact, I envy you. It's just so difficult, not knowing what you should be doing with your life. Right now, I feel like I'm flailing around on a rudderless ship in a storm that I can't escape."

Her heart went out to him. She'd been there, just before Dotty had offered her the chance to lead a tour through Budapest two years ago—a decision that had changed the course of Lana's personal and professional life for the better.

"Things will improve. You will find your place in this world. You just need a little more time to figure out what it is that you want."

Alex stared at his hands. "It's just frustrating that this didn't work out. Being a guide is everything I thought I wanted—travel, adventure, and flexibility. Yet it wasn't exactly what I'd envisioned. Part of me is relieved that Dotty already made up her mind, but another part feels like I'm giving up too soon. I haven't even completed two tours, and I'm already throwing in the towel."

Lana smiled gently. "I can understand why you would feel that way. And if I thought you just needed to get used to dealing with all of the personalities you'll encounter on a tour, I would say to give it more time. But if it doesn't feel right, why push it?"

"True. But what do I do now? I have to earn a living."

"Now is not the time to make any more life-altering changes. Maybe you need some time away, to think things through, with no pressure to decide?"

"Like you did in Iceland?"

Lana chuckled. "I guess so."

When Alex's expression darkened, she squeezed his hand. "So where do we go from here? After this tour ends, would you like to go back to Seattle or take a short trip with me somewhere in Central America first? I have two weeks free before I lead a tour in Switzerland."

Alex took her hand and gently kissed her fingertips. "Honestly, as long as we are together, I don't care where we go. I just want to be with you."

Lana's heart flooded with joy. They were going to get through these tough times together, as any loving couple should. "Being with you is the best destination of all. I love you, Alex Wright."

"And I you, Lana Hansen."

THE END

Thanks for reading *Death by Oxcart*!
Reviews really do help readers decide whether they want to take a chance on a new author. If you enjoyed this story, I hope you will leave a review on BookBub, Goodreads, or your favorite retailer's website.
I appreciate it! Jennifer S. Alderson

Acknowledgments

Dear reader, thank you for encouraging me to write another adventure featuring Lana Hansen! Because my followers on Facebook are the ones who pushed me to write another book in the series, I let them help me decide where she should travel to next and what kind of tour she would be leading. It was a fun experience, loosely collaborating on the premise of this book, and I hope to continue this tradition next year!

Unfortunately, caught up in the moment, we all forgot that in two previous books I had briefly mentioned Lana having led a tour in Costa Rica, right after returning from Hungary (her trip in book one, *Death on the Danube*). I only discovered the mistake after I'd finished writing *Death by Oxcart*, which meant it was too late to change the location of this book.

Instead of rewriting *Death by Oxcart*, I decided to replace the four mentions of "Costa Rica" with "Portugal" in Books One and Two. By the time this book is published, those earlier novels should be updated.

That means, if you have an older copy, it is now a collector's item!

As always, I am deeply indebted to my family for giving me the space to write. My editor, Sadye Scott-Hainchek of The Fussy Librarian, does such a wonderful job of polishing my manuscripts until they shine. My cover designer, Elizabeth Mackey, delights me with her fabulous and fun covers ever time—and this book's cover is no exception.

Costa Rica truly is a paradise for lovers of nature and adventure, it and holds a special place in my heart. My month-long trip to the county is one I often think back on fondly, thanks to the stunning landscapes, the incredible flora and fauna, and the many warm-hearted people I met along the way. If you ever get the chance to visit—grab it and go!

Until next time, happy reading and travels.

About the Author

Jennifer S. Alderson was born in San Francisco, grew up in Seattle, and currently lives in Amsterdam. After traveling extensively around Asia, Oceania, and Central America, she lived in Darwin, Australia, before settling in the Netherlands.

Jennifer's love of travel, art, and culture inspires her award-winning Zelda Richardson Mystery series, her Travel Can Be Murder Cozy Mysteries, and her Carmen De Luca Art Sleuth Mysteries. Her background in journalism, multimedia development, and art history enriches her novels.

When not writing, she can be found perusing a museum, biking around Amsterdam, or enjoying a coffee along the canal while planning her next research trip.

Books by Jennifer S. Alderson:

Carmen De Luca Art Sleuth Mysteries
Collecting Can Be Murder
A Statue To Die For
Forgeries and Fatalities
A Killer Inheritance

Travel Can Be Murder Cozy Mysteries
Death on the Danube: A New Year's Murder in Budapest
Death by Baguette: A Valentine's Day Murder in Paris
Death by Windmill: A Mother's Day Murder in Amsterdam
Death by Bagpipes: A Summer Murder in Edinburgh

Death by Fountain: A Christmas Murder in Rome
Death by Leprechaun: A Saint Patrick's Day Murder in Dublin
Death by Flamenco: An Easter Murder in Seville
Death by Gondola: A Springtime Murder in Venice
Death by Puffin: A Bachelorette Party Murder in Reykjavik
Death by Oxcart: An Independence Day Murder in Costa Rica

Zelda Richardson Art Mysteries
The Lover's Portrait: An Art Mystery
Rituals of the Dead: An Artifact Mystery
Marked for Revenge: An Art Heist Thriller
The Vermeer Deception: An Art Mystery

Standalone Travel Thriller
Down and Out in Kathmandu: A Backpacker Mystery

Collecting Can Be Murder

If you love strong and resourceful heroines, puzzling mysteries, and a dash of art history, you'll probably love reading about Carmen De Luca's adventures!

Coming out of retirement can be deadly... After tragedy struck three years earlier, art sleuth Carmen De Luca vowed to never work in the field again. But fifty is too young to fill her days with water aerobics and bingo, so when her former partner calls and begs for her help, Carmen gladly agrees.

Yet after their first assignment—the recovery of a rare medieval prayer book from an eccentric collector living in rural France—goes horribly wrong, Carmen ends up in the crosshairs of both the local police and a murderer!

With her target dead and the stolen book missing, she and her partner will have to pull out all of the stops to sleuth out the true killer's identity—before their stay in France becomes permanent.

Excerpt from *Collecting Can Be Murder*
Chapter 1: Wakey Wakey

"Carmen—wake up!" A light slap greeted my return to consciousness. All around me, voices were crying out, gasping in fear or surprise; I couldn't tell for certain which. But their anxiety was audible.

I opened my eyes and saw a fuzzy version of the Baroness, my favorite partner in crime, hovering over me.

When she raised her hand to strike my cheek again, I caught it midswing. "I'm awake."

"Talk to me! Who are you?" Lady Sophie—or the Baroness, as I called her—knelt down, the hem of her aquamarine ball gown spreading out around her like a silky pool of water, and grabbed hold of my shoulders, shaking me as hard as her social status allowed.

"Carmen De Luca, art sleuth," I mumbled as I ran my fingers over my temple, wincing when I hit broken skin. "Why is there a baseball growing out of my forehead?"

"It looks like you got hit by a whole lot of books. Those covers aren't soft at all. Or maybe the bookshelf nicked you."

"The bookcase!" My last memory before I lost consciousness was of a mass of books racing towards me. I sat up far too quickly, jarring my bruised skull. Several hardcovers slid off of my chest, adding tiny bruises to my list of injuries. I squeezed my eyes shut and lay back down.

"I guess it did hit me. How's Harold?"

The Baroness's eyes widened slightly, enough to tell me something was very wrong. "He took the brunt of it."

My brain screamed for me to remain still, but I had to see what had happened to my target. I pushed myself up onto my elbows and followed my partner's gaze over to the ceiling-high bookcase that had been filled with hundreds of rare first editions when I had entered. It was now lying across the room, its valuable contents strewn over the floor and furniture.

The legs of the chair that had been closest to the bookcase had been crushed by the heavy planks, as if they were toothpicks. Sticking out from under the shelving were a pair of burgundy pants and alligator-skin boots—the same ensemble our party's flamboyant host, Harold Moreau, had been wearing this evening.

Neither the legs nor boots were moving. Billy, a museum curator from the East Coast, and two of the collectors invited to the private viewing were busy clearing the many books covering Harold's body, chucking the pricey volumes behind them in their rush to reach his face.

Several almost nicked Harold's wife, Tammy, who was pacing the floor, seemingly unaware of the heavy books being thrown in her direction.

"I told Harold that bookshelf was top-heavy, but he wouldn't listen. Instead, he kept buying more and more. It wasn't a hobby anymore, it was an illness. No wonder it toppled over!"

"That's not right. I saw a pair of arms pushing the bookcase, just before everything went black," I muttered, too softly for the anxious wife to hear.

The Baroness leaned in close to my ear. "Are you sure? That would mean…"

"That someone intentionally pushed it onto Harold. He was sitting in that chair when it fell." I groaned when a horrible thought struck. "He wouldn't have been able to react and perhaps save himself, either, thanks to the chloroform I'd administered. But why would someone want to harm him?"

I studied the scene before me. The books that had tumbled from the fallen bookshelf littered the floor in piles several volumes deep. Our host had boasted that the case held his most prized first editions. They weren't as valuable as his multimillion-dollar collection of medieval prayer books, but were still worth a pretty penny and far easier to sell off than the ancient volumes. If someone had intended to disarm Harold so they could steal them, they had botched the job.

So if that wasn't their goal, what was?

When I took another gander around the space, something else sent chills up my spine. Several of the books of hours that had been displayed in the glass cases lining the back wall when I entered were no longer there. I scanned the volumes scattered all around me, but didn't see any of the illuminated manuscripts' gold- and silver-lined covers shining back at me.

"Baroness, several of Harold's prayer books appear to be missing." When I jiggled my head towards the closest display case, it felt like someone was taking a hammer to my skull.

My partner grabbed my arm, her nails digging into my skin. "Where is the Avron book?"

"In my purse."

"Why is it in your purse?" The Baroness's voice rose an octave as her face paled considerably. "You weren't authorized to take it."

I tuned her voice out as I reached for my bag, luckily still by my side, expecting to feel a hard lump where the illuminated manuscript should have been. All I felt was overpriced leather and my hairbrush. I rubbed gingerly at my forehead, trying to recall my exact movements, until those final moments before I lost consciousness replayed in my mind. Of course the book wasn't in my purse—I had been preparing it for transport when the bookcase came crashing down on me.

"Baroness, we have a problem. Mission not accomplished."

She nodded towards Harold. "We have more than one, by the looks of things."

The three men were still busy removing the mountain of books smothering our host, their tempo bordering on frantic as Harold's face finally came into view.

"Harold! Can you hear me?" Billy what's-his-name screamed, but our host didn't respond. My memory was not great at the best of times, but jet lag and the blow to the head had worsened it significantly.

"I've got a bad feeling about this," I whispered to my partner. She squeezed my hand tight as we watched the others tend to our party's host.

When Harold's face was clear, one of the guests shoved a mirror under his nose, while another searched for a pulse.

"How is he doing?" I dared to ask.

Billy leaned back on his haunches and shook his head. "Not as lucky as you, I'm afraid. Harold is dead."

* * *

If you are enjoying the story so far, why not purchase *Collecting Can Be Murder* now and keep reading? Available as eBook, audiobook, paperback, large print edition, and in Kindle Unlimited.

www.ingramcontent.com/pod-product-compliance
Lightning Source LLC
LaVergne TN
LVHW041703070526
838199LV00045B/1177